BLUE
and
LIES

Helen Paish

Copyright © 2020 Helen Paish

Helen Paish asserts the moral right to be identified as the author of this work.

All rights reserved.

No part of this publication may be reproduced, stored or transmitted in any form or by any means, electronic, mechanical, photocopying, recording, scanning, or otherwise without written permission from the publisher. It is illegal to copy this book, post it to a website, or distribute it by any other means without permission.

This novel is entirely a work of fiction. The names, characters and incidents portrayed in it are the work of the author's imagination. Any resemblance to actual persons, living or dead, events or localities is entirely coincidental.

A catalogue record for this book is available from the British Library

IBSN 9798647896384

First published independently in 2020

Front cover photograph by Alexandru Zdrobău

For my mother and father, forever there to inspire.

To Yvonne and Simon, always there to support and to all my family and friends who have encouraged me to keep going.

"To every action there is always opposed and equal reaction."

Issac Newton

Part One

Ask No Questions

The day ended very differently from the way it began. A black body bag unceremoniously dumped into the sea, bound in thick black tape to remove any air and weighted down with chains. The corpse inside just another 'disappeared' whose solitary resting place would be the bottom of deep Mediterranean waters off the Southern coast of Spain.

1

One Went Missing

April 2008

The mountainous backdrop of La Concha grew smaller as the luxury ninety-nine-foot Ferretti yacht navigated its way seamlessly out of the port, leaving behind the designer shops, restaurants and supercars that bordered the famous frontline playground of Puerto Banus on the Costa del Sol.

The sun was sparkling on the water like diamonds on indigo silk as the pilot headed for the open sea, picking up speed He was the only official crew member. His view of the guests onboard would be confined to those using the sunbathing area across the bow, to the front of the pilothouse window.

The sounds of popping champagne corks and the

clinking of ice cubes dropped into crystal tumblers carried across the water as a party of seven gathered at the stern on the flybridge deck. A mix of Hip Hop and Indie Rock was pumping from the sound system. The guests included the owner of the yacht, his business partner and one other man. Although casually dressed, their money was on display, from the Ralph Lauren polo shirts down to the Gucci loafers, Ray-Bans and Rolexes. They sat relaxed next to the bar on white sofas shaded from the sun and looking on with mixed interest at three beautiful girls. Two brunettes and a blonde were dancing, wearing only bikini bottoms; their long hair carried in the breeze as their seductive figures moved to the rhythm of the music.

A fourth man, Sergiu, presided over the scene. He had an air of control and self-importance attached to his large frame which seemed to exude a natural force field against anyone who might think to approach him. Dressed all in black, he kept himself detached behind his dark glasses, monitoring the guests' every move. It was he who selected the girls to entertain the men, though he knew it was no pleasure trip.

Now in his early thirties, Sergiu had forged a career by exploiting the misfortunes of others. As a young boy growing up in Bucharest he was encouraged to take up boxing by his father, he had demonstrated considerable potential as a boxer but he quickly learned he had other skills which were more lucrative and exciting. He was good looking, ambitious and knew the ways of the streets as well as being smarter than most his age. The petty rivalries between local gangs did not interest him unless he could see an opportunity to use them. He was an expert in manipulation and what he could not achieve by a natural advantage in intelligence, he could solve by brute force.

His roots lay in Sector 4 of the city, home to various neighbourhood gangs, many of whom were former sportsmen; boxers, wrestlers and rugby players. They joined forces with a hierarchy of Steaua Bucharest football ultras and it was within this inner hardcore that Sergiu promoted his talents. He impressed his bosses with his ability to network and expanded their empire of organised crime through blackmail, racketeering, contract murders and robbery. He ordered punishment beatings, orchestrated public order disturbances and developed a lucrative business from breaking and entering, all of which flew in the face of a defective and corrupt Romanian law force.

Over fifteen years the gang successfully branched out to human trafficking, prostitution, drug trading and IT crimes which spread across international borders, particularly Spain where Sergiu was now reaping even more rewards. He had worked his way up over the years and provided he continued to deliver what they asked he could enjoy a lifestyle most would envy. It wasn´t about trust, no one could trust anyone in his business but there was a code. If you crossed any lines, you did not survive.

Today's voyage would end with a satisfactory outcome for his bosses and a handsome paycheck for his services. The instructions from the boat owner and his business partner were precise and Sergiu was confident everything was organised.

Before boarding the girls were treated to a

shopping spree accompanied by their prize clients, blending in amongst the happy tourists with money to burn enjoying a day out in Marbella. They would be well rewarded in cash at the end of the excursion. Sergiu instructed them to remain on the flydeck, to entertain the men and ask no questions. Each was carefully chosen not just for their looks but also for their reliability. To be at the top of the game needed control and experience, to be a professional was to know the limits when it came to drink and drugs and to deliver a service without emotional compromise from either client or provider. He had taught them well.

Of the three girls, one was taller and particularly striking. Mihaela was blonde, with piercing blue eyes and a teasing smile that was bait for anyone with deep pockets. Her body was tanned and toned, her breasts so natural and appealing that any man would feel his hands drawn there as if they were magnetised. She was keen to maximise the opportunity to earn any extra money and getting close to being able to go her own way.

Two of the men were strictly off-limits, the boat owner and Sergiu's boss, an ugly brutish man whose head shone like a polished Faberge egg. She had seen them several times in the Casino in Puerto Banus but Sergiu, who monitored all her clients, had told her to stay away. He boasted how important these men were to his success as if that mattered to her anymore.

She concentrated on the third man who was happily deep sea fishing the contents of a whiskey bottle. Surely there was no harm in tapping him for a bigger tip! She sashayed her way over to a buffet of fresh seafood jewelled with fine pearls of caviar. While slipping a sideways glance to see if she had attracted the right attention, she selected a morsel of creamy white fish, dropping it between her lips and teasingly licking her fingertips. Like a purring lioness, she purposely made her way over to the man whose eyes met hers. It was just having fun, flirting, playing the game. She cupped one hand around the back of his neck and lowered her pink-clad bottom playfully onto his lap. The two of them were laughing, enjoying the cocktail of sun, sea and music.

Mihaela was toying with him, continuing to flatter him, parting his open white shirt to reveal a hairless chest and a tattoo in the shape of a heart, with the name Mihaela running through it in a ribbon. He told her it was his wife's name, joking that although she shared the same name; she neither looked nor behaved like his wife. The boat owner was smiling, amused by the play but his partner was listening and studying more closely. She was conscious of his disapproval, as he turned his scarred bald head toward her and signalled her to move away, suggesting she would be more entertaining if she went back to dancing, where they could all appreciate her.

She gracefully lifted herself off, brushing her hand gently across the man's chest, pouting with a disappointed 'another time' expression. The man with the tattoo objected to her departure, slurring his words as he spoke to his host. 'Felix, you are too serious, relax everything is fine.' The bald-headed man smiled but then glanced toward Sergiu who flicked his head in warning at Mihaela. She immediately retreated. She liked an audience but perhaps this was not the time to be in the spotlight.

By mid-afternoon, the entertainment was over and the girls were dismissed to the front of the flydeck. They lay like mermaids, side by side, stretched out on the sun mats cushioning the front of the pilothouse as the yacht continued to glide through calm waters. The music changed from dance beat to lounge chill out. The men made their way down to the saloon on the main deck.

After several minutes, Sergiu returned to the flybridge deck checking the bar area which was empty apart from leftover food, several upturned champagne bottles and one empty whiskey bottle. The girls were quiet and out of the way. Satisfied, he returned to the real purpose of the excursion.

Mihaela turned onto her back staring up at the sky but after a while, she began to feel unwell. Her companions seemed to be sleeping but Mihaela was restless. They had been told not to go down while the men were at business but after champagne, music and dancing there was a call of nature that needed a bathroom. She would be quick!

Her bare feet padded silently down the stairs to the starboard corridor. There were two choices, either to make her way along the outside to the stairs of the lower deck, passing by the large windows of the main lounge or to be cheeky and cut across the dining area to the portside guest bathroom. She hesitated, knowing it was against orders but her pressing need for the toilet was worth the small interruption. However, as she peered in towards the seating area during her seconds of indecision, she froze. Felix was standing with a gun pointed at the forehead of her laptop muse. 'Good riddance, Stefan,' Felix muttered, as he released two successive shots at close range. It was like a scene from a movie, the pop-pop of a gun with a silencer and the thump of a body onto the floor. Mihaela panicked stepping back, hoping she had not been seen but there was a flash of blonde and pink detected from within the room and she sensed it.

She fled up the steps two at a time, in shock at what she had seen and grabbed a bottle of water from the bar where they had been partying earlier. The sounds of muffled voices were coming from below and she was sure someone would come up. She sprinted back to the girls lying in the sun, seemingly oblivious to anything. Footsteps followed on the stairs as she sat with her eyes fixed forward on the open sea, unscrewing the top of the water bottle and taking a sip. It was Felix who came up the stairs, helping himself to a drink and turning up the music. She nervously tilted her head sideways, relieved to see the top of his bald head disappearing back down the stairs. As the yacht began to change direction, there was the heavy impact of something hitting the water. It was no ordinary splash.

As they got closer to port, Sergiu appeared and told the girls to get dressed and gather their things. Once they were moored up, he made sure they disembarked first, escorting the three of them onto the jetty, before turning back inside.

They strolled along the waterfront, this time only browsing in the shop windows. From the far side of the marina, Mihaela could see the yacht and the men preparing to leave. She counted the pilot, Sergiu, Felix and the boat owner but she did not see Stefan, the man with the tattoo she had been entertaining. She was far enough away but sure that Felix was staring directly at her. Even from behind his dark glasses, his gaze held, somehow singling her out from the crowd like a lame sheep amongst the flock. He commented to Sergiu and by one nod of his head in her direction, she knew they had seen her on the main deck, in the wrong place at the wrong time. A chill of fear passed through her. These were people who could make you suffer for their own pleasure and she couldn't trust Sergiu to make excuses for her. He would follow whatever instructions they gave him. For all the planning she had secretly been making, it was now impossible to wait any longer. She needed to run.

After she left Puerto Banus, Mihaela returned to the large villa she shared with the team of girls. The villa was sectioned into two halves. Each girl had a private room with a shared kitchen while the other half contained a high-end brothel with further bedrooms and a lounge. Mihaela worked under a different set of rules to the other girls whose job was parading in front of the men who called by, seated in the blue-lit lounge with their drinks viewing the girls one by one until they made their choice for their hour or two. As Sergiu´s preferred pet, he was more selective in whom she performed for, taking pleasure in lending her out as a favour to his special friends.

He commanded a higher price for her services. He paid her well, even continuing to lavish gifts on her and offered her a private apartment but she refused. Mihaela knew if she moved into a place of her own, he would take advantage to come and go as he pleased, so she told him as he was away so much it was better to have the company of the girls. Sergiu never came to the brothel. She went to his luxury apartment, a penthouse overlooking the beach on Marbella's Golden Mile.

Sergiu would summon her from time to time to suit his own needs. In the beginning, she had thought herself in love with him, now she hated him, despite the good money he gave her. He had complete control over her and the higher up he progressed in business, the more aggressive and arrogant he seemed to become. She knew how to service his ego and was smart in getting what she wanted. He had been using her more for hosting at private clubs or luxury villas along the coast where he could keep a close eye on her, trusting her to gather information on what she had heard or seen. Her work had become more like corporate entertaining with many hours spent just languishing by poolside listening in on conversations and teasing for snippets of dirt she could feedback to Sergiu. From her observations of these people she soon learned they did more business when they were relaxed after several drinks than they did behind the closed doors of a meeting room but she had grown tired of the games.

She had wanted out for a long time but the events on the yacht were a catalyst. She wanted her freedom back, to be rid of her controllers, to come and go as she pleased without being constantly answerable to Sergiu. It was no longer enough to have a wardrobe of designer clothes and access to Marbella's glamorous town. Now her escape had to be quick. If an order came from above that she was in any way a liability, it could only turn out badly for her. She would stand no chance unless she could get to safety fast and in secret.

She went through the motions of having dinner with the girls then let them know she was going out with friends in Marbella and did not know what time she would be back. They wouldn't think anything strange about this as the girls were entitled to two nights off a week and she was more independent than most. They were all gathered in the kitchen with "Madam" in their dressing gowns, doing their nails and chatting over coffee or on their laptops waiting for the bell to ring with prospective clients. She excused herself to get ready.

She had returned to her room and was packing when her mobile rang. She hesitated before answering. It was Sergiu. Be smart, she thought. They had arranged to meet that night for dinner. She dealt with it, promising she would be there then quickly returned to her packing leaving out much of the expensive garb from her wardrobe, taking more casual clothes and only a few of her designer label dresses. Her room needed to look like she was coming back. She could buy more once she got home.

She then packed all the jewellery that she thought she could sell if needed, except for one piece, a silver Edwardian Alpaca locket enamelled with a single pink rose set above the elaborately engraved initials "A" and "C." It was something she treasured, handed down from her German grandmother, from whom she had inherited her blue eyes. Her grandmother was called Ana and her grandfather was Claus. She fastened its delicate silver chain around her neck, taking care to pack the blue velvet box with its love letter written by her grandfather to her grandmother folded inside. Her mother always told her how much she resembled her grandmother. In her generation, her grandmother had been a free spirit. She loved to travel and dared to go against convention. Mihaela had never met her but somehow with the stories her mother told her she was an inspiration.

She placed the suitcases just outside the patio door leading to the garden and returned to say goodbye to the girls. No one was paying much attention. She was dressed for a night out, carrying just her handbag, her passport tucked safely inside. She passed through the door, retrieving her suitcases from outside, pressed the buzzer on the security gate and slid into the backseat of the taxi she had ordered.

From the villa, she headed for a private apartment, just East of Marbella, to a client she met two or three afternoons a week and who regarded her as his mistress. She had met him in a nightclub three months before and he was captivated by her. He knew little about her; he didn't need to and she was good at convincing him she worked in a beauty salon and was saving up to go to University. It was convenient for him, no strings and they could meet up at the apartment, just the two of them. He was generous to her and gave her good money which she kept in a safe in the bedroom. She liked him and more importantly, he was malleable, flattered by the attention she paid him. Jan the Swede couldn't get enough of her. If Sergiu ever found out, it would have meant serious trouble as it was against the rules to have a private client but up until now, she had managed to keep the liaison secret. It gave her some satisfaction to think she could get away with something behind his back and extra finances to see her way out.

She stripped out of her Marbella party dress and put on white jeans and a low-cut top. She began to prepare herself for the call she was about to make to Jan on the mobile he had given her. Working up false tears she pressed the speed dial. He listened to her distressed voice telling him how she had to go home at short notice because her grandmother was dying.

He came straight to the apartment to see her, gave her cash without question and then left on the promise she would return, which she had no intention of doing. She had money stashed and with what he had given her now she had nearly three thousand Euros, more than enough to get home.

She went to the local store and bought hair dye. On her return, she used the same mobile Jan had given her and dialled the police headquarters in Bucharest. She gave no name, speaking to whoever picked up the phone and left a cryptic message, to be delivered immediately to Razvan Ionescu, the one policeman she could trust. She could not risk being anything other than an anonymous informer. Only he would understand her message. He called her straight back. They hadn't spoken in a long time and she didn't have much time now. Instinct told her Razvan knew what she did for a living and she had avoided contact with him up until now when she needed him.

She told him what she had seen. He had to help her! She knew he was working his way up the ladder in the Romanian police force and she could trust him. He was her brother, after all. Surely what she could tell him would be useful? At first, he told her not to panic, to act as normally as she could, that he needed time to arrange things. He couldn't just have her turning up like that but she insisted she didn't have time, she was coming home! She pleaded with him and in the end; he gave her strict instructions, buying himself some time.

She then took the scissors to her hair carefully disposing of the strands of blonde that fell around the bathroom and the bottles of hair dye that had given her a new look. Her own mobile rang, startling her. She had to answer, as Sergiu's number appeared ominously on the screen. He would not be at all happy to be kept waiting. She should have been the one waiting for him. She pulled off the best deception she could think of then smashed both Jan's mobile and her own with a cocktail ice pick from the kitchen. She added the remnants to the garbage bag with the hair dye and dropped them in the communal bins as she headed to the local taxi rank. The taxi to the airport couldn't go fast enough for her.

2

Poison Apple

Sergiu had been last to leave the yacht. The words Felix had whispered in his ear regarding Mihaela were penetrating his thoughts like a larva that had infected his eardrum. It had been a simple request that he needed to reign in his girlfriend. No woman could be trusted and with informants everywhere prying into their business, it was up to him to get rid of any bad apples. 'Deal with her,' Felix had told him. Sergiu knew what that meant. Business was becoming more difficult and this was a test of his loyalty. He had a reputation to maintain and most importantly bosses who expected him to deliver. He had something to prove. Perhaps he had kept her too long. He could not afford to make any mistakes, or his bosses would make him pay in the same way he dealt with inconveniences.

He called Mihaela's mobile just before he disembarked, sounding calm and sticking to the plan they had already discussed, that they would meet for dinner. He instructed her to wear the cute tight-fitting red leather dress she had bought earlier in the day as he planned to peel it off her later. He had cause to celebrate and he wanted her looking sexy. She told him she would be there, the lady in red. He made a very unfunny parting comment, meant to tease her that what he had in store for her required no lady.

The plan was to meet at Buddha Beach in Puerto Banus. Newly opened, it was the hottest beach club on the coast. Sergiu had taken his time showering and getting changed formulating a plan to dispose of the Red Delicious. She would soon be apple sauce.

He planned to spike her favourite cocktail and get his driver to take her further down the coast to a lock-up where he would arrange for her to be sold off to the highest bidder, one that wouldn't treat her as well as he did and one who would probably make her life not worth living. No one would find her. Mihaela the beauty queen, the shopaholic, would be sent to the trash like something past its sell-by date.

He had his driver collect him, dropping him off at the front entrance of the club which was already full of party-goers rocking to the sounds of a top guest DJ. Cocktails flowed and the waiters were practically running from table to table. He took his time making his way over to the space reserved for him. He shook hands and passed some social comments to a few people he knew on the way to his table which was just far enough away from the main crowd to enjoy the show but not to be overlooked.

He had expected Mihaela to be seated there, poised for his appearance but there was no sign of her. Maybe she was in the powder room. He looked at his watch then ordered some drinks. He was growing impatient. He called her mobile again. After several rings, she picked up. 'Where the fuck are you? I'm sitting here with an expensive cocktail for you and the ice is melting!' he barked over the loud music.

She sounded upset. 'I'm so sorry Sergiu, I was on the way but I was sick in the taxi. I threw up twice. I think I ate some bad fish or something, the boat made me queasy and I started my period too! I had to turn round to get changed again. I'll get there as soon as I can.'

Sergiu was boiling over inside. He had wanted to conclude business for the day as quickly as possible and now she was messing him around. She would know she was in trouble and therefore she was avoiding him. He'd already spotted a pretty girl eyeing him up. He wasn't going to allow Mihaela to spoil a good evening and he needed to release some of his frustration on someone who would happily unzip his trousers for him. Let her stew a little longer he thought, best to play it cool, not to startle her. Mihaela was used to him protecting her. Let her think things might go back to normal, he could play games too. He would get to her tomorrow. He smoothed the way.

'It's not like you Mihaela to let me down like this. Go to bed. We will meet tomorrow instead. I will have my driver pick you up. You can come to breakfast at my place, just the two of us. Maybe then shopping if that will make you feel better. Be ready at ten in the morning.'

'I'm sorry, Sergiu. It would be no fun for you when I am feeling like this. I will see you tomorrow and I promise I will make it up to you!' she whimpered. He could hardly hear her over the music, hanging up before she had even finished talking and signalling for the girl he had seen to join him.

The following morning he was up early, keeping the same routine he always did, with a two-hour workout in Macklin's boxing gym in Marbella at seven in the morning followed by a cold shower and a breakfast of steak and eggs. He assumed Michaela would be joining him.

At 9.45 his driver called him. Mihaela was not at the villa. Madam had gone to check her room. Maybe she had overslept. After all, she had said she was going out the night before. There were still clothes lying around the room and makeup on the dresser. She didn't think it was so unusual if Mihaela had stayed over somewhere else. She reported this to the driver who then informed Sergiu and alarm bells started going off in his head. He tried Mihaela's mobile. No reply. She had gone out and she had lied to him. He called Madam demanding to know where she had gone.

'She didn't say, just that she was going to Marbella. Try Helena. She often meets up with her,' she had answered truthfully. Sergiu immediately pressed hang-up and dialled Helena. She was one of the girls he had selected to come on the yacht along with her roommate, Celeste. He needed to stay calm. Helena answered and he asked as casually as he could if Mihaela happened to be with her. Helena replied that she hadn't seen her since they left the yacht.

'That's a shame,' he said. 'I have a very lucrative job lined up and I have been trying to get hold of her. I believe she went to Marbella last night but she isn't picking up her phone. I need two girls now. Have you any idea where she might be?'

Celeste had been listening in enough to realise there was a chance for her to take advantage of the fact that Mihaela wasn't available. She had no loyalty to her, shortchanged continuously for work over those sickening blue eyes. She seized the opportunity. She grabbed the phone from Helena.

'I can be there, Sergiu. As for Mihaela, I have no idea. We went to Olivia Valere last night. It's a favourite of ours but she didn't go last night. You should also know I think she is seeing someone. Maybe she is with him. I have seen her leave there a couple of times with him, a Swedish man, I think he is called Jan.'

Celeste was satisfied she had set a cat among the pigeons but when she asked where and when she and Helena should meet for the job he had Sergiu just hung up.

Time was moving on. He was due to meet his bosses that afternoon and Felix was sure to be asking questions. He made some more calls and by midday, he was on his way to an address of a villa in Nueva Andalucía. Driven by total anger, he needed to take direct action. Could this Jan be harbouring her?

3

Gate Crasher

His driver pulled up outside a large white Andalusian styled villa surrounded by tall walls heightened by masses of pink overhanging Bougainvillea. He told his driver to wait and went to the gate entrance. There was a party going on as he could hear pop music and the voices of a happy crowd along with the smell of a barbeque. To his surprise, the gate just buzzed open. Perhaps they were expecting more guests. He strolled in through the open front door, making his way to the terraces that overlooked the Los Naranjos Golf club.

He had walked in on a children's birthday party with girlie Disney balloons festooned around the garden. The heated pool was full of noisy children with parents milling around, some with plates of food and drink in their hands, or idling poolside keeping watch over their offspring. A woman approached

Sergiu, the hostess he assumed. She looked like a typical Princess, probably never done a day's work in her life while her wanker banker husband brought in the money. Sergiu had already found out that Jan was married with two children and manager of a portfolio of high-end clients of a Swiss Bank.

Princess appeared unsteady, spilling her drink from the fluted glass she was carrying. She had the customary straightened blonde hair with good skin for her age. Sergiu thought she was probably in her mid-forties and dressed like most Scandi women he had met, in white linen with some tasteless forged metalwork around her neck and gold flat sandals on her feet.

'Good afternoon, Can I help you? Do I know you?' she asked innocently, smiling at the formally dressed man before her.

Always such nauseatingly polite and boring people thought Sergiu to himself.

'I'm so sorry to intrude,' he replied. I was looking for your husband. His office told me he was at home today and I tried to call him but there was no answer. I have urgent business regarding one of his clients. Therefore, I came directly.'

'Oh, I see. Most unusual! It must be important. What did you say your name was?'

'Carl. Please, I promise not to take up too much of his time. I can see you are in the middle of an enjoyable party but this is a matter that must be dealt with as soon as possible,' said Sergiu.

The Princess nodded. Her husband's business was his business though it was annoying someone would call at her house uninvited. She looked across to Jan busy in conversation with two others as he tended the barbeque. She thought how good looking he was, even when wearing an apron printed with Disney Aladdin motifs and flipping hamburgers.

'Jan, someone to see you!' she shouted.

He raised a glass of beer and signalled for them to come over but Sergiu stood where he was. Jan handed a spatula to a friend and removed his apron, making his way over. He was waiting for an introduction from his wife, not recognising the large man that stood before him.

'Sorry, what did you say your name was?' Princess giggled.

'Carl,' repeated Sergiu fixing his eyes on Jan.

Jan extended his hand out in greeting.

'Pleased to meet you. Now what can I do for you?' he asked.

Sergiu returned the handshake, not too hard. 'I'm sorry to interrupt your party but I had no choice. I am representing one of your main clients and need to speak to you urgently on his behalf. Is there somewhere private we can go?'

'Of course,' replied Jan wondering what could be wrong and more specifically, what this man with an Eastern European accent wanted from him. He took his mobile from his pocket and noted he had not received any missed calls from the main office warning him someone was coming. He placed it back in his pocket and led Sergiu to his office inside the villa.

Rows of bookshelves full of travel volumes and classic novels surrounded the walls, all too neatly arranged to think they would ever be read. The blinds were drawn against a window in front of which was placed a minimalist white desk, no papers, just a phone and pictures of the happy wife and children.

Sergiu didn't waste any time. As soon as the door closed and before he could even offer him a seat, Jan found himself grasped from behind, one large hand over his nose and mouth and another with a vice-like grip around his testicles. The pain was excruciating and Jan was left powerless to struggle, his cries suffocated.

'Listen you Skitstövel,' growled Sergiu in a low voice, using the one Swedish word he understood that translated as motherfucker. 'You are in deep shit. It seems my girlfriend has been entertaining you regularly and I am not happy to learn this and neither will your wife. You disgust me with your nice villa, loyal wife and sweet children and yet you feel the need to poke someone else's woman from the comfort of a little love nest. Now here's the thing. My girlfriend isn't taking my calls and I think you might have some answers.' Sergiu twisted Jan's balls even harder. Then he let go. Jan crumpled onto the floor, rolling around the white fur carpet trying to breathe, holding his privates in torment. Sergiu kneeled over him. 'So, what can you tell me? Did you see her last night?'

Jan hardly had a voice. He knew straight away Carl was asking about Mihaela, there was no point in pleading ignorance. He could only nod, yes. Sergiu demanded to know how long the affair had been going on. What could Mihaela possibly see in a wooden top like him, except to use him for money?

Jan drew himself onto all fours, like a scolded cat.

'About three months. I'm sorry I didn't know she had a boyfriend. She told me she loved me, no strings, she just wanted someone to treat her nice. It suited me. She was always saying how she wanted to improve her life, get a real job, go back to studying and learn to drive. I was helping her.'

Sergiu started laughing. 'Helping her? For God's sake, she's a whore! You seriously fell for that crap? She has played you for a fool I can tell you. That girl only studies shopping channels and how to milk spineless men like you!'

Jan was trying to stand up. Sergiu changed tack, playing him for a fellow victim. 'I'm sorry she has played us both for fools. Do you know where I can find her?' He said, pulling Jan to his feet.

'I met her last night, at my apartment. She was upset. She told me she was going home, to Bucharest. Her grandmother was dying. I gave her money because she said she didn't have enough and wasn't sure how long she would be away. She was going to stay at the apartment and leave in the morning for the airport. I didn't stay with her. I needed to get home.'

'Her grandmother is dead! Did she say which flight she was catching?' demanded Sergiu.

Jan shook his head in a no. 'I have been a fool, haven't I,' he said, standing up fully. 'I will try and call her. I gave her a phone.' He moved to his desk and took out a mobile from the drawer and dialled. There was no reply, not even a voicemail. Sergiu knew she would have ditched the phone. The last thing she would have wanted were messages from a doomed lover.

Sergiu was losing precious time again. He needed

to bring the meeting to a close, no need to be polite, at which point he threw a right-hand jab straight at Jan's nose. Jan reeled backwards, feeling his shattered nose and the warm fountain of blood that followed. Sergiu then marched him by the collar of his Hugo Boss polo shirt and pushed him straight into the pool. The party stopped. Music was playing but the audience's attention had turned to the water now turning crimson as Jan floated up to the surface.

'Your husband is a cheat and a liar,' Sergiu shouted for all to hear. 'He's been shagging my girlfriend for three months behind your back,' he continued, staring at the Princess. 'I suggest you call a good divorce lawyer,' and he turned and walked out leaving the guests to extract their screaming children from the bloodied water whilst the Princess stood among the shattered shards of her Prosecco glass, her mouth gaping open in shock like a displaced fish.

Sergiu was already on his phone when he got in the waiting car. He called in his spies in Bucharest to watch the airport for the arrival of one major blonde bitch coming in from Malaga. Now he had to face his bosses. He had to buy some time. He would say he had it under control and that he was dealing with it personally. He would divert their attention to more pressing matters, especially the recent moves by police to shut down their operations on a local level. Mihaela wouldn't be highest on their list of priorities. He gave Mihaela no credit for intelligence. She would be retreating to her family, he was sure. He just needed to get to her and he had plenty of reliable contacts.

His patience reached breaking point when days

later, there was still no trace of her. Somehow, they had missed her arrival in Băneasa airport but then they wouldn't have known to be watching for a brunette coming in via Manchester, Amsterdam and Berlin. He had people watching her family house but there was no sign of her. Sergiu was wondering if she had gone to Bucharest after all. She could even have lied about that to Jan, or maybe Jan had lied. He didn't think so but he should have ripped his testicles off anyway and he planned to do even worse to Mihaela when he caught up with her.

4

Chameleon

Mihaela bore no resemblance to the glamorous girl she had bid farewell to in the bathroom mirror two days before. She had disembarked from the plane at Băneasa Airport in Bucharest and made her way to baggage claim keeping her eyes hidden behind a plain pair of cheap tinted glasses. Her hair was cut to a length just below her chin and was the colour of autumn brown. She wore dark denim jeans, worn converse pumps and a black leather jacket, the antique locket hidden beneath her cream blouse.

It had taken only thirty minutes to arrive at Malaga airport where she paid cash for an airfare, running to check in her bags before the gate closed for the flight to Manchester. Razvan had told her the connections and to pay for a ticket in cash at each arrival. With three flights over two days, she finally arrived. She had given no thought to the position she must have put her brother in, only caring that she reached home. It had been a dramatic and impulsive move.

She passed through customs and passport control without any delay. Her passport photo resembled her more when she had left Romania four years ago at the age of seventeen compared to how she looked when she was living in Spain. She headed for the left luggage lockers, depositing her suitcases as Razvan had instructed before making her way through the terminal to the taxi rank. She had thought she was coming home and there would be someone to meet her at the airport but Razvan had told her this wasn't possible. He would take care of her but she needed to stick to his plan.

The taxi ride was brief, heading for the Băneasa Shopping City that had just opened its doors in April. So much had changed in the landscape with new developments and faster roads. It felt unfamiliar. She had butterflies in her stomach and wrung her hands in nervous anticipation. She was feeling alone and just wanted to get to her brother. She avoided the glances in the mirror from the taxi driver who was trying to strike up some polite conversation with his passenger. She wished he wouldn't bother and just returned his interest with simple responses.

She was thinking about her parents. She had been rehearsing a reunion in her head since boarding the plane from Malaga wondering what she would say to them after so long and why she had returned home. There would be more lies. She had telephoned her parents from time to time but the calls were short. She had nothing in common anymore with their life in

Bucharest and was selective in what she shared with them about her life in Spain. She had grown further and further apart from them, especially her mother. As a child, her mother had indulged her, cherishing the little girl that would grow up to have a bright future with all the things she had been denied growing up under communist rule.

Mihaela was barely two years old when finally, the Ceausescu regime was brought down in 1989 with a people´s revolution. December 21st, Bucharest was a much bleaker place, the air filled with soot and murky from the burning of soft coal in the winter. There was little on offer in the shops except for Chinese canned sardines and cabbage with very little sign of meat, fresh fruit or vegetables and yet Ceausescu stood on the terraces of the People´s Palace in front of what was to become Revolution Square and gave his speech on what a great harvest there had been, what excellent relations Romania had with the rest of the world and how he would keep Romania safe from backward trends that were like a disease infecting other countries and might spread to Romania. He wanted to chastise the recent participants in riots that had broken out in Timisoara. Of course, there were no official statements or broadcasts following the protest on December 16th in Timisoara. They say the military and Securitatea killed hundreds of people and by word of mouth, news spread to the capital.

As Mihaela´s parents stood in the square they had joined in the booing and chants from the angry crowds that forced a shocked Ceausescu to retreat inside, his propaganda irrelevant and treacherous to the population. They actively joined the mass riots that followed. They had experienced the chaos, the gunfire, watched the blood of friends and colleagues soaking into the roads and pavements, unsure who was shooting at whom and from where.

Ceausescu and his wife were forced to flee. Unable to escape, they faced a hasty trial and within an hour, were executed by shooting. It was Christmas day. The death penalty was abolished in Romania shortly after.

Mihaela would have no recollection of the bloodied and terrible times that surrounded this. Her parents never spoke of it. She had grown up ignorant of the people who had suffered during his time and continued to endure the consequences of change, the un-seen poverty and deprivation. She was part of a new generation fortunate to be on the right road to progress. Her parents were both respected teachers and for them, education was the passport to the future.

During her years growing up, Romania fast-tracked into industries like IT, engineering and medicine. Her two older brothers had done well living up to everything their parents had fought for. They assumed she would follow in their footsteps studying towards a career but Mihaela was rebellious believing there was more to life than working hard at school. She had a taste for the bright lights and the new material world on offer. She had been spoiled, used to attention with her stunning looks and doting brothers. Her mother battled with her teenage moods and finally turned to her eldest brother, Razvan, to take her under his wing.

At seventeen, she moved in with Razvan, his wife and baby son. They found her part-time work as a waitress in one of the fashionable cafés in the old town. She loved the city, known as 'Little Paris' with its wide boulevards and mix of old and new architecture. She could continue with her studies close to where they were living and they could keep a close eye on her. She seemed happier and settled but within three months their great plans were fractured, on the day Sergiu walked into the café.

The taxi drew up outside the mall with its impressive glass façade leading inside to avenues lined with white floors, full-sized trees and fountains. Michaela was not impressed by these features. She was used to the famous brands and big-name stores. For Bucharest, they represented a new era, a burgeoning market in a country that had been clawing its way back to European economic recognition after twenty-four years strangled in the talons of a dictatorship.

She followed the signs to the food hall, pausing a little distance away from the Burger King restaurant, the first to be opened in Romania. She had not seen her older brother Razvan in four years and wondered how easily she would recognise him; there had just been a few photographs. She took in the faces seated at the tables tucking into their fast food but she could not make him out from the crowd. Unknowingly, he was already observing her from a distance. Finding an empty table, she took up a seat and checked her watch. It was six o'clock in the evening and she was tired of travelling and the plans formed previously. Maybe she was early. The taxi from the airport had only taken a few minutes after all.

A hand on her shoulder and a voice she recognised

immediately brought her out of her thoughts. Razvan gently spoke her name and sat down opposite her so as not to startle her. He was six years older than her. He looked larger now with broad shoulders, a man with three children she didn´t know and a successful career.

Razvan had two paper bags of food and two coffees. He slid over one of each for her and was smiling like they were new acquaintances. She felt a little disconcerted. She had pictured in her mind a happy reunion where she would put her arms around him and confess all her sins. He would understand and forgive her, just like he used to when she played up but it couldn't be that way.

Razvan had trained his way up the police ranks and now a career ahead of him working with the Romanian Intelligence Service. She was his only sister but she was also part of the underground world he was working to cleanse. She would have no idea, at such short notice, of the lengths he had gone to, to try and protect her.

'Well, my little one, good to see you and how was your journey?' he asked.

'Long, with many changes,' she replied, sensing he was not just asking about her journey of three flights across two different countries.

Their conversation was polite as they ate, talking about the weather and the new mall. As they finished their food Razvan casually passed her a serviette, indicating there was a drop of ketchup on her chin. She felt the envelope hidden in the folds and slipped it into her handbag, removing the left luggage key she had from the airport and sliding it discreetly towards him. Razvan stood up.

'Give my regards to your brother when you see him,' he said wryly and patting her hand lifted the key unnoticed before he disappeared into the crowd.

Mihaela sat for a few moments finishing the last of her coffee then headed for the large department store Peek and Cloppenburg. As a distraction, she took her time purchasing some extra clothes before making her way to the restrooms. Razvan had told her on the phone to move freely and not leave anywhere in a hurry and not to follow him.

As it was, she could still be just like any other visitor until they could get her to a safe place. Once in the toilet cubicle, she opened the envelope which contained a small piece of paper with an address she did not recognise. She was to make her way to the northern part of the city again by taxi. It would take around thirty minutes. She was anxious knowing by now her presence would be missed back in Marbella. The trail would be alight. She had no choice but to put her trust in her brother and she had no idea what was ahead of her.

5

The Interview

The taxi drew up outside a smart new apartment block, built over four floors and set on streets lined with trees and manicured garden entrances. It was a quiet residential street. Most people would be behind closed doors out of the cold and dark end of the evening. She paid the taxi driver, waiting until he pulled away and made her way to the entrance gate punching in a key code. There was a click and the gate opened. From the elevator, she made her way up to apartment 3C and rang the bell. The door opened almost immediately. Mihaela was glad to step inside to what she hoped would be some sanctuary. Razvan closed the door behind her, guiding her through to the living room.

'Is this your apartment?' Mihaela enquired looking around the modern furnished space.

'No, it belongs to the police. We use it for various reasons, including for people in your situation.'

'Is this where I will be staying?' she ventured. The apartment seemed surprisingly homely.

She began to explore the rest of the two-bedroom apartment, thinking how much closer she would be to her parents and her family, how they would all protect her, how pleased they would be she had come home.

'Only for tonight, Mihaela, you have no idea how difficult it was for me to arrange this without warning. For me to take care of you, I have had to be careful. No one can know you are back. It is because you are my sister that I have been working hard to pull some strings and ask favours. My superior will come shortly. I trust him and he has agreed to help in exchange for the things you can tell us. I don't want you to be involved in this but I have convinced him you can be useful to us. There is an in-depth investigation going on, some of which includes your people in Marbella.

He seemed so clinical with his statement only minutes after opening the door to her.

'Please don't refer to them as my people, Razvan. I want nothing more now than to leave all that behind me,' she replied with some abruptness.

Razvan looked into her blue eyes. She was still the same little sister, oblivious to how her behaviour affected those around her, always willful, thinking everyone would dance to her tune but the reality was very different. He loved her and any judgment of her, he felt, was overruled by the need to protect her, to get her on a sensible path again for his parents' sake.

He sat down next to her on the sofa taking her hand, the first real sign of affection he had been able to show his only sister. He hated what she had done, leaving them all the way she did, with just a note. She had been so carefree growing up, always the light of their household but full of mischief too. She knew how to taunt her older brothers and get away with it. He loved her for her charm and spirit. His parents had no influence or control over her. They were always of the belief that she would settle eventually so long as they were all there to guide her. If asked by friends, her mother would say their daughter was running a beauty business in Spain. She was so busy she didn't have time to come home, sending pictures of sun-kissed beaches and groups of her friends together in fancy restaurants wearing expensive clothes.

'I understand what happened to you, Mihaela,' said Razvan. 'It's an easy thing for certain types of men to persuade young girls like you to trade in their ordinary lives for a dream. That is their business. I know they did not force you. You left by your own free will but you were seduced, then brainwashed, like so many. I was angry after you left, frustrated with myself for being powerless to stop it. It's not like you came from a poor home or had no one to support you.'

Mihaela, the victim, nodded, as tears began falling from her cheeks. She leaned her head against Razvans' shoulder.

'It was like a dream in the beginning. Sergiu was different. From the moment he entered the café, I felt drawn to him. He was a man, not a boy. He seemed to be important the way he spoke to people and I could see he had money by the way he dressed. He paid me a lot of attention and I started to look forward to him coming into the café each day for his coffee. He always gave me a big tip! I was flattered when he started to take me out to dinner and different clubs. He treated me like a grown-up. Over the weeks he convinced me I could be something more, a model perhaps, that he had contacts and I believed him. We became lovers and I thought I was the only girl in the world for him. How crazy that seems now.'

She sat up staring into an invisible world she thought Razvan could not possibly fully understand.

'I'm sorry for all the lies,' she continued. 'For all the things I didn't tell you. I wanted to follow that dream and I knew you would stop me. I was selfish but I learned to look after myself. I learned to make it work for me even though I wasn't making the decisions anymore. Once you are on that path, you feel you cannot turn back. It's like being in a forest that grows forever about you; the branches become strong hands, twisting and thickening, so you only see what they want you to see.' She emphasised her words, curling her fingers, reaching out and seeming to pull at imaginary roots.

'Listen Mihaela, said Razvan, bringing her back to reality. 'You could have stayed in Spain and done nothing about what you saw. But I think you are scared and had reason to run and it took courage to do that. The problem is now you have created a risk, to yourself and our family. You have lit a fire on the edge of that forest and the flames will fan a smoke of mistrust on those you have left behind. I will do what

I can to keep you safe but promise me that you will do whatever I say. I will help you make a fresh start somewhere else but you must on no account make contact with anyone from your past life or speak about the life you have left behind. Not even mother or father, though I know that will be the hardest thing. The first place these people will look for you is through your own family, so they must know nothing do you understand? Things are happening. There are others, women who were trafficked against their will, not chasing a dream, like you, being persuaded to come forward but we need all the evidence we can get and it takes time. There is still so much corruption and these organised crime groups think nothing of the law. They have contacts at every source and many prosecutors fear for their lives just trying to bring justice.'

He looked at his watch and right on cue, the doorbell rang. Mihaela was not sure what to expect when Razvan´s superior walked into the room. He was considerably smaller than her five feet eight inches, wearing a long heavy coat which seemed to shorten him further. He had a head of thick black hair, slicked back with gel and a pointed, narrow nose supporting thick black-framed glasses over small beady eyes. He removed his coat under which he wore a full dark suit and tie. She immediately sensed his business-like approach and more than that, despite her brother's good reputation, she had the feeling he viewed her as a second-class citizen. It was true. The man had no interest in whose sister she was. Any information she could give him to add evidence and help to rid his country of the vermin that discredited it worldwide would be helpful and maybe she would turn out to be bait for the bigger fish. It was the real reason he was here and why he had agreed to Razvan's request to look after her.

He placed his leather-bound briefcase on the coffee table and took up position on a hard chair opposite to the sofa where Mihaela was sitting. Without even looking up, he addressed her brother.

'Razvan, would you bring me strong black coffee, no sugar.'

He merely nodded to Mihaela as he took up his seat and now sat sizing her up and down. It was in no way a flirtatious study, more of a cold examination. Mihaela was not used to this type of reaction but then she was no longer the blonde in Marbella. She was now just an exhausted and fragile girl. Perhaps she was not what the Superior expected either. Razvan disappeared into the kitchen to make coffee. There was no introduction. The man opened his briefcase and took out various folders and envelopes which he arranged in an orderly fashion on the coffee table.

Over the next two hours and several cups of black coffee, he systematically went through the files. There were numerous photographs. He wanted only the briefest of answers to his questions. If Michaela elaborated, he chose to put up his hand to dismiss information that was of no use to him. He would question her for specific names, dates and places.

Mihaela found herself reliving those early days and what events had led her to this point in time. When she had left Romania four years ago, she and Sergiu had first travelled to Germany. Once there they had rented a small apartment near Berlin. He had lavished attention on her, introducing her to the cafes and nightlife in the city. As his lover, he taught her everything she should know about how to please a man, introducing her to games and toys only she imagined were exclusive to them. He regularly took cocaine but always refused her curiosity to try, saying it would damage not only her brain but her beautiful looks too. He had seen others ruin their chances of success and he did not want to see her waste her potential in the same way. She liked the protected status he gave her.

During the days when he went out, on business, she shopped, open to new styles and spending all the cash he gave her on things to please him. It was Sergiu who suggested she go blonde. She wore makeup every day and heeled shoes or boots rather than her flat boots from home. Always he promised her the right connections and flattered her constantly. If she continued to follow his advice, he would genuinely take her places. She was eager to please and so the first time he suggested she should leave a club with a different man other than him she convinced herself this person would be one of those good connections to open doors for her. It seemed to excite Sergiu.

It became a pattern and each time she spent in another man's apartment or hotel, Sergiu would collect her. She stopped questioning him with time. After all, he told her he loved her and he took good care of her. She felt she had left the girl behind guarded by parents and was making her own destiny and she liked it.

Finally, after four months in Germany, they

travelled to Spain. They stopped in Madrid for a couple of days. It had been an exciting time exploring the city, just the two of them together. She never questioned how he earned his living and was contented to continue to spend the notes he gave her. But in the evening when they left Madrid she got some glimpse of the other world that occupied his time. They stopped at a gipsy camp just on the outskirts of the city with its sprawling shamble of makeshift homes, a mix of concrete and corrugated iron clinging to the landscape without order.

Grubby faced children were running around amidst the rubbish and roaming dogs. Older women sat in clusters by open campfires and young girls, no more than teenagers gathered in groups listening to music, smoking and drinking in the warm Spanish night air. Their clothes lacked any style except to make them appear older than their years.

Mihaela watched from their Mercedes car as Sergiu made his way over to a larger band of men. They seemed to be celebrating. There was a lot of talking, slapping on the back and shaking of hands and cash changed hands. Eventually, he returned with two extra passengers. Both girls, who looked no older than thirteen, climbed into the back seats of the car. They were excited and incessantly chattering as they drove away; waving as they left the camp behind them. Mihaela had no idea what had transpired. She had never mixed with these types of people. Hers was a very middle-class background with southern roots. These were gipsy people, Roma, whose origins could be traced back to northern India a thousand years ago but who had dispersed throughout central, eastern and southern Europe. They were an alien culture to her. Even those born in her own home country, many considered were not Romanian and suffered heavy discrimination.

Mihaela was sure she was on a different level to these girls. She chose not to involve herself in their coarse conversations. She would learn later that their parents had sold them into marriage. As young children they were brought up to thieve and would work the streets of Madrid, loitering by cash machines in groups of two or three, distracting the bank customer, to pick their pockets or brazenly snatch their cash. The police were virtually powerless to detain them. As minors, they would reappear on the streets unaffected by any warnings.

For these young people, prospects were few. Being sold at a young age into marriage was a step forward and an accepted part of their culture. They might be excited by the prospect of leaving the camp but men and a hierarchy would always control their lives. It probably would not expand much beyond a lifetime of petty theft, begging or childbearing, within an order going back centuries. If they were lucky, they would make some money and be content within their own culture.

Sergiu's interest could only be that these people were just another resource, a recruiting ground that fed into a self-perpetuating system; the winners were the dealers and gang leaders who were accumulating wealth back in Romania, establishing elite neighbourhoods by building huge elaborate houses, each trying to outdo the other, flaunting their success and wealth.

Mihaela was just another example of human trafficking that would be feeding into the same system though she wouldn´t see it that way. These two young girls were born into it and would never aspire to anything. Michaela thought herself educated and she was hungry for the material things in life. She was easily dazzled by the prospect of the lifestyle Sergiu promised.

Once they moved down to the Costa Del Sol Mihaela was just carried along with the current. She savoured the lifestyle enjoying the money she had, the shopping, the parties and the excitement of life on the Mediterranean. She hardly gave a second thought to those she left behind. Sergiu treated her differently to the other girls, she was his property but after a while, his demands and constant checks began to annoy her. The novelty began to wear off. He saw other girls, at first she was jealous and then she was glad it was somebody else, not her. She still toed the line; he had a temper and increasingly she became aware that beyond his pride, she meant little else to him. She had seen other girls take refuge in drugs or drink. She thought herself smarter than that and she needed to stay at the top. If you didn't, you were ruined, or handed over to be managed by a lesser mob. She had a talent for teasing and making men feel good. However, she hadn't expected to find herself so close to the precipice as on the day she boarded the yacht.

Her account finished with the description of that day. Of particular interest to the Superior was the identification of tattoos and names she could associate with the events on the yacht. Already it seemed a million miles away from where she was now.

Razvan remained quiet during the interview. In conclusion, the Superior thanked him formally for his time, gathered up his papers, thick coat and left.

Mihaela was feeling drained. Razvan poured them each a large brandy, about to say something when the doorbell rang again. She sank back into the sofa and closed her eyes as Razvan went to answer. Someone was dropping off her cases collected from the airport. They were alone once more. Razvan could speak now.

'The men you were with on the yacht, Mihaela, are all part of a big organisation we have under surveillance. The one you identified as Felix is a key player. You did well. Stephan, the man who unfortunately did not get off the yacht, was a rat and they rumbled him.'

'Who was he?' she asked curiously.

'He was once a promising university student back in 2003 but like many young Romanians back then he was frustrated with the lack of opportunities and job prospects. He was as you might describe him, an internet geek and because of the people he mixed with back then saw he could make big money. He was one of the first to get involved in setting up something called 'phishing.' Three years ago, in 2005, there was a report to the FBI in Connecticut, America, which alerted the authorities to emails being sent to people asking them to click on a web link. It would say that their bank account was locked and to unlock it they should click on a web link. If the person did this, it opened a page that appeared to originate from a bank called People's Bank. Any personal information or financial information given could then be sent back to individuals in Romania or to a 'collector' account, which was an email account used to amass all the information. Crimes like this use technology that makes it a global problem. Part of what I am involved in now in my work is improving cooperation between authorities like the SRI, the FBI, Scotland Yard and various European Police agencies. Spain was to be a big earner for these people, along with other crime rackets like drug smuggling and human trafficking. This man bit off more than he could chew as although he was very successful; he was becoming greedy. He mixed with dangerous people who had little regard for anyone but themselves. We caught up with him and persuaded him to work for us.'

Mihaela was even more curious. 'Why did he suddenly start to help you?'

'The tattoo you identified on his chest, the one that shared your name was not his wife's name. It was the name of his sister. She was found about two months ago in a garbage container in some Spanish village. She had been raped and murdered. They say she was on drugs but it was all the same people involved, they had sent him a message not to mess with them. She was his only family.'

There could be nothing else to talk about following Razvan's explanation. The brandy had served its purpose like an aesthetic, helping to dull the impact of his words. By now, Mihaela was too tired to take in any more. Her way of life in the last few years had been influenced by material things, money, good times and a life in the sun, with no connection or thought given to those caught in such a cancerous web.

She would do whatever Razvan asked of her. She

did not want to jeopardise the one chance she had of freedom. He warned her of the shadows that would find her if the rules were ignored. So far, she was just glad to have made it home.

6

Becoming Ana

Mihaela could have slept longer. She felt safe with her brother there and comfortable in the bed she had fallen into the night before. Razvan pulled back the curtains. Dawn was breaking gaining light with the promise of a blue sky to come. He was dressed casually in jeans and a sweatshirt, resembling more of her brother than the policeman he had become.

'Come on, Mihaela. We have things to go through and not much time before you leave.'

She showered and dressed, choosing to wear blue denim jeans and a comfortable Nike sweatshirt. She repacked her case and went to join her brother at the small breakfast table. He had boiled some eggs and put out a plate of different breads, jam and hot coffee. She was ravenous and ate without interrupting his briefing.

'In exchange for your cooperation, my Superior has arranged a contact. The man is a lawyer here in Romania. He has worked with us closely on many legal issues and our work with other organisations. His name is Andrei. You can trust him completely. He has arranged for you to stay with friends of his who run a small hotel. You will have work and a place to live, you are lucky he could do this for you.'

'Where?' she asked as she licked the jam from her fingertips.

Razvan handed her a serviette. 'It is a mountain area near Brasov.'

'Brasov? Mountains? That´s in the middle of nowhere! It´s miles away! I won´t know anyone!' she protested.

'Precisely, It´s for the best until this thing has run its course.'

'How long will I be there? I want to come home and be with you and mama and tata!'

Mihaela once again was sounding like the little sister he used to know who pouted and stamped her feet when she didn´t get her way. Razvan was finding it annoying, after all the trouble he had taken.

'Mihaela, you have to appreciate that you can´t just come home and drop into a job. Your resume´ wouldn´t look very impressive to most legal employers!'

Razvan realised how hurtful he must have sounded but she needed telling.

'Listen to me. You coming back means other people are involved and that opens up more risks. Think of them! You cannot stay here where you are known and who knows you might decide you like it in this new place if you try and make it work. It is a new start for you and I have pushed to help you. If you want to go back to what you were doing, be my guest but do as I say and you have at least a chance to choose!'

It was enough to silence her and he was able to continue with his instructions. He took her passport from her and gave her a new one. He told her from now on she was Ana, taken from her middle name and not to give away any details about exactly where she was from or anything that might give some link to Spain or her family in Bucharest. Her story would be she was a student looking for a career in the hotel industry and this job was to gain experience. She would be helping in the hotel working for the owners David and Maria. They had recently taken over the place and had big plans to make the most of the increase in tourists coming to the region of Transylvania.

'They are happy to have a good worker to help them so if you have to clean toilets, wash glasses, or sweep the floors, just do whatever they ask!' Razvan added impatiently.

Mihaela had visions of an old-fashioned place where she would be wearing a shabby uniform, forced to do manual labour for a mean matronly boss that would be barking orders at her from dawn till dusk. It would be like Cinderella in reverse going from riches to rags!

'Andrei has a son, Alex. He is collecting you and will drive you there. He has been studying here at Bucharest University. Alex is also close to David and Maria and I understand he is setting up his own walking holiday company during the summer months. He will be good company for you. His father has told him nothing about your situation, just that he is doing a favour for a friend and he should look after you.'

'I don't need a minder! I can look after myself and I might not like him. I like to choose my friends.' Mihaela said stubbornly.

Razvan reminded her again of his conversation with her the previous night, of the sister found in the garbage bins. He made her promise she would try hard to make this work, not to let him down. She finally stopped arguing and agreed with him, putting her arms around him and hugging him tightly.

They cleared away the cups and plates enjoying all too brief a time to talk about the family and reminisce about old times when the gate buzzer sounded. Razvan pressed the entrance button to the apartment block and Mihaela took up position behind her brother, peering past him to the door. Sunshine flooded in as he opened the door so that only a silhouette of the young man could be seen, hiding his features until he stepped in and the door closed behind him. The first thing she noticed was a friendly smile. Razvan greeted him, shaking his hand warmly.

'Hi Alex, I am Razvan, thank you for helping us out by driving today. I hope you found my place okay from my directions. Your father is a good friend of mine. Alex, this is my sister, Ana.'

Alex shook her hand, politely. She could see that Alex was very good looking, athletic in build with an air of vanity about him. He was dressed casually in jeans and a polo shirt, tight enough to see the outline of a broad-shouldered, well-muscled body. Here was a confident young man who she decided was probably a good friend to have looking out for her. Other than that, she formed no further opinions, keeping herself guarded and occupied only with the journey ahead.

Alex was equally polite. His father had told him to stop by and pick up an extra passenger on his way home to Brasov, that he had organised a summer job for a friend's sister. He was happy to oblige, especially as this girl seemed very attractive.

Razvan offered him a coffee keeping the introduction casual and giving no clue that they were in an apartment owned by the state police that had been the scene of an interrogation of his sister the night before.

'She is looking forward to starting her new job. I understand you know just about everything there is to know about such a beautiful place, so I hope she will allow you to show her some of the sites and make her feel at home. Your father tells me you are starting your new walking holiday company this summer. I wish you every success.'

Over coffee Razvan kept the conversation focused on Alex´s plans for the summer before he said his goodbyes to Ana, prompting their departure with the excuse they should avoid the traffic out of the city by leaving early.

Razvan did not leave the apartment. Ana fought back a few tears of frustration. It was not what she had imagined, being banished to some mountain fortress, unsure of when she would see her family again or under what circumstances.

Alex did not miss the expression of uncertainty on her face and assumed it was merely, as with anyone else, the feeling of a first day at school. He kindly gathered up her things and they left together in silence. They walked to his car parked on the street. She recognised the old model, Dacia 1300, as one that her parents had also driven before she had left Romania. As she stepped into the front seat, she glanced up towards the apartment giving a silent wave but she could not see her brother. Having put her cases in the rear boot Alex slipped into the driver's seat and started up the engine, patting the dashboard affectionately as they set off.

'Come on old girl, let's go home.'

7

Road to Reinvention

They navigated their way along the busy roads skirting the city´s Sector one area heading for the northern route towards Brasov. The land was flat with fewer buildings. There were more green spaces, interspersed with traditional houses and a few industrial sites but nothing very scenic. Then the road began to climb and the scenery changed as they headed for the mountains.

Ana gazed out of the window not really taking in anything and preoccupied with her thoughts. Just days before she had been sailing under Mediterranean skies and now she was headed to some back of beyond place to stay with a bunch of strangers. Maybe she had been impulsive to leave and perhaps she had overreacted. It had crossed her mind to stop everything and go back but it was too late now. She had shared intelligence with the authorities. Razvan was right. Her actions might now cause more trouble than if she had stayed in Spain. She knew Sergiu would be furious to lose her this way, he owned her and everyone knew it. He would feel mocked in front of his peers having lost control over her and without doubt, would have his spies out trying to find her. She was scared of what was behind her and equally scared about what was ahead of her.

She began to realise how difficult it was going to be not to give anything away about who she was. One slip of information and someone might see straight through her. She had to concentrate on becoming Ana. She would do her best to keep herself to herself, do whatever it was she was meant to do and lie about everything else until her brother could give her the all-clear to go home to the city and back to her own family. She wasn't looking forward to getting involved with any of these mountain people whom she imagined would have nothing in common with her.

Alex was making various attempts at conversation with his passenger, politely inquisitive about her but he soon realised Ana was not interested in talking about herself. That was fine by him as girls who were only full of themselves had no appeal to him. On the other hand, she did not seem very interested in him either or where they were going, which he found rather annoying. They had been travelling for over an hour continuing towards Sinaia when Alex asked her if she wanted to make a stop.

'If you haven't been there before its one of the most picturesque towns I know. We could stop by Peles

Castle if you like.'

He did his best to paint the picture of the rainbow-coloured wooden houses of the town nestled in a valley of fir trees and set against the jagged backdrop of the Bucegi Mountains. Its fairytale castle was a magnet for visitors from all over the world who came to see the Carpathian Pearl.

'It's one of the most famous and oldest mountain resorts in Romania,' he added.

Sightseeing was the last thing on her list to do but she did not want to seem impolite either and hesitated before answering him.

'I´m sorry Alex, I´m just keen to get to the hotel, I´m looking forward to it,' she said, trying to sound convincing.

Alex smiled at her, dismissing the idea with a friendly shrug of his shoulders.

'We should be home in about an hour. Perhaps another day when we have more time. There are so many things to see and do here, besides everyone is expecting us for a lunchtime birthday celebration!' he said.

Ana was thinking to herself, home for Alex perhaps but a long way from anything she was familiar with and now she was going to walk into a party!

'So whose birthday is it?' she asked, wishing she had made more effort to dress smarter and put on some makeup instead of arriving in her baggy sweatshirt and jeans.

'It is Maria's´ birthday and everyone loves Maria! I think there will be various family and friends dropping by during the day but at lunch, it will just be Maria's´ husband David, their two twin girls Sasha and Brigit, her parents and my father Andrei who is godfather to the girls, me, you and my best friend, Mattei. He is the chef there, so I hope you are hungry as he is the best there is! He trained in one of the best hotels in London and we are lucky he chose to come home and make a name for himself here.'

Alex told her there were two tour groups booked into the hotel that he would be organising walks for and that she was welcome to join them if she had free time. Despite her very casual clothes, he could see she was quite fit-looking, probably with great legs he thought, glancing sideways at her. She caught the look he gave her and replied with her eyes fixed on the road ahead.

'I´m not really into hiking but thanks for the offer,' she said politely.

Her body was toned and fit from training in the gym and jogging along the Paseo Maritimo beside Marbella's´ beaches in the early mornings stopping for a fresh-squeezed orange juice along the way followed by a warm shower and light breakfast. Her vision of groups of walkers in the mountains consisted of dreary people in heavy boots marching around with walking poles and snapping pictures of birds along the way. It was not her idea of fun.

'If you are going to be working with us you should know something about the area, guests like a bit of local knowledge and Maria is keen for you to feel part of the family. My father recommended you to her because we have different nationalities coming and we heard you studied English, German and Spanish, which could be very useful! Is that true?'

Ana didn´t respond immediately. She needed to think carefully about her answers when someone was asking her about anything that might reveal her past life. Razvan had told her Andrei knew most of her story but he could be trusted. She was to say she was a student looking to go into hospitality as a career. In some ways, this was true as she had picked up languages during her travels from the people she met and she had worked in hospitality, just not the kind that most people would imagine. The irony made her smile.

'I am certainly not fluent in all of them but I can get by. I understand more than I can speak but I hope I can be helpful.' She knew how to play the game. Alex smiled.

'I am sure you will be just what we need. Maria and David have worked so hard to drag the place into the 21st century. They bought the place just over a year ago to be close to her parents who have a house nearby. It had changed very little over the years but you should see it now! They gave up their jobs in Germany where they were living and working in banking and have put their hearts and souls into the place, even selling their family home to fund the improvements. You name it, heating, new bathrooms, a fully equipped kitchen, they have done it! We are all excited to put Casa Flori on the map. For me, it realises a dream. I was one of the first people to get my license as a mountain guide. I love the outdoors and I know every inch of the mountains around.'

They had turned off the main road signed towards Brasov, just north of Sinaia and the landscape became increasingly wild as they dissected their way through the Transylvanian mountains. They passed through a few villages lining the roadside banked by thick woodlands as far as Ana could see. There were a few hotels and pensions dotted along the way but gradually it became more and more sparsely populated. She wondered where on earth they were headed.

'So who else works at the hotel?' she enquired.

She was hoping he would say there were at least a couple of girls similar in age to her but was disappointed when he told her there were just two older ladies that took turns to help with cleaning and laundry.

'It´s why we are more like a family, everyone pitches in so you can see why Maria is pleased to have you aboard, it´s not easy to get regular people.'

Staring at the empty countryside around her, Ana could understand why. Who would choose to live so far from anything? Alex knew why she was asking.

'Don´t worry Ana, we get time off and Brasov is only half an hour away. It has some great clubs, restaurants and cafes. My father lives there and we often stay over after a late night. He enjoys the company too. Plus, we are close to Bran, Rasnov and the ski resort at Poiana. I work there in the winter as a ski instructor.'

A glimmer of hope thought Ana. She couldn´t live with the idea there would be no shopping and she would need money. She was not going to risk using cash machines, preferring to make a personal withdrawal from the account she had set up a couple of years ago. When Sergiu had asked her what she did with her money, she had told him she sent it home to her parents. In reality, it didn't go to them. Instead, it accumulated as savings for herself but he never questioned it as many of her friends sent money home.

Alex was nursing the Dacia around a series of hairpin bends concentrating ahead for oncoming traffic which he warned had little respect for anything else on the road. Ana had closed her eyes and squeezed herself into a ball at one point when they passed one truck veering perilously close to them, which he found highly amusing. Eventually, the road flattened out and the valleys widened with very little to see except fields and open space. They bypassed Rasnov before heading south again towards the historic town of Bran. About fifteen kilometres before Bran they turned off onto a narrow road peppered with traditional houses and farmsteads until they reached a sign pointing to the hotel.

Alex turned the Dacia into a gravel drive and came to a stop outside the hotel. It was larger than Ana had imagined, built in a Germanic style traditional of ski lodges with a mix of natural stone, white walls and a roof like a toboggan run. Pretty wooden shutters decorated its timber frame and baskets of bright flowers hung in masses from the balconies of each of its four levels, greeting visitors with a waterfall of colour.

'Welcome to Casa Flori, Ana.'

8

Casa Flori

Ana stepped out of the car, pushed her sunglasses on top of her head and stretched her arms. It felt good to get out of the car and breathe in the clear mountain air. Alex had retrieved her bags from the boot and with a nod of his head indicated her to follow him to the main entrance door with its pretty painted welcome sign. They walked into a bright sunlit foyer at the end of which was an ornately carved reception desk. The polished wooden floors smelled subtly of beeswax and along one side of the walls hung a series of neatly framed antique maps opposite a cushioned bench seat in the same style as the desk. Alex placed her bags down and they headed for a room to her left from where they could hear the sounds of chatter and laughter.

Ana took in the room with its lemon painted walls

animated by traditional stencilling and hand-painted quotations written in varying calligraphic styles. It was a large open lounge with a wood-beamed ceiling falling from a double-height towards a set of terrace doors that welcomed in the sunshine.

The furniture was a mix of antique pieces blended with modern sofas and comfortable chairs arranged in four or five seating groups, their plumped patchwork of cushions inviting the visitor to sink into comfort at the end of a satisfying day. In one corner of the room, a stone fireplace housed a wood-burning stove, its inglenooks housing vases of fresh flowers that filled the air with their natural fragrance. There were pretty lamps on side tables and books and magazines scattered on coffee tables resting on thick cream-coloured rugs. Ana was used to more modern city hotels from her days spent in Germany and Spain rather than this rustic style but she had to admit to herself it was very tasteful.

They continued out onto an elevated stone terrace which ran the whole length of the building. A magnificent view stretched across a palette of undulating green fields dotted with haystacks and wooden railed fences finally ending with the towering backdrop of the Bucegi Mountains. Her attention turned back to the group of people seated around a long wooden table. Her first introduction came as a surprise when Maria stood with open arms to welcome her. Her trim figure dressed perfectly in tailored white trousers and an Escada tee-shirt accessorised with a silk Dior scarf. In her kitten heels and with her long straight hair pulled back into a simple ponytail, she was certainly not the domineering matriarch Ana had imagined. She immediately wished she had made more effort to look smarter herself and apologised to Maria for arriving empty-handed when she now knew it was her birthday.

'You are my birthday present! You have no idea how difficult it is to get help! What a surprise!' she laughed.

Maria then took it upon herself to go round the table with her to shake the hands of her parents, Raluca and Vlad, her seven-year-old twin girls Sasha and Brigit, her husband David and finally Andrei. His presence made her feel transparent but he was just as welcoming, passing her a glass of cold Prosecco and raising a toast to the team.

A voice emerging from the opposite end of the terrace interrupted them.

'Wait for me! We cannot all be sitting idly in the sunshine. You think this food will get to the table all by itself?'

Maria made her way over to Mattei, the Master Chef that Alex had described to Ana during their journey. He appeared in his kitchen whites with a black bandana tucking in a thick head of curly hair. He was handsome with a tanned youthful face, dark brown eyes and a charismatic, cheeky smile that made him instantly likeable.

'Mattei you are teasing, as usual, here let me help you!' said Maria taking one of the two large platters of food he was carrying.

She introduced Ana as they placed the platters one at each end of the table. Mattei had been expecting a greasy-haired local busboy for the low wages offered when Maria told him how Andrei had managed to find extra help, so he was taken aback when he shook Ana by the hand.

'Nice to meet you, Ana, welcome to the team. Where did Andrei find you?' he said, laughing.

Mattei had not missed one inch of Ana´s attractive qualities, her hands were smooth, her nails painted perfectly, she didn´t look like a worker and he just hoped she would fit in for Maria's sake. They had all been stretched to get the hotel ready for its first season and what they needed was someone who was prepared to get stuck in.

He produced a bottle of Tuică from his chef's coat pocket and placed it alongside the small glasses that waited be filled to accompany the Mezeluria, the selection of appetisers similar to the way Spanish would have tapas. There were different meats and sausage, a selection of cheeses, devilled eggs stuffed with homemade pate and beef salad served in miniature pastry baskets, all beautifully arranged and enticing. The twins tried to be the first to help themselves but Maria reminded them gently that among guests, they must remember their manners.

'Don´t let these two run rings around you, Ana, they can be full of mischief at times,' said Mattei fondly as he tussled the hair of each of the girls. They responded by tickling him in the ribs, clearly enjoying his attention.

The next hour passed so pleasantly Ana had almost forgotten where she was or why she was here. It had been a long time since she had joined in any family occasion and with Maria being the centre of attention, they were less curious about her. Mattei asked her to help him clear some of the plates and glasses that had accumulated and she followed him towards to kitchen entrance.

'Don´t worry,' said Mattei, 'We will soon give you the full tour and get you settled in. We only have nine people in so far and today is their free day, so we have the place mostly to ourselves until they return later. The idea is that we have one day when the restaurant closes, so they have to fend for themselves! I think most of them have headed into Brasov. However, in the next weeks, we are almost full. David is mainly responsible for that. He is an internet genius. With Alex´s input, we have visitors arriving from all over, thanks to their websites and advertising. We have fifteen bedrooms and one cottage that sleeps up to six people so if the restaurant is full, we need to cater for up to forty people, sometimes maybe more if people come from outside. I want to make this one of the top restaurants in the region. We have seating for sixty!'

The kitchen was immaculate, newly fitted he explained with all the tools he needed.

'Good food comes from a clean and precise chef. That is one of the first things I learned. If the kitchen is messy, the food will also be this way. I have prepared some traditional Romanian dishes for us this afternoon but I like to put a twist on things.'

He was clearly passionate about what he did telling Ana how Romania had such a variety of foods because of the influences of so many other countries, from the ancient Greeks and Romans that they traded with, to the Saxons who settled in Transylvania, neighbours from Slavic countries, Turks from the

Ottoman Empire, Hungarians all had their influence in the different regions.

Mattei was easy company and clearly at home surrounded by an impressive array of kitchen gadgets. He didn't ask her too much about herself other than her interest in food and if she had ever done any cooking, curious to know how useful she would be and if she was at home in a kitchen or preferred to work front of house. He was assuming she had some experience. Ana told him she had been lucky to do some travelling and was quite accustomed to hotels and what people expected as customer service.

She allowed him to do all the talking with Mattei happy to describe his days growing up in the village and how inspirational his mother had been in his passion for food.

'My mother was a good cook,' he told her. 'She taught me many things but cooked with too much pork fat and salt like all the locals do! Thankfully she was a great believer in fresh produce and vegetables. I grew up spending as much time helping her in the garden as in the kitchen.'

Ana helped him plate the dishes for the main meal. They would start with Ciorba de Perisoare, a sour meatball soup and Mattei described the process to make his own Bors, the souring agent that gives the soup its unique taste.

Everyone helped themselves ladling out the broth and soft, delicate meatballs from a decorative ceramic tureen. Ana helped plate the next course, put together under close instruction. In the centre was a neat round layered stack with a base of creamy polenta topped with Samarle, parcels of minced pork, rice, herbs and spices wrapped in pickled cabbage leaves. She poured over a smoky, fresh tomato-based sauce and topped each dish with a parmesan wafer. She was surprised by the sophistication of the food which she was used to eating but not preparing and thought to herself she would manage just fine if this was all that they required of her.

The meal ended with dessert with Mattei serving up a Savarina, the Romanian version of a french Rhum Baba for the grown-ups and the girls had their favourite Papansi, doughnuts filled with jam and sour cream.

The conversation continued around the table with David taking on the role of topping up everyone's glasses of wine at regular intervals. The girls had disappeared further down the garden with their grandparents. The sun began to set and the remaining party began the task of clearing the table, gathering in the kitchen to wash the remaining pots and load the dishwasher.

'Quite an introduction for you and all at once, Ana! You must be ready to see your room and take a break from us. Let me show you,' said Maria.

Ana followed her, not back into the hotel but outside from the kitchen where a stone stairway took them down to another garden level with a play area for children and two outbuildings that looked like old barns.

'We thought you would have more privacy down here away from the main house. We have been renovating these buildings to put in a sauna room with a Jacuzzi and extra accommodation or a reading room. We haven´t quite finished yet, so I hope you will be okay here,' explained Maria.

She opened a small doorway into a studio room. It had a small kitchenette, a sofa area with a television and what looked like a wardrobe.

'We brought this back from Germany where we used to live and it is very comfortable' said Maria as she reached up to a handle and pulled releasing a drop-down bed.

'There is a bathroom and a shower for you, though you might find storing your clothes a bit tricky. Tomorrow Mattei says he is bringing a storage closet for you from his house. Typical you leave things to the men to finish but they don´t think about the practicalities!'

'It´s fine thank you, I appreciate all the effort you have made and I´m looking forward to settling in.'

Maria smiled at her new protégé. 'I´ll leave you to get some peace then. When you are ready, come back up and join us if you like. Tomorrow I will give you the grand tour!'

Ana closed the door after Maria and sat on the edge of the drop-down bed surveying the room around her. It was better than she had expected with a small window looking to fields behind.

With the combination of wine, great food and conversation, she was starting to feel sleepy. She had been travelling nonstop. It was beginning to sink in that she was very much on her own, away from her friends back in Marbella, having to be someone else. She sighed, staring at her bags which had arrived earlier. There was no point in unpacking just yet so she decided she would at least take a shower and change.

The shower was soothing and it made her feel even sleepier. She lay on the bed, wrapped in the soft white bath towel provided for her and soon fell fast asleep. By the time she woke up and reached for her watch, it was after eleven o´clock at night. She lay back down again, pulling the damp towel from underneath her and curled up in the crisp cotton sheets. She closed her eyes and drifted off to sleep again. Tomorrow would come soon enough!

9

Working Girl

Ana was roused from her sleep by a soft but steady tapping at the door. It took her a few moments to remember where she was, opening her eyes she was expecting to see daylight instead of the darkness of the room. She glanced at her watch. It was six-thirty in the morning.

'Who is it?' she called out nervously.

'Alex', came the reply.

'One moment!' she said hastily wrapping the discarded bath towel around her. Without putting on any lights, she fumbled her way to the door, opening it just far enough to peer outside.

Alex caught just a glimpse of a bare shoulder, tousled hair and blue eyes blinking at him in the dawn light. He was standing only a half meter from the entrance holding tightly to the collar of a massive black furry dog; it's large frame straining towards her.

'Ana, I hope you slept well, we missed you last night but understand you must have been tired. We are breakfasting at seven, so I thought I should come and wake you! I was taking Baloo here for a walk.'

Ana couldn't take her eyes off the dog.

'Yes, of course, I was just getting up, thank you,' she said, closing the door on Alex. She leaned against it in silent surprise. She was more used to coming home at this kind of hour than thinking about getting up for work. As for the dog, she had never seen such an animal, with a ruff of black hair around its neck like the mane of a lion and paws like a polar bear!

She hurried back to shower, then tipping the contents of a suitcase untidily onto the bed she selected a pair of black cropped trousers, white blouse and flat ballet pumps that she thought would be more suitable for working. She was not sure what exactly she would be doing. Her hair was just long enough to tie back, held in place with a beaded scrunchy. She added a little makeup to take away the early morning tiredness. At five to seven, she made her way back up towards the kitchen entrance, greeted by the smell of fresh coffee and baked bread. She could hear voices and following them walked into the dining room where Alex, Mattei, Maria and two older ladies were seated around a table set with cups for coffee and a platter of cold meats, cheeses, fresh rolls and jam.

'Good morning Ana, did you sleep okay? Help yourself to coffee and join us,' said Maria. 'We meet most mornings to go through the agenda for the day. Meet Elena and Alina who help us with the housekeeping!'

Ana took up a seat returning a polite response to the two ladies who looked like they would eat her for breakfast, resembling more of what she had imagined Maria was going to be, better at home in Cell Block H as prison warders than hotel cleaners. They just stared at her, with what was probably for them a smile. She could see their yellowed teeth which seemed to blend in with their floral housecoats. There was no way she was going to wear one of those!

'Be nice to my girlfriends, Ana!' Mattei joked, noting her silent appraisal of them. 'Each of them is very special to me because they also take care of my house and I wouldn´t do without them.'

The two ladies nodded in agreement, commenting that he needed looking after. His house was one of the most disorganised in the village and he should be looking for a good strong woman like them to take care of him. Mattei teasingly agreed.

Maria was going through the guest list and which rooms would need cleaning first. Elena and Alina then excused themselves to get on with their morning's work. Mattei went through the menus for the day, who was having dinner, who had ordered packed lunches and what supplies were needed. He then headed for the kitchen as the first guests arrived to begin their breakfast. There was already a buffet of hot and cold beverages, breads, meats and fruit laid out but the guests could choose to have a hot breakfast made and so Maria suggested Ana follow Mattei to the kitchen to collect herself an apron and start by taking breakfast orders.

'Just make our guests feel welcome, Ana. Ask them about their plans for the day and how they have been enjoying themselves. I´m sure you know what to do. We like them to feel at home with us. Mattei will guide you and when you have finished the breakfast sitting, I will show you around the rest of the hotel.'

Ana was glad she could be of immediate use. At least waiting on tables was something she knew how to do even though it had been some time ago when she worked in the café in Bucharest. She put on the blue apron and picked up a pad and pen, popping it into the front pocket.

Guests were helping themselves to breakfast juice and hot drinks, some piling plates with fruit or bread and jams. She greeted them one by one introducing herself and making pleasant conversation. Some were chattier than others, with a mix of Romanians, Danish and an English couple who were delighted she could speak to them in their preferred language. She took a few orders relaying them back to Mattei in the kitchen and bringing out the hot plates of food.

By ten o´clock, as instructed, she had cleared away plates and tidied up the long table where the buffet had been. She was feeling tired again, wondering how much more she would have to do. Mattei had already started on prep for the evening meal when Maria returned asking if all had gone well.

'Maria, she has done just fine, she's a fast learner!' he said kindly.

'Well, you just be careful not to overwork her, Mattei. I don´t want you to turn into a fat idle chef,' Maria joked.

'Come on, Ana, let me show you around and then we can take a coffee.'

They started on the first level, Maria showing her

the different rooms that they were able to enter. They were individually styled with a blend of old and new that kept the character of the place but with all modern comforts, as tastefully done as the lounge area, Ana had admired.

'My father and some of the local carpenters made many of the pieces of furniture you see,' said Maria proudly.

'Did you live here before?' asked Ana.

'No, my parents have a house close by that has been in the family for years. They moved to Germany when I was young and my sisters and I grew up there but each summer we would come back for the summer holidays. I always loved coming here but back then the hotel was quiet, really only open for the winter and the ski season. It became quite run down and when the last owners put it up for sale, I persuaded David to buy it. We have done so much to it. My parents have helped us, taking care of the girls or pitching in with whatever they could manage. My father likes to stay active, so this has turned out to be his ideal retirement!'

'Are your sisters living close by too?'

'One of them is living in Germany still but she comes to stay quite often. She has two children, both boys similar in age to my girls. The other sister went to live in America, a total career girl working in banking the same as I used to but she hasn't married yet. We maybe see her once or twice a year. What about your family Ana?'

Ana liked Maria, imagining she was the sort of person who you could lunch with, talk about fashion and have a fun time with but here she was, Ana, just a lowly employee. She held back talking about her family, not wanting to encourage more on the subject, agreeing that like Maria's family, her two older brothers had busy careers, so they didn´t get the chance to meet up very often. As for herself, she had done some travelling and was hoping now to settle on a career in hospitality. It was just as she had been briefed by Razvan to keep it simple. They had made their way to the top floor and Maria was able to show her one of the studio rooms they had only just finished.

'This is my favourite room,' she said and Ana could see why. It had a high-pitched roof just like the lounge with wooden beams sloping towards a balcony with breathtaking views. The bed was a sumptuous king-size complete with four-poster carved frame and soft drapes falling to the floor. There was a pretty seating area arranged around a wood-burning stove and a bathroom with a Jacuzzi bath and separate walk-in shower. It oozed luxury details from the fluffy white towels to a built-in bar.

'It´s lovely Maria,' said Ana and she meant it.

Maria beamed with pride, smoothing the covers of the bed. 'The only problem is the stairs. It was just too expensive to have an elevator installed but being as most of our guests are fit outdoor types we think we can get away with it! I´m just sometimes worried Alina and Elena find it hard but then they are built like little oxen and never even mention it!'

She went through the housekeeping routine showing Ana where the linen was stored and how the inventory was kept. The idea was for Mihaela to take over some of the duties and allow Maria more free time, especially with the girls after all the hours they had sacrificed to get the place ready for the summer season.

Finally, they went out to the garden area where Ana had her room. There were other outbuildings, one of which was converted into an office for David. His desk had two computers; one he explained was the engine for the hotel and the other was his real work. They joined him for coffee.

'He still works as an investment consultant for the bank. He hasn't been able to give up the day job just yet!' explained Maria, giving her husband an affectionate hug.

The morning had gone quickly with a lot for Ana to take in. She was feeling hungry. The kitchen was empty when they returned. Mattei had a few hours off in the day unless he was going into town to get supplies. Maria suggested she go with him one day and have a look around.

'I understand you will not have much in the way of provisions in your little kitchen so we have a staff fridge here and you can help yourself to whatever is in it. You have seen what Mattei cooks, so I´m sure you will enjoy helping yourself. He always makes some extra so that none of us go hungry. We start serving in the evening about seven o´clock so I will see you at about six to run through the routine then. Take some rest now Ana but if you need anything just let me know, tomorrow we will go through the reception process,' and she left Ana to herself.

Ana was glad to have some space and opening the fridge, selected some salads, cold meats and potatoes and sat quietly at the little staff table enjoying her food. Once she finished, she headed back to the sanctuary of her room. There was so much to take in, feeling there was an assumption from Maria that she knew what she was doing. It was real work. She wondered what Andrei had told Maria about her.

She was surprised to see the door already open and peering tentatively inside caught sight of Mattei and Alex manoeuvring a pine wooden wardrobe into one corner with a small chest of drawers just squeezed in beside it.

'Looks like you might be glad of this,' remarked Mattei glancing at the upturned contents of her suitcase piled on the bed, including her underwear and a box of tampons which she immediately grasped in a bundle feeling a little embarrassed.

'I am, thanks,' she replied, refusing their offer to help her any further. Both Alex and Mattei seemed to be enjoying her moment of awkwardness. After they left, she tidied away her things and decided there was enough time to take a siesta before the evening shift began.

She set the alarm on her watch just in case, not wanting to invite any more knocks on her door or strange encounters with big dogs but instead of dozing off her mind was in hyperdrive. So much had happened in such a short space of time, leaving Spain, meeting new people, starting a real job. No one except Razvan knew where she was or what she was doing. She needed to keep reminding herself why she had ended up here, to stay safe and for that to happen, she needed to be good at her job. She would adopt a new persona.

She decided Ana should be mature and capable,

friendly but also businesslike. After all it was to be a temporary role. Apart from that, she had no idea what she wanted for her future. At least so far this had turned out better than she had imagined but deep down, she felt uneasy. She was harbouring secrets and out of her comfort zone. She wondered just how long she could live like this.

10

Overcoming Obstacles

As it happened, her first evening shift went smoothly. She followed Mattei's instructions, taking orders and bringing out each dish with its intricate layers of flavour, delicately arranged.

'Where did you learn to do all this Mattei? I can't imagine there are many places around here offering food as beautiful as this!' she enthused.

Mattei was flattered, happy to tell her his story as they plated up together. 'In London, I got a job in quite a small place, at first as a pot washer and then a waiter. The chef was a crazy Scottish guy who treated me like a simpleton because my English wasn´t good but he was difficult to understand anyway! He used to call me cabbage boy because he thought that´s what we ate in Romania! He was always shouting at me but he was also a roaring drunk so one night I had to help him get all the food out and I did well. I impressed the owner and got promoted! I´ve always loved being around food. In London, I would spend hours in my spare time checking out restaurants, looking at menus. I must admit I was pretty obsessive at the time but it worked out as I got a job in one of the big London hotels. I soaked up everything I could like a sponge. After two years I got a call from Maria asking if I wanted to come home and help plan the restaurant here, it was a perfect opportunity so here I am!'

'So, you didn´t go to college or university to study then?' asked Ana thinking of her own shortcomings when it came to studying.

'No.' Mattei laughed, 'I wasn´t good with the academic side of things, I didn´t like school much. I couldn´t wait to leave, unlike Alex, who was always top of the class. So, I am self-taught but I also believe if you want something badly enough, you will find a way to get there and I have been lucky too.'

They had finished for the evening but rather than leave for home Mattei suggested they take a beer and sit outside on the terrace at the back of the kitchen. The evening was warm and he had no problem keeping company with Ana for longer.

Mattei sat opposite her opening the beers. 'To answer your question,' he said, clinking his bottle to hers, 'there are more and more restaurants opening here and the quality of the food is getting better. It used to be pretty basic, just traditional foods but that´s changing as we have more people from different countries coming all year-round. I go to Brasov quite often to get supplies but you should let me show you the town and maybe sample some local eateries. It´s good to check out the competition from time to time!'

Ana nodded, 'That would be nice plus I need some time to go shopping, get to a bank that kind of thing.'

'Well, I don´t know about the shopping part. It may be better to ask to go with Maria but I´m happy to show you around.'

'Thanks, I'll take you up on that!' said Ana.

'Another thing,' continued Mattei, 'It can make you a bit stir crazy being in the hotel all the time, so you are welcome to join Alex and me at my house for a change of scene instead of going back to your room. It´s just along the road here.'

'I appreciate that Mattei. So Alex stays with you?'

'He does and you take us as you find us! We are not the tidiest of people as you learned from Elena and Alina this morning! I heard you met our other house companion, Baloo this morning. Are you okay with dogs?'

'I´m okay with dogs but that was more like a bear!' exclaimed Ana, throwing her arms open as wide as she could to show she meant large.

Mattei laughed. 'He´s a Romanian breed, a Raven Corb, all black fur. I named him Baloo after the bear from Rudyard Kipling's The Jungle Book. Do you know it?'

'I know it from the Disney cartoon film. Is he friendly or always on a tight leash?' she added, looking more serious.

'If you are a friend of mine, then he will be a friend to you. Maria's children are crazy about him. They are always asking for me to bring him over to play. They are common around here as guardians for livestock. If

Baloo needed to, he could tackle a bear himself and his bark can travel miles. He can sense the difference between good and bad, so I have to be careful to keep him away from the hotel guests just in case someone gives off the wrong scent! Alex likes to take him out early in the morning, that´s why you had the pleasure of seeing him first thing. I´ve had him from a puppy. My parents always had a dog on the place.'

Ana was curious as Mattei talked of his parents. She couldn´t help but ask.

'Is it just you, Alex and Baloo? Are your parents close by?'

Mattei nodded. 'Yes, in a manner of speaking. My parents are buried in the cemetery in Brasov. Alex, Baloo and I live in the house where I grew up.'

'I´m sorry' said Ana.

'It´s okay. I adored my parents, I don´t mind talking about them. They were both just so full of life! They had been away visiting family near Cluj. The roads in parts were abysmal, not maintained since the end of the communist rule. It was evening and dark and quite isolated. They had swerved to avoid an oncoming car which was travelling too fast. Their car spun off the road, tipping over and rolling several times. It crumpled like a tin can with no escape for them. My father died instantly but my mother was still alive. There was one witness who heard the noise of the crash, just some poor person who didn´t even have a telephone who went out to see what had happened. They could do nothing except comfort her as she lay trapped. Then someone passing just happened to see the wreckage and stopped. They called for help but the emergency services could not get there quickly enough. She died there.' Mattei paused. Ana sat silently, waiting for him to continue.

'I stayed in the farmhouse on my own for a time, not knowing what I wanted to do. I couldn´t think straight. Eventually, with support from my friends, I decided I needed to make a fresh start and that´s when I went to London.

'You seem so positive and cheerful, it must have been such a shock for you,' Ana sympathised. She couldn´t imagine what it would be like to lose either of her parents, let alone both. She just took it for granted they would always be there.

'We were all shocked at what happened. To lose both my parents when they were relatively young was tragic. I was only eighteen. We all miss them but as they say, life goes on!' Mattei smiled gently. He gathered up the empty beer bottles, returning to them to the kitchen. 'It has been a long day for you. I should let you get some sleep.'

Ana allowed him to bring the conversation to a close. 'Thanks again Mattei, for helping me settle in.' She felt he would have talked more but he seemed to want to change the mood. His face brightened.

'Well, don´t forget our invitation to call in whenever you like. Alex and I will be glad to have younger company around! There isn't much fun listening to Elena and Alina droning on!'

"I can imagine!' replied Ana, genuinely. I will come and you can introduce me better to Baloo, so he knows I´m a friend and not his breakfast!' she smiled, wishing Mattei goodnight.

11

Getting to Know You

Nearly a week had passed with Ana settling into her new routine. Maria suggested she take time to go with Mattei to Brasov. 'It was his suggestion and she thought it was a good idea.

'Take as much time as you want. You don´t have to be back for the evening with the restaurant closed tonight.' Maria reminded them as they were leaving.

'Thank you, Maria, I think we know that!' Mattei blushed.

They set off just before mid-morning in Maria's´ Opel Zafira which Mattei used when he needed to pick up supplies. It felt good to escape the hotel for a few hours and Ana was looking forward to spending time in a place that had shops and bars with people who wore something other than country walking gear. She chose to wear a dress and sandals, making the most of the dry, sunny weather.

They headed for the Eliana Mall on the outskirts of Brasov, with Mattei sympathetic to her desire to do some shopping saying he also had to pick up a few supplies for himself.

'When we have finished there, we´ll head for the old town and have a good look around. I would also like to treat you to dinner.' said Mattei.

The only thing she was worried about was getting to a bank. She needed to have plenty of spare money, just in case she needed to run again. She needed to convert more euro into lei. Mattei had said there were cash machines but she insisted she had other things to sort out and needed to go to Unicredit Bank in person.

'No problem, Ana, there is one right in the centre where we are going anyway. We can head there first though I can lend you some money if you need it.'

'No but thanks anyway, Mattei and it´s nice of you to offer to take me to dinner but I can pay my way,' she insisted. He looked disappointed.

'It´s my way of saying, thank you for all your help back at Casa Flori, so let me have the pleasure.' He was genuinely pleased to be taking her out. She was pretty and there was something different about her compared to the local girls he met. She had style and seemed more grown-up for her years than most. It had been a long time since he had taken anyone out and it would do him good he thought.

He parked the car in the underground car park and they made their way to the information point where Ana could locate the shops she needed. They agreed to split up and meet back in an hour. She flew round returning to the meeting point on time with several shopping bags containing two navy pencil skirts, four blouses, two pairs of low-heeled shoes and a pair of clear black-rimmed glasses she thought would give her an efficient appearance when she was working in reception.

Mattei was impressed by her punctuality. 'Most girls I know would have said an hour and meant at least two when it comes to shopping.'

Ana laughed. 'That's true but you don´t know me well enough yet. I would probably take three hours normally and have my nails and hair done but I´m happy to be out in the sun now and ready to explore Brasov so let´s go!' The truth was she was disappointed how lacking the stores were but it would have to do for now.

Mattei was true to his word and once he had found a space to park, they made their way to the bank located in the Piata Sfatuli, the picturesque square in the heart of the medieval town. It had a fairy-tale quality to it with baroque German styled architecture and old merchant houses with bright red and orange rooftops.

'Legend has it that the Pied Piper and his young wards surfaced in this very square after leading the children underground from Hamelin,' said Mattei pointing the ancient town hall with its Trumpeters Tower warning the townsfolk of any approaching danger. 'You can take the cable car up and look out over the whole town! Maybe you would like me to take your photograph next to Brasov's equivalent of the Hollywood sign.' Ana realized he was being serious. She was not sure she wanted to spend her free time sightseeing.

'You are like a professional tour guide, Mattei. Have you got a second job or something? I could really do with a coke and a sandwich right now,' she said, glancing around at the inviting cafes with their open terraces.

'You're right, it´s the perfect place just to watch the world go by but I´m determined to show you some of the sights but maybe the cable car another day,' he agreed.

Once they had finished at the bank, Ana was happy to sit and soak up the atmosphere in the bustling square. It was good to be back in civilisation, she thought. They chose one of the pretty cafes and ordered their drinks and food, observing the passers-by, some tourist taking lots of pictures, others just going about their daily business. The café was busy but Ana´s attention became focused on a man who sat down on his own to the side of them. He ordered a black coffee and opened his newspaper, his head concealed behind a double sheet spread. It was within reading distance and she could see the front-page article, the word 'Spain' catching her eye. She began reading, Mattei´s voice temporarily fading into the background.

"Spanish police have broken up a gang of Romanian human traffickers who were faking identity documents and credit cards. Twenty-two people have been arrested, the majority of them Romanians, between Valencia and Alicante in southeast Spain. In the past month, police have broken a similar gang involved in prostituting Eastern European women who were brought to Spain on false pretences. The investigation began in 2003 after a

Romanian girl claimed a gang had forced her into prostitution. The gang specialised in bringing Romanian women, often under-age girls, to Spain to force them into prostitution, using fake documents. Police seized false passports, identity papers, credit cards, scanners, computers, printers and one firearm and one fake gun."

Mattei was waving his hand and calling her name. 'Hello, earth to Ana, shall we get going?' She stopped reading.

The man peered around his paper as he turned the page. He cast a glance at her as the pair prepared to leave the table. She was intrigued by the story, maybe it was a sign, things were coming to a head and she might soon be free from her forced hiding. She rose from the table, turning away from the man as he continued to stare after her. Mattei put some cash on the table and hurried after her.

The next couple of hours they spent sightseeing and she indulged Mattei allowing him to guide her around the main points of interest. He was so enthusiastic she couldn't help but enjoy most of it. They visited the Black Church, home to the largest church bell in the country, which Ana joked would come in handy to know one day. They visited the Black Tower and the White Tower along the defensive walls; Catherine's Gate and the Shei Gate and meandered along the main street, Strada Republicii, with Ana eventually managing to drag Mattei into a few shops to look at jewellery and clothes.

'There is more to this town than history and I think you need reeducating, in the art of shopping,' she teased, picking out a couple of tee-shirts for him to try.

With a couple of purchases, they ventured off to explore the quaint cobbled alleyways pausing to take a beer and finishing with a walk through Strada Sfori, one of the narrowest streets in Europe. Their shoulders touched each other as they squeezed through its close walls.

To finish off the day Mattei had chosen to take her to dinner at Bistro Del L´Arte with its cosy vaulted rooms, art gallery and jazz music. The food was excellent and the conversation easy. Ana felt relaxed and it was nice to be able to switch off from everything. They returned to Casa Flori long after dark. Mattei dropped her off and as she made her way to her room, she thought about her childhood. Her parents had always loved going to look at churches and monuments when they went on holiday but she had been bored by this and never made much effort to show any interest. What would they think of her now? She smiled to herself, surprised at how much she had enjoyed Mattei's company.

It was a few days later that she decided to take up Mattei´s invitation to join him and Alex for a beer. They had finished earlier than expected. Alex had offered to give them a hand, his hikers having taken dinner quite early and retiring to the outside terrace where Maria was serving them coffee.

The evening was still light as they made their way to the farmstead that was Mattei's boyhood home. Ana was quite familiar with the rustic style of country houses but she had never been in one. It was as if time had stood still, with structures of forest wood married together to form a one-story house, a couple of barns, all enclosed by a woven picket fence. The roof gated entrance had a circle carved into it, a traditional symbol of regeneration, the repetition of seasons and the death and rebirth of nature.

Mattei led her up to a wooden veranda which ran the length of the house while Alex went to release Baloo off his chain. They could hear him wining with delight as he anticipated their arrival. The next thing she knew Baloo came bounding up the steps making a beeline for her. She was in his territory, with his master and smelled familiar, so she must be a friend. He bounded over, his shaggy tail beating like a branch in a hurricane, thrusting his face into Ana's lap and knocking her sideways. Mattei sent out a command immediately and Baloo retreated giving her space to recover. The dog stood on his hind legs with his front paws resting on Mattei´s shoulders like they were dancing partners with Mattei roughing up his fur and making a big fuss of him. 'Sorry Ana, he´s as soft as they come once he knows you. He won´t forget you now.'

Ana brushed off the black hair she was covered in, trying to compose herself.

'Let me give you the grand tour,' offered Alex.

He led her through an area kept for growing vegetables, a small orchard of fruit trees and rows of old vines with their gnarled branches supporting a healthy promising crop. The old barns were mostly empty apart from a collection of antique farm implements. To one side stood an unused pig pen and a chicken coop with a variety of poultry inside pecking at the dirt or roosting in small nest boxes. It had a farmyard smell which she found disgusting, placing her hand over her nose.

'We have more than enough eggs and Mattei takes them to the hotel, along with herbs and vegetables he likes to use in his cooking. It´s all about fresh produce he says but I know he takes pride in keeping the garden like his mother did.'

They went back up to the house and inside it was the same, like nothing had changed for generations. All the textiles were hand embroidered, a colourful collage of woven curtains, tapestries and rugs telling the stories of ancestors before. Plates decorated the walls and baskets hung from the low beamed ceilings, interspersed with dried flowers tied together with ribbon. The only evidence of modern living was the typical bachelor's collection of books and papers, a play station, a sound system with huge speakers and a new flat-screened television. The kitchen was old but there was an up-to-date fridge and cooker. A laptop was open on the dining table. Of the three bedrooms, two were in use and untidy just as Ana had been warned, with laundry on the floor and unmade beds but the third was made up in a way she thought had probably been Mattei's parents' room. She wondered if they had been the last people to use it.

Alex put some music on and sitting out on the veranda with the sounds of Coldplay and Shakira drifting through the windows the three friends settled into easy banter. Alex and Mattei reminded her of her brothers in the way they joked with one another, with just a hint of rivalry as to which one of them was smarter or faster or fitter. Baloo had curled up beside her on the front step. The Costa del Sol seemed even further away than the stars that filled the night sky. She could not imagine Sergiu would ever find her in a place like this.

12

Bear Country

Ana went for a run each afternoon. It gave her some space and time to think. She liked to stay fit in addition to her work routine, which had her climbing the stairs of the hotel several times a day. She might be in the countryside but she didn't have to let herself go! She had stopped by Mattei's house a few times to take Baloo with her. She had warmed to him and the dog seemed to be content to fall into stride with her, staying close as she attracted the attention of a few locals raising their eyebrows as she jogged by in her cropped top and Nike running shorts.

Alex had mentioned several times that she should join him on one of his hikes. She had politely declined saying she preferred running.

It was her fourth week at Casa Flori. May was melting into June and the hotel was full. She built up a good rapport with most of the hotel guests, always remembering names and quickly learning how they preferred their morning coffee or what newspaper they would read. At least one skill she could excel at was how to keep a customer happy.

There was one couple that arrived who seemed to take a particular shine to her, especially as she could speak in German to them, even if just simple conversation. They were a mature couple, in their mid-fifties who had retired early to follow their passion for wildlife and walking. Fritz and Ina had managed to waylay her a few times with tales of their adventurous holidays. However, in the three days since their arrival, she was finding them rather dull and at times annoying.

It was an evening when Alex was giving a talk in the lounge that she got involved in yet another of their stories. Ana was serving coffee. Between Alex, Maria, Fritz and Ina attention became focused around her lack of enthusiasm for hiking. She was feeling under pressure and looked to Alex for support but he was not going to help her with the situation that was evolving.

'You can take the girl out of the city but you can´t take the city out of the girl. Is that what you are saying Ana?' quizzed Alex good-humouredly. He thought it was odd she liked to go running but wouldn´t try hiking. There was a little arrogance to her he decided; something about her couldn't put his finger on. His father had said very little to him about her. He and Mattei had talked about her. He could see Mattei was attracted to her, who wouldn't be? But Mattei denied anything teasing Alex that he was jealous Ana and he seemed to get on so well.

Fritz and Ina were smiling convincingly. They had boxed her into a corner. She was trying to think of an excuse not to spend an entire day in the company of two Bavarian explorers.

'I don´t have the right gear, nothing to wear on my feet!' she proclaimed but Maria was already sizing her up.

'Don´t worry. You are similar to me, I think. I have several pairs of walking boots and some other things you can borrow, so I am sure you will be as prepared as everyone.'

Maria was delighted she would be going but Ana was having nightmare visions of trekking into the unknown with Fritz and Ina in their jolly matching outfits, guiding her through the wilderness by prodding her with their walking poles.

The next morning arrived too soon for her. A group of nine guests gathered in reception, collecting their packed lunches and adding them to knapsacks already pre-packed with binoculars, cameras, spare socks and waterproofs in case the weather turned.

Ana joined them wearing tight-fitting tracksuit bottoms, a white tee-shirt and the sturdy walking boots borrowed from Maria. She didn´t have any of the extras these veteran walkers carried and stuffed her packed lunch into the borrowed knapsack which also contained a ghastly pink kagool.

Fritz and Ina were there to reassure her that they would take lots of pictures. They took her under their wing like a baby bird, bustling her into the waiting minibus and helping her with her seat belt. She was cringing, hating every minute of it with the two

Germans keen to tell her what they had learned about for the day ahead. They passed her little pocket guides and pamphlets of bird species she might like to study.

There was a journey of fifty minutes to endure, heading around the edge of Brasov then south through the Piatra mountains where they would stop to pick up the trail to Canionul Sopte Scari -The Seven Ladders Canyon. Alex was doing a commentary on the way which was far more interesting than listening to Fritz and Ina and fortunately they were polite enough to pay attention as did all the others.

'The first thing you will see when we arrive is a sign warning about the bears. We have the largest population of Brown Bears in Europe, thanks partly to Ceausescu's passion for hunting which forbade anyone else to hunt them in his grounds which covered miles of this terrain. They are protected now with hunting licences only granted if they pose a threat to human safety and property. Unfortunately, some hunters still search for them deep in the forest to kill them for their skins but we are starting schemes to collar and tag them in order to protect them. There are sites which are deliberately set up for them where they put food out but I believe there is a fine balance between interference and tourism. You probably won´t see any today as they tend to hide deeper in the forest and they are quite solitary. However, at this time of year, there may be young cubs with their mothers or males that are looking to mate again so you have to remember they can be aggressive. There are rules, make a noise to alert them you are there. If you meet one close up, do not turn and run as they can travel at up to twenty-five miles an hour. If attacked, curl up in a ball and protect your face. Last but not least, abandon everything at the first sign of trouble, including your belongings!'

Everyone seemed to be very excited at the prospect they might see bears, except for Ana, who hoped the bears would be somewhere else other than where she was. There were lots of questions and Alex shared stories of his wildlife encounters, not just with bears but with wolves, lynx, chamois. He told them of the variety of birds to spot.

Eventually, they arrived in a flat green area where they would leave the minibus. Everyone climbed out, making sure cameras and binoculars were at the ready. The weather forecast had predicted rain for later in the day but so far, the skies were clear and bright.

'Don´t worry Ana. I have firecrackers in my bag to scare the bears away, though Fritz and Ina are enough to scare any animals away. Have fun!' Alex said quietly to her winking as he strode to the front of the pack.

'Not funny,' she muttered just as Fritz and Ina took up position beside her.

They set off across a concrete bridge that led towards a woodland path. The first animal life they came across was a horse, harnessed to a series of chains dragging felled trees down the hill; its owner doffing his cap as they passed by. Fritz and Ina had their cameras out trying to persuade Ana to stand next to the horse for a rustic shot but there was no way she was going near the black beast which had attracted flies and smelled of sweat. She carried on walking, catching up with the others nearer the front of the group.

The path grew stonier continuing uphill with the forest of pine trees standing like centurions. Sunshine permeated the green canopy and the rush of water from a rocky stream below grew louder as they walked. As they reached the start of the Seven Ladder's Canyon, they paused so that Alex could explain a little of what was ahead.

'Please take your time with the bridges and ladders, not too many at one time on any crossing. It looks precarious in parts but as long as you concentrate on where your feet go, you will be fine! If you can, watch be fine! Watch out for Wall Creepers. You will see these little birds fluttering their wings like butterflies against the rock walls. Chamois could be looking down on you too though you are lucky to spot them, they are well camouflaged. Once we are out on top and in the open, we can stop for lunch. Ana, you can join me at the front if you like. Is everyone ready?'

The group organised themselves into one line and waited for Alex to take the lead. Ana joined him.

'I'm afraid of heights, so when you start talking about ladders just exactly what am I doing here? You could have told me a little bit more before I agreed to come along,' she moaned, feeling like she was on the end of some practical joke.

Alex just grinned, insisting that nothing would go wrong.

'Facing your fears is how to overcome things. Lots of people make this walk so if they can do it you can too! I´ll be right with you Ana, as will we all, isn´t that true everyone?' Alex piped up for everyone to hear.

A little cheer and punching of fists in the air from the group meant Ana had no choice but to move on, cursing under her breath as she made her way along a rough wooden planked pathway. Its single rustic rail was the only barrier between her and the gushing river below. There was another sign indicating that the walk would take two hours. The canyon was one hundred and sixty meters long with a height up to fifty-eight meters and the highest waterfall was thirty-five meters. She suggested to Alex that perhaps she should turn back but he was determined to challenge her.

'Come on, Ana! You should stay with us. If you go back by yourself, who knows, the bears might have you!'

'You cannot be serious Alex!' she exclaimed. Neither bears nor ladders were a good option, so she decided if Alex was going to play the hero, she would let him and stay with the group.

They came to the first ladder, eight meters of rusty looking steel attached to rough limestone walls. Alex went first and as if by some grand plan, she found herself sandwiched between Alex and Fritz with no choice but to keep going. She took hold of the handrails and began one foot at a time to make her way up keeping her eyes fixed ahead at the rock face, its' prehistoric formations smoothed by thousands of years of water erosion. How anyone was going to be looking for birds and attempting this, she had no idea.

At the top of the first ladder, it got even worse with an old metal-framed gangway missing several of the planks of wood on which they were to cross. She could see the river far below in the gaps, a cauldron of frothing water fighting its way through the sheer-sided canyon walls. Ana was petrified while everyone else seemed to be unconcerned about the dilapidated state of the bridges.

The next ladder rose above her, leading to yet another narrow platform. It felt tight and enclosed with a waterfall thundering its way down the crevices. The noise was deafening as it echoed off the rock walls. No one could hear her muffled cries of panic. She had made it to the third ladder with its thick spout of water raining into her and climbed about halfway up the fifteen meters when a wave of confusion hit her. The water sped past her and the walls of the cavern loomed above her. She felt the ladder shaking and froze where she was. Her cold, white fingers clung to the slippery rails. She glanced below and began to feel dizzy. She closed her eyes and hung there, not knowing what to do. It was Alex that drew her glance back upwards, calling to her not to look down and she could hear Fritz encouraging her to keep going. She released one hand shakily, reaching to pull herself upwards. It seemed an eternity before she made it with Alex helping her make the last step.

'Well done Ana, three down and four more to go! That is the most spectacular waterfall and climb. From now on it will come easier.'

She couldn´t believe she had managed it, daring to look down into the abyss where she could see the others making their way up one by one. She trusted Alex was right and they continued through the maze of rock and water eventually coming out to the top of the canyon and the open sky. The group was full of excited chatter; each feeling the trip was one of the most memorable. Ana had to agree it wasn´t something she would ever forget but unlike the others, she would prefer to forget it. Her clothes were soaked and she was starting to shiver. Ina took a spare sweatshirt from her knapsack and insisted Ana wear it along with the pink kagool to warm herself up. She gave her a friendly hug squeezing Ana like a favourite niece before offering her a sip of brandy from a flask that appeared from her windbreaker pocket.

'Just for medicinal purposes, you understand!' Ina chortled.

Ana was feeling a tinge of guilt that she had been so dismissive about Ina and Fritz, laughing behind their backs when really, they were being kind. The group had stopped on a rocky outcrop overlooking a clearing in woodland, tucking into the packed lunches of freshly made wraps, cheeses and pickles that she had helped Mattei prepare earlier. She wished she could take off her boots, feeling the blisters forming on the back of her heels but said nothing as she loosened the laces a little. Alex came and sat beside her, allowing the others to relax and enjoy their food.

'So how do you feel now you have come this far? I could see you struggled with some of those ladders and the crossings are pretty worn out but you were courageous, like a little mountain goat!'

Ana wasn´t sure she liked the comparison to a goat. She wished she had been as stubborn as one and just refused to go. Her limbs were aching from muscles she didn´t know she had. Her feet were sore and her clothes and hair clung to her body like cling film. Alex's comments didn't make her feel any better.

'One day soon they will replace the entire old framework as more and more people are coming here but I think it has a level of charm right now for the real adventurer! I´m sure I can convert you to hiking if you let me. I do like a challenge!'

He still seemed to be mocking her but she wasn´t going to give him the benefit of knowing how terrified she had been, especially in front of the other guests who were all enjoying the trip as if it were a Sunday stroll.

'I appreciate your enthusiasm, Alex but let me get through this day first before you start planning any more surprises!' She wasn´t going to give him credit for making her do something she hadn´t wanted to do like he was some Sherpa god.

There were still another two hours of walking to get back to the minibus, so everyone gathered up their things and set off down a narrow track. Ana just about managed to tighten her laces again and hobbled into position behind Fritz and Ina.

The weather was closing in and a mist like a pale silk scarf was floating down the mountainside. The pathway was well marked, cutting through the trees and giving them more shelter from the winds that were picking up and threatening to bring rain. Ana was keeping her eyes trained on Ina in front of her, concentrating on the direction they were going when the line stopped abruptly. She leaned to one side, peaking past Ina, to see what was ahead. They had reached a frothy stream with an assembly of boulders dotted across from one side to the other, their shiny black surfaces arching out of the water like the humps of the Loch Ness monster.

'You have got to be kidding me,' she muttered to herself. By now, her feet were throbbing inside her boots.

One at a time, everyone picked their way across the stepping stones. Ana was second last to go with Alex bringing up the rear. She took a deep breath and reached a foot out to the first stone, slowly bringing her other foot on and balancing momentarily before continuing to the next. It seemed to take forever with all of the others standing opposite on dry land watching her. She was managing just fine until the middle point when she paused to look up at the waiting team. Her facial expression morphed into a look of horror as she realised she was losing her balance. Her body wobbled backwards and forwards, her arms stretched out to nothing, she was desperately trying to keep her feet where they were but she couldn't control them. She let out a high-pitched whimper and side-stepped off the rock into the stream. It barely came up to her knees but she was unsteady grasping the slippery surface as the water gurgled spitefully around her.

'I'm okay, I'm fine, I'm fine!' she shouted to the rock, cursing over the three manicured nails she knew had broken.

No one could contain themselves and they all burst out laughing at the sight of Ana in her pink kagool frozen like a statue in the water. She was fuming and felt utterly foolish.

Alex reached out a hand, pulling her back up. Her boots were heavy and her legs felt ten times their normal size. He guided her safely across like a fireman rescuing the damsel in distress. The others reached out to settle her onto terra-firma. She felt even worse as they fussed over her admiring her efforts.

The rain began to bite down on them as they continued back to their starting point. Once there Ina helped Ana by peeling off the pink kagool. Her hair stood up in a frenzy of static. Ina then took off the boots and rolled up her tracksuit bottoms just above her knees, replacing the sodden footwear with an oversized pair of Fritz's thick woollen socks. Ana was past caring how she looked. She sat in the minibus, sandwiched between Ina and Fritz. Her eyelids grew heavy and her head rolled to one side, resting on Ina's shoulder. The voices became a murmur in the background and sleep enveloped her even before they had left the car park. The girl from Marbella had undergone a baptism in humility.

13

The Shepherd's Hut

It took Ana several days to recover and Maria had been very sympathetic, feeling guilty that she had literally sold Ana down the river. She had been almost unrecognisable when she had returned to the hotel. The hotel guests, however, were full of compliments about her triumph over adversity. They adopted a nickname for her, Canyon Annie, with Fritz and Ina leaving a comment in the hotel guest book.

"We will always think of you in the pink! Thank you for joining us and making the Seven Ladders one of our most memorable trips. Forever in our hearts Canyon Annie, we will be back to conquer more!"

Ana could not imagine repeating the experience, nor did she appreciate her new nickname. The image of the efficient, neat and tidy Ana she liked to portray lay shredded after their return. She hadn´t enjoyed it, deciding her trekking days were over and she would stick to gentler pursuits, so when Mattei suggested a leisurely walk and lunch one free afternoon, Ana happily accepted.

Once she finished her morning duties, she waited in reception for Mattei. Alex arrived to collect his group of six guests that would be heading along a route to Bran. They would be spending the afternoon there exploring the historic castle with its mythical associations with Dracula, before returning to the hotel for their evening meal.

'It is a pity you aren´t coming with us, Ana. It´s such a pretty walk along the edge of the Bucegi Massif, not anything like as difficult as you experienced before and you have time to explore the town.'

'Thank you, Alex but I think I am happier to stay closer to home today. Mattei is taking me for a picnic and has already promised me I won´t need big walking boots.'

Alex just shrugged his shoulders, reminding her to watch out for bears that might be interested in the treats Mattei would have prepared. Ana was pleased to say they were taking Baloo and she was sure Mattei would not put her in any danger, reminding Alex that when she had gone with him, she had ended up with blisters and nearly died of pneumonia.

'That is true,' he laughed. 'I´ll bet he is taking you to that little wooden cabin of his. It is where he hides from us. He says it's where he gets his inspiration from, disappearing to dream of opening a restaurant of his own one day! I´m sure he will be good company talking about his menus all day!'

There was a hint of sarcasm in his remark that Ana could only see as jealousy that she would be enjoying herself in the company of his best friend. It didn´t matter to her what they talked about, so long as it was a break from the hotel guests and her regular conversations about other people's holidays. Mattei had already told her where they were going and the cabin Alex referred to was a shepherd's hut only half an hour of easy walking distance from his house. He had promised the most amazing views. She was happy with that.

Mattei, like her, had changed into shorts, tee-shirt and running shoes. They headed off passing by Mattei's house to collect Baloo on the way. Baloo knew where they were going and raced in front, turning back now and again to check they were still following. They had turned off the road onto a cart track with a gentle gradient that ran parallel to an area of dense woodland. To their left, the views looked towards open countryside. The weather was perfect with a blue sky stretching way above them. She had nothing to carry as Mattei had everything ready in his knapsack. Contrary to Alex´s comments, Mattei led the conversation telling her a little more about where they were going.

'The shepherd's hut is part of the farmstead. They would gather the sheep there in pens for handling at different times of the year, much closer to home. Most of the year they were grazing up in the mountains.'

'Was your father a farmer, then?' asked Ana.

'No, my grandfather and his forefathers before him

were farmers and shepherds. It was a way of life, quite nomadic. Most of the time they were away tending the flock so there are huts dotted all over these mountains where they would stay. My grandmother stayed at the farmhouse and took care of the rest of the farm. She grew vegetables and looked after the poultry and a few pigs. The bigger jobs were mainly handled by the men, like haymaking and harvesting. It wasn´t an easy life, especially when the Russians took over.'

'What happened then?' asked Ana.

'Did you not learn any history at school, Ana, or were you a daydreamer at school?' he teased.

'History wasn´t my strong subject but then they never made it sound as interesting as you do!' she prompted him.

'Well in 1949 the Russians took Romania under their control, after the second world war. Of course, they were communist and so enforced their ideals onto everyone. Generations had been farming here in the same way quite happily but they marched in and took everything away, animals, carts, ploughs every instrument large or small, even seeds and stored produce. They took it all to a collective farm. They left no choice but for the farmers to work for them. Otherwise, you starved. They still needed the people to tend the animals, so my grandfather just carried on even though everything they produced had to go to the collective. In 1965 Ceausescu took over but things continued to run under a communist fist. My grandfather encouraged my father to work hard at school. He didn´t want him to be a farmer even though my father loved these mountains and knew them just as well as his father, he became a dentist of all things!'

'He must have worked very hard to achieve that!' remarked Ana.

'Yes, there were a lot of sacrifices along the way and they had five children to take care of, none of whom became farmers. They had four daughters and one son. My father was the eldest. The daughters all got married eventually and moved away.'

'What happened to the farm then?'

'Well finally in 1990, after the fall of Ceausescu they gave the land back to the rightful owners but without any money or tools to make it profitable. It was all my grandparents knew, so they continued to live here but they were getting older and not able to continue as before. By then, my father had a successful dental clinic in Brasov and could afford to take care of them. They promised him they would leave the farm to him. It was his boyhood home, after all. I was brought up a country boy but went to school in Brasov, where I met Alex. He spent most of his spare time here, with us.'

Ana was listening to the story intently, trying to work out all the connections between everyone and how they had all become so close. She asked about Alex and Maria.

'Alex often stayed with us. His father was going through a nasty divorce. His mother was English. She left Andrei for someone else and went back to England. She didn´t want anything to do with him, so Andrei easily got custody but he worked long hours. Our house became like a second home for Alex. Maria's family has been here for generations. They were close to my grandparents and parents and all descended from the original Saxons. They were all German-speaking. After Ceausescu's departure, there was a mass ethnic migration back to the fatherland. The German politician Hans-Dietrich Genscher persuaded many that they would be much better off going back to West Germany. No one really reported it but at the time ninety per cent of the German-speaking population upped sticks and left here for a better way of life. However, these lands have a gravity that draws you back, so you see why Maria has returned to her roots and her parents also.'

By the time Mattei had answered most of Ana's questions, they had arrived at the hut he had described. It was built entirely from the natural resources of the nearby forest, like his house, though its wooden frame was more weathered. It had a narrow inverted 'V' shaped roof which kept the snow from collecting in the winter. On one side three steps led up to a door and a small veranda overlooked the sheep pens, long since out of use. The view stretched for miles with a carpet of flowered meadows dotted with haystacks laid out before them. Ana could see the bright gardens of Casa Flori and Mattei's farmhouse in the distance. It felt so tranquil. The air was soft and fragrant from the breeze that whispered through the nearby trees. There was the sound of a running brook nearby.

Baloo settled himself just outside the door, panting in the heat of the summer's day. 'The door is never locked,' said Mattei, 'No need up here and I always have Baloo with me. Once inside you can pull a metal bar across though that's more to stop the bear's from getting in!' Mattei laughed, leading Ana inside.

There were two rooms, each with handmade furniture. The main one had a small log burner in one corner, a table and chairs and an area that could be used to prepare food. Some shelves stored a few heavy black pans, a cast-iron cauldron and some plates. The second room contained a single bed and a washstand with a chamber pot placed beneath it. A small window overlooked the path they had come. It had a homely feel, decorated with various hand-woven textiles in traditional patterns and colours just like the ones Ana had seen in Mattei's house.

'It is primitive as you can see, no electricity, no running water, just a kerosene lamp to light at night but I love the simplicity. If you need a pee in the night and you don´t want to venture out, there is a pot, handy in the winter months! Cooking is mainly done outside over a fire which is dug into the earth and surrounded by stones but when the log burner is going you can warm up the best coffee!' Mattei beamed.

Ana had never even been camping before but she thought if it was like this, she could be quite comfortable. It was like a child's playhouse.

He began unpacking the contents of the knapsack, asking if she was hungry. She followed him outside, taking a large blanket as directed and spread it over the grassy bank. Baloo settled on it, taking up more than half the space.

'Baloo! Sorry, Ana, he´s used to being the centre of attention here as I am usually on my own,' said Mattei, attempting to roll Baloo off the blanket.

He opened two beers and they both relaxed,

enjoying the food he had brought. Mattei turned the topic of conversation back to her family.

'You don´t say much about yourself or your family, Ana, not that you have to!' Mattei was curious as to how she came to be working at the hotel especially after speaking with Alex. Maybe she was running from something, maybe even a broken heart but he didn´t want to seem too nosey. His nature was always to think the best of people.

'You are asking how I ended up here, aren´t you? I have family and I also adore them but I was a bit of a rebel growing up. I am not like you, or Alex. I haven´t figured out exactly what I want to do yet and I suppose they thought a complete change would do me good. My brother helped to get me this job, away from the city and temptation,' she joked.

'So how do you feel now that you have joined us? Do you still think we are all peasants?' He asked her light-heartedly.

'It´s nothing like I expected. I miss the city but I´m glad I have come here. I´ve done things I´ve never done before,' she answered honestly.

She volunteered more. It felt good to talk about her early years growing up, how she was the youngest of three and how her two older brothers always took the blame for any trouble she created. Once upon a time, she was that carefree girl and she missed it.

'You and Alex remind me of my brothers. Were you an only child Mattei?' she asked, realising that although he had told her a lot about his family history, he had never mentioned any brothers or sisters.

Mattei was unusually quiet for a few moments.

'Not exactly, nothing is ever quite as it seems,' he said hesitating as if he wasn't sure what to say next.

His remark took her by surprise. She immediately thought she must have given something unintended away about herself but to her relief, Mattei smiled at her and spoke again.

'I told you all about my parents, my grandparents and growing up here. I had a happy childhood and then I found out something that turned all that on its head. I don't talk about it much, like you, there are things I'm still trying to work out.'

Ana couldn't think what he was about to tell her but she stayed quiet and waited for him to continue.

'When my parents died, there was so much to go through, paperwork, wills, that kind of thing. Andrei was a huge support taking care of most of it but it was during this time that I found out I was adopted. I thought I was an only child, no brothers or sisters. I never really thought about why they only had me. We were always happy. It was such a shock. Everything I had known and assumed became a falsehood. I didn't know who I was anymore. I was angry, not only had I lost two people that were the most important to me in the whole world but they had kept something from me, something I felt they should have explained to me years ago. Other people would have known but for whatever reason, no one ever explained it to me. For a while, I was bitter, resentful. I started to look at myself in the mirror, knowing that I couldn't be a mixture of the two of them which I had always assumed. I didn't resemble either of them directly. I was someone else's child and I had no idea why my birth parents had given me up. Leaving for London was part of the healing process, not just about having an adventure or taking up a different career path. I was trying to avoid a lot of emotions. It took me a while to get over things but eventually, true love conquers and I realised that my adopted parents had only ever wanted the best for me. The way they brought me up and the things they taught me meant I did have so much of them in me even if it wasn´t their blood.'

'So, did you learn anything about who your real parents were once you found out you were adopted?' Ana continued curiously.

'Not at first, I felt it would have been a betrayal to papa and mama but after a time I began to think about it and I did want to find out why I had been given up. I asked Andrei to help me and we tracked down the adoption papers and names of my birth parents but it was like a needle in a haystack. They left me in a state orphanage when I was barely three years old. I didn´t remember anything from that time, or I didn´t think I did. Sometimes growing up, I had strange dreams but I never associated that with the real truth. We couldn´t locate my birth parents, only getting as far as knowing they signed some papers and left the country with two sons, my brothers. We think they went to Italy but then lots of Romanians migrated at that time. I know they were poor because the village they lived in was just a series of shacks close to Craiova, so we assume they left to escape poverty. I found out that a lot of people, like my birth parents, were conned into selling whatever they had to get to other countries. They were promised a better future by unscrupulous gangs that never delivered. I hate the bad name people like that give our country and how they treat our fellow countrymen. It was hard when I was living in London, the amount of prejudice. People hear you are from Romania and straight away think we are all criminals, pickpockets or prostitutes! It is true, the gangs that operate are greedy and exploiting innocent people but no one seems able or willing to stop them. If it weren't for them, maybe I would still have my real parents. Bastards, all of them!' he retorted.

Ana flinched at his remarks as a shadow of Sergiu. crept into her subconscious. She had never seen Mattei lose his patience or show any temper but clearly, he felt strongly about the subject. She felt sorry for him.

She thought about the Romanians she had seen on her travels in Germany living hand to mouth in cramped rooms or on the streets and camps in Madrid. She had ignored them and even looked down upon them. Now she had met someone who had a real family probably reduced to hopelessness thanks to the likes of Sergiu. She knew many of these people were off the radar, so it was no surprise they were difficult to trace.

'So, you have no idea where they are or what happened to them?'

'No but I did find out I wasn´t alone when they left me behind. I had a sister called Christine. She was left behind at the same time, in the same place. Somewhere deep in me, the strange dreams I was having started to take on more meaning. Odd memories came back to me, though distant and hazy.'

It was mid-afternoon and time was passing by very

quickly. Mattei suggested they start to head back, so they gathered up the things and made sure the hut was tidy.

'Are you sure I´m not boring you? I haven't talked about all this for a while but it feels good to tell someone,' he said to her. Ana assured him that she was happy to listen if he needed to talk more.

'I have decided to look for her but it is hard when I don´t have much to go on, no photographs, no real information. David is helping me being a king of technology! He has put out notices to different charities, missing persons, at least with a name, how old she would be and the fact that she was in this orphanage. All we can do now is wait and see if anything comes up. I tend to come up here to think things through but on my own usually. It has been so busy getting the hotel and the restaurant going and always so many people around. Maria and David are great but they have enough to think about and I don´t want to load anything more on to them. Of course, Alex lives with me and he´s like my brother but he doesn´t know what goes around in my head exactly. He said I should just let sleeping dogs lie and move on but now I feel like some part of me is missing and I would like to find that piece.'

Ana was sympathetic. 'I can understand why you would want to find her. It´s easy for Alex to say let sleeping dogs lie. I´m sure he thinks he´s protecting you after everything you have gone through.'

'You are a good listener,' said Mattei moving his hand to her face to brush away a lock of her hair that had fallen across her cheek. Ana pulled back just a little, arranging her hair in place, caught out by his sudden but gentle gesture.

'Sorry, it´s nice of you to say that.' she blushed.

He was so honest. If Mattei knew the truth, he probably wouldn´t even speak to her, let alone trust her with his feelings. She shouldn´t misinterpret his action. It was kindness to her, as Ana.

They headed back down the path, falling once again into easy conversation; Mattei joking that anytime she needed to go to the 'think house' the door was never locked. They both had an evening's work ahead of them and so she left Mattei to take Baloo back to his house and headed to Casa Flori by herself.

She wanted to call Razvan to ask him when she could come home. Mattei had stirred up new emotions in her reminding her of the lies she invented. She had to admit to herself she wasn't the ideal daughter, trying to impress her parents about how happy and successful she was, always too busy to talk for very long on the telephone. It was the same with her brothers, not taking much interest in their day to day lives.

She kept herself in a bubble, maybe in denial about what she had become and too stubborn to think she couldn´t handle things herself. It wasn't her fault she was forced into hiding. Maybe after a little more time, no one would be thinking about her or care anymore that she had bolted from Spain. Surely, she wasn't that much of a risk. She would show him she could behave differently. She could be Ana for longer.

She made her way back to her room and picked up the mobile Razvan had given her. He was cheerful when he answered, listening to her talk about the friends she had made and how the work was going. He noticed a change in her just by her questions. How were his children, were they enjoying the summer and what had they been doing? She asked about all the family and he had laughed, saying the mountain air must be making her dizzy, to ask so many questions. 'I've changed,' she told him, 'I'm ready to come home.' She attempted to sweet talk him.

'I know but it's complicated. Remember, this isn't just about you. Eventually, you may be summoned as a witness. You have to appreciate we can´t just go out and arrest the bad guys. We are covering international borders, gathering as much information as we can. Prosecutors work in fear of their lives. It all takes time. Maybe I shouldn´t be telling you this but I want you to remain cautious. Sergiu has been back to Bucharest. Word has it that he was trying to find you but of course, there is no trail to follow so be patient and you will stay safe. We are tracking his people. Things are moving along but I can't say how soon it will be over.' Razvan was well aware his house was under surveillance and his parent's house too. So far, he was content they were wasting their time.

Ana could only promise she would be sensible but for the first time in years, she was feeling homesick. She took out her locket from its blue box and held to her heart. Her balloon filled with dreams of a happy free life had been deflated, leaving her frustrated. She needed to snap out of it she told herself and concentrate on being Ana.

Over the next week, she did just that. She threw herself into her work, making herself busy, even doing extra hours, offering to help in any way she could. There wasn't much else to do. Maria was becoming concerned that Ana was wearing herself out.

'Ana, you shouldn't feel like you have to be on duty, twenty-four-seven! You are not here to be a slave and I want you to enjoy working here. I will be so sad when the time comes for you to leave. Andrei told me when we took you on that it would probably be just for the summer but I wish we could keep you! Alex mentioned to me that he thought you were ready for a break and I agree. He suggested you deserved a proper night out!'

'Maria I'm fine! I enjoy what I do. It doesn't feel like work. Well, sometimes if there is the odd grumpy guest but I'm learning all the time and that is what I'm meant to be doing so I'm just making the most of it!' Ana reassured her. The truth was that the harder she worked, the easier it was not to worry about what was happening back in Spain or the fact that she had no contact with either her friends or her family apart from Razvan.

She enjoyed the time she spent with Alex and Mattei. They were a distraction, always making her laugh. They were both serious about their work and both ambitious but they were also young and good company for her so when Alex asked her to join him on a Saturday night out to a club with friends she could see no harm in it. Maria was right. She couldn't bury herself entirely in Casa Flori. She missed nights out in Marbella when she and the girls would head for the clubs. The heady mix of moneyed visitors provided them with free nights out in exchange for a little flirting. There were afternoons spent at Nikki

Beach and Ocean Club where they would hire a cabana bed for the day, drink champagne and enjoy the music while bitching about the assortment of outfits and fashions on parade.

She wasn´t sure what to expect in Brasov and she was sure Alex wouldn´t be ordering champagne and cocktails but either way, it might be a chance to meet more people of the same age and she intended to make the most of it.

14

Dancing Among Wolves

Saturday night arrived and she had spent time doing her nails and hair and trying to decide what to wear. She chose a casual little black dress. Surely you couldn't go wrong with that! She kept her makeup light but allowed herself some heels since she had worn nothing but flats since her arrival. Her glossy hair had grown to her shoulders and she had parted it to one side, tucking it behind one ear, adding a simple pair of pearl earrings.

She made her way up to reception where Alex was waiting for her.

'Wow, you look amazing, Ana,' he said.

Mattei had ventured out from the kitchen, as had Maria.

'Is this okay?' asked Ana knowing how attractive she was. She was looking to Mattei for approval. He merely nodded before disappearing back to the kitchen. Maria caught her look of disappointment.

'Don't worry Ana, you look lovely! Mattei is just a bit put out he's not coming with you.'

She meant it as a placatory comment but Ana couldn't hide her feelings that Mattei didn't share her eager anticipation for the evening ahead. It was the first night out she'd had in ages. Alex had offered to take her out. It wasn't a date as far as she was concerned but there was a slight air of awkwardness as Mattei left the room. Alex was already on his way out, opening the car door for her.

It was dark when they reached Brasov. Alex parked the car outside his father's house and they made their way to one of the café bars in the Piata Sfatului. They took up a table outside and ordered a beer each, enjoying the warm evening and watching the town hall square fill up with a younger crowd. Alex had arranged to meet some friends. After a few drinks, they would head over to one of the clubs where he said he was a regular.

As they arrived, he introduced them, four boys and two girls about the same age as Ana. Alex explained that they had all been in school together but he had been the only one to brave University. His friends enjoyed teasing him about his new business as a mountain guide.

'You are like Bear Grylls!' one of the boys joked. 'Always off in the mountains and saving the forests. We never see you for days on end! Tell us, Alex, have you not yet shown Ana our famous bears in Brasov. You do not need to go to the forest!'

Alex took the bait, replying defensively. 'He is

120

referring to the bears that come close to the town where the forest meets an area of garbage dumpsters. People have been encouraging them, feeding them watermelons and taking pictures. A film crew from Australia came to report and put our little town on the international map but I do not agree with it. These bears are wild, not some cute teddy bears in an open zoo. They should have reported on the real efforts to protect our wildlife.'

'Relax, Alex, get off your soapbox. We are winding you up! You know we respect what you do!' they all chorused, breaking into laughter.

They passed an hour or two catching up with the events of the summer. Ana joined in with stories about the guests at the hotel, keeping the conversation general and careful to avoid how she came to be working there. Alex let slip her new nickname, Canyon Annie which she did not appreciate but she went along with it. Everyone else seemed to find it funny. Eventually, they all made their way to the Hacienda Club.

A wall of sound from the resident D.J. hit them as they entered. The club was characteristically dark except for the flashing of multicoloured lights that sped about the room. A young woman made her way through the crowd, clearly on a mission, as the group gathered at one of the seating areas. Alex introduced her to Ana, who was expecting a greeting in the same way as she had met the others. Instead, the girl whispered something in Alex´s ear as she gathered her hands around his waist. She then sauntered off, giving Ana a frosty stare. Alex was grinning.

'Don´t mind Sophia. I think she´s a little drunk

already. She is an ex-girlfriend. We split up when I went to University but she thinks she can pick up where we left off every time I come back to Brasov. She will be jealous of you for sure but I´m not going to tell her you are working for us. Let her think what she likes!' said Alex.

Ana wasn´t as amused as Alex. She had no intention of allowing this girl or any other to think she was Alex´s new girlfriend. She wanted to enjoy herself and she didn´t need Alex to hang on to her all night like a trophy.

A stack of beers, vodka shots and bottles of water filled their table. Ana sat herself down on one of the sofas helping herself to a vodka shot. Alex took up position next to her, a little too close, she thought as he stretched his arm across the back of the seat behind her. She felt he was showing off and adjusted her body in the direction of the girls in an attempt to make some distance. Luckily the girls were friendly enough even remarking that Alex was up to his usual of charming the girls. After a couple of shots of vodka, Alex suggested they head to the dance floor. Ana liked the song that was playing and led the way.

Most of the girls danced with their feet rooted to the spot, doing a gentle grind and waving one hand from side to side in the air, looking about the room to see who was watching them. Alex was enjoying himself in the spotlight with Ana. She began to drift into the rhythm of the music, the effect of the alcohol taking its course. Some admirers were moving closer and she was enjoying the attention, wanting to detach herself from Alex's attempts to stay in the limelight. She was used to making a show and stood out from the crowd, aware that she was the prettiest girl in the room.

As she surveyed the scene, she singled out one man leaning on his elbows with his back to the bar, who couldn't seem to take his eyes off her. He cut a handsome figure in jeans and a white shirt as he toyed with a lowball glass of whiskey. She started doing some distance flirting but then her mind began to race. Supposing someone recognised her? Sergiu had contacts in every corner and now she realised that something of Mihaela was starting to show itself in her actions, in her laugh, in her eyes. She became very self-conscious, catching the eye of Alex's ex still whispering in the ears of other girls. She left the floor abruptly, retreating to her seat and taking up one of the bottles of water. The room was suddenly full of wolves.

'Are you okay Ana?' Alex shouted over the music.

This time she was glad he came over, feeling he was protecting her. After a time, she allowed him to take her by the hand back on the dance floor with Ana adopting a more moderate style of dancing that blended in with the others.

In the small hours, people began to filter out onto the street, noisily saying their goodbyes and making their way either to other bars or home. Ana was glad they were heading straight back to Alex's father's house. Her feet were aching and she felt light-headed. She noticed the man that had been at the bar was taking the same route. Was he following or was it just a coincidence? She took Alex's arm keeping her head down and after a short time saw him turn off and head in a different direction. It was probably her imagination. She let go of Alex.

A feeling of relief passed over her, as they entered the house, its silence was welcoming. Andrei would be asleep. Alex kicked off his shoes and made his way to the kitchen.

'Are you hungry Ana?' he asked as he opened the fridge door and helped himself to a plate of cold meats and cheeses and a tall glass of fresh milk. It was nearly three o'clock in the morning.' Better to eat now than try to face a breakfast in the morning,' he said.

Ana was content with water, wondering how soon she could get to bed and let her head meet a soft pillow. Alex invited her to sit down.

'You made quite an impression on everyone tonight, Ana. I don't think my girlfriends are used to someone like you commanding all that attention,' Alex said, half-joking.

'Girlfriends, how many are there, other than the lovely Sophia?' she mocked.

'Probably too many,' he laughed. 'I'm not looking for a steady relationship. Not yet. There are too many things I want to do and some of these local girls are just too willing to tie you down. It was fun to have you around and stir things up a bit!'

I didn't intend anything,' she said defensively. 'I was just having fun.'

Well, I am sure you must have broken some hearts on your travels,' he added. Ana had been giving him mixed messages all night, sometimes keeping him almost intimately close and the next pushing him away.

He could not be further from the truth, Ana thought. She had never had a real boyfriend, just a controller in Sergiu, who fooled her into thinking she was special. She had been in bed with more men, of all ages, over the last few years than Alex could ever have had girlfriends but she had not broken any hearts. Where men were concerned, she had been taught to keep her emotions at bay, never allowing herself to be close with anyone. It was just business, keeping the punters happy. Sergiu made sure of that, he hadn't broken her heart either but he had hardened her soul.

She changed the subject, bringing the conversation casually round to Mattei.

'Well, since you ask, he spends too much time thinking about food,' Alex smiled. 'He has ambitions, just like me but he´s not interested in playing the field and having fun on the way. We go out together but maybe to different places. He doesn´t like the type of place we went to tonight. He says it´s a pick-up joint and I always beat him to the girls anyway! He likes good music, eating out and we have a good group of friends but he´s not looking for anyone. I suppose one day someone will come along and cupid will hit him with an arrow where it hurts! He´s that type of guy, always laughing, making the jokes but underneath he is as vulnerable as they come. He´s like my brother. I wouldn´t ever want to see him get hurt.'

Alex was looking directly at her, his comment piercing her skin like a warning shot. It was true she got along so well with Mattei but who wouldn´t? She hadn't done anything wrong and she wasn´t leading him on. How dare Alex think she had any intentions on him? She changed the subject again.

'It was nice of you to bring me along tonight. I can

cross off one thing on my list of things to do in Brasov and that is to avoid places full of your ex-girlfriends! It would seem you have broken a few hearts,' she teased, 'as for me, I have no idea what I want to do.' she smiled, trying to keep things neutral. Alex reached for her hand across the table, adding 'Some people should just stick to being friends.'

Ana felt annoyed. Alex had flirted with her and even been happy to give the impression to some of his friends that there was more going on between them. He had no right to form any judgment on her. Maybe he was disappointed she hadn't responded to his charms like the other girls did but that was his problem she thought. It all seemed a bit juvenile to her; she no longer cared if she went to another Brasov club or not.

She helped him clear up the remains of his supper and then he showed her to the guest room, leaving her to her thoughts. She took off her makeup and finally lay down, thinking about Mattei. She was flattered he confided in her. He was interested in what she thought. So what if she did like him? He made her laugh a lot and feel good about herself but she had to let her head rule. She couldn´t forget neither her past nor what she was hiding from and tonight there had been a little reminder she wasn´t entirely free. She switched off the sidelight, turned on her side and was soon fast asleep.

15

Smelling the Coffee

A draft of sunlight peeping through the curtains fell like a spotlight on Ana. She lay in the bed, stretching her arms and yawning as she roused herself from a good night's sleep. She could hear sounds from the kitchen with the enticing smell of coffee and toast wafting through to her room. It was already mid-morning and she immediately felt hungry. She pulled on a pair of shorts, a spare baggy tee-shirt, ran a brush through her hair and ventured out.

Andrei was frying eggs and buttering thick slices of toast. There was no sign of Alex.

'Good morning, Ana. How was your night out?' he asked her.

'Fine,' she replied.

'Just fine? That doesn´t sound to me like you had

any fun. Has my son not exercised his usual charms on you or was Brasov nightlife not what you were expecting? He's not up yet and so you can be honest with me,' he smiled, pouring her a mug of coffee.

'No, it was a good night, it's just that I've become so used to the countryside. I'm beginning to think I prefer it. I met some nice people and I know it did me good to get out for once, so I am glad Alex took me.'

Andrei placed a mound of buttered toast on the table. 'I must admit I was a little reluctant when Razvan called me asking if there were any contacts I knew of to help you out. I was unsure how it would work, placing you with people so closely connected with me given your situation but he is a good man and he promised me you would make it work. I know Maria is glad of the help and from what I hear you have made a good impression on her. Do you like it there?' asked Andrei.

Ana thought about how things had worked out. She hadn't known what to expect but at least there was no heavy manual work. She helped out with the breakfast shift, handled the reception, did room checks and worked in the restaurant in the evenings. There was nothing to complain about, especially when everyone accepted her so readily. She was unsure what Andrei thought of her but felt Razvan would have explained she was a victim, unlucky to be in the wrong place at the wrong time. She was grateful to have a job and it was only temporary before she could get back to the city, back to shopping and being with her friends.

'Yes, I enjoy the work and I'm learning a lot! I appreciate the chance, thank you. I miss my family and I do want to be able to move on,' said Ana truthfully, switching her gaze to her coffee mug.

Andrei nodded sympathetically.

'Speaking of family, I spoke to your brother. He was somewhat concerned you and your blue eyes would be out amongst the lights of Brasov.'

Razvan's conversation with Andrei had been to the point. After all the trouble he had taken to make sure she kept a low profile, her decision to go clubbing wasn't a good one. He didn't want Ana causing any more complications.

'What did you tell him?' asked Ana.

'I told him you were out at Alex´s invitation. He knows he can´t expect a young girl to be staying in every night with a good book to read but he is right, you do need to be wary. It´s quite touristy here, which is a good thing as you can blend in but like anywhere there are eyes and ears about that will report to bad company, especially if they think there is a reward involved. Alex has good friends, so you needn´t worry on that score.'

Ana was feeling uneasy thinking about some of the people in the club who had not been so friendly. Was it true there was a reward out for her? Razvan hadn't said anything.

Before she had time to ask him what else her brother had told him Alex appeared. She and Andrei stopped talking.

'Have I missed something?' asked Alex. He was wearing old jogging bottoms and was bare-chested, his hair uncombed and face unshaven.

'Alex, you could have made more effort to tidy yourself up when we have company,' said Andrei, avoiding the question.

'Trust me I've seen Ana first thing in the morning, so I'm sure she's not going to be offended by me!' Alex helped himself to toast and eggs, winking at Ana.

She knew he was teasing his father and put the record straight that he had knocked on her door on her first morning at Casa Flori and terrorised her with a dog.

They finished their breakfast then showered and changed, ready for the return to the hotel. As they were leaving Andrei, put his arm around Ana's shoulder reassuringly and checking Alex was out of earshot, he quietly told her to keep following her brother's advice and she would be fine.

They headed out of Brasov and as the countryside began to roll out its carpet of green Ana felt some relief. Alex turned down the radio so they could talk more easily. He had enjoyed taking her out but was still curious and his father didn't tell him much. He was sure she was no criminal but he had his suspicions; she was mixed up in something. It couldn't just be his father doing a favour for a friend in giving her a job. There was something about her he couldn't quite put his finger on.

'My father seems to like you, like a baby bird he has taken under his wing,' he said jokingly. 'He even told me to keep a special eye out for you. Do you need protecting Ana?' he asked, cheekily.

'Of course not, why should I?' she answered almost too quickly.

'Just asking, you don't say much about yourself, you are a bit of a conundrum as they say.'

'Well, isn´t it true that a little mystery makes us more interesting?'

He laughed but chose not to pursue the line of conversation any further. He wasn´t interested in getting involved in whatever Ana was keeping secret, nor should Mattei. He changed the subject back to day to day things for the rest of the journey.

That afternoon Ana was out on the terrace watering some of the flowerpots for Maria. Mattei had arrived earlier than usual for the evening shift catching her by surprise. He seemed in a buoyant mood. She sensed something had happened. He asked her politely if she had enjoyed her night out. Alex had already told him about the evening and the impression Ana had made on his ex-girlfriends and to every male in the club.

'I'm telling you there is a different side to that girl but not my type' he commented.

Mattei thought that Alex must have fancied his chances with Ana. He was always first when it came to leading the way when girls were around and she had looked amazing on her way out. It was strange Alex had chosen not to pursue her. At least there would be no rivalry between them. For now, he just wanted to share his latest news with her.

'Something has happened, what is it Mattei?' She asked, setting aside the watering can and sitting down next to him at one of the tables.

'I had a phone call last night, from a woman called Julia. She said she thought she knew my sister from some of the adverts that David had placed for missing persons. She seemed pretty sure and she´s asked me to meet her.'

Ana was surprised. 'Wow that is good news. What else did this woman say?'

'Not much, I was quite taken aback. I didn´t know how to respond. I feel excited and nervous at the same time. We have agreed to meet next week.'

Ana was delighted for Mattei but immediately thought how he would feel if it turned out to lead to nothing. Wasn't it strange she wanted to meet him without saying very much else?

'I know it´s early days to be surmising,' said Mattei 'but I have to go, it´s a start at least. She said it was important to meet me in person rather than talk on the telephone. I have nothing to lose in going. Would you come with me? She lives near Ploiesti.'

Her heart went out him. She thought for a moment. She couldn´t just set off roaming about the country even if she wanted too, besides this was about Mattei´s family and something he should follow up, for himself.

'Mattei, I´m pleased you asked me. I know how important this is to you but I think this is a first step, one you should take on your own. This woman is expecting to meet you, not your entourage. Find out what she can tell you and I will help you in any way I can, if it turns out positive.' she added kindly giving him a friendly hug.

He was sure she would have offered to go with him but maybe Ana was right, it was a first step and he shouldn´t be building up his hopes too soon. Time would tell.

16

Julia

Mattei had been full of anticipation all week. He was not sure what to expect from his meeting with Julia. They had only spoken on the telephone once more after her initial call, to confirm a time and how to get to her home. It was the first time in months of searching that he had finally uncovered some concrete information that could lead him to his sister. He was unsure just how much he could trust this woman. Maybe she would have the wrong person and the trip would be a wild goose chase. Julia had said she was sure she knew his sister as she had worked in the orphanage where both he and Christine were left. From Mattei's research, he knew there were nearly two hundred children housed there during the 1980´s. How could she remember him or his sister and how after nineteen years might she still have any real information on where she was now?

Julia lived halfway between Brasov and Bucharest in the commune of Bucov, one of several rural villages making up the county of Prahova. The closest large town was Ploiesti, the county seat a few miles away. He had borrowed Alex´s trusty Dacia for the two-hour trip, taking in little of the journey south as he analysed what possible outcomes there might be from this meeting.

Julia was reluctant in their second conversation to go into any detail even though he had asked. She had insisted they meet before she would say anymore, perhaps also wary of Mattei's intentions. Maybe she did know more than she was saying and wanted to protect his sister in some way, after all, she didn't know him either. These were thoughts that ran through his mind, like trying to connect the dots on a puzzle, not knowing what the picture was.

He drove around the outskirts of Ploiesti and followed the main DN1B that took him through Bucov, slowing down, to look for the roadside supermarket where she had told him to park.

A mix of one and two-storey buildings lined the road with a few houses, a beauty salon, a pharmacy and an animal feed store. They seemed run down, with assorted signage and flaking paintwork. Mattei saw the small supermarket and pulled into the car parking area bordering the road. It was just after ten in the morning. The sky was grey, the landscape flat and the whole scene very different from his home. He wished Ana had been able to come with him.

He locked the car door, taking the brown envelope of photographs from his years growing up that Julia had suggested he bring. There were a few people around mainly with their heads down, going about their daily business. None of whom took any notice of him. He was fifteen minutes ahead of their scheduled time but decided to wait by the car, hoping she would make herself known.

After several minutes he became aware of her. She was smiling at him as she approached. It had to be her. She appeared older than he imagined, dressed in a loose-fitting blue garment that women of a certain age seemed to wear to disguise a lost figure. Her hair had remnants of an added colour but mostly it was grey, permed and thinning. As she came closer, her smile revealed a kindness, tinged with a mix of recognition and caution. He could see the lines etched on her face like a palm reading telling a life history. She was small standing next to him.

She studied him, taking in his height, his face and his eyes.

'You are just as I imagined you would be,' she said, 'I am Julia. I thought it would be easier to meet you here and then we can walk to my house. I am not very good with directions and you would not know which my house was!'

Mattei responded politely extending his hand and thanking her for her invitation. They walked for several minutes along the main road. The cars and trucks speeding past made any conversation difficult. They turned off onto a quieter side street and began to exchange pleasantries about the weather and how different Bucov was from Brasov. They passed a general store with its display of fresh tomatoes, melons and onions. A horse and cart stood outside, its driver loading what looked like sacks of flour onto the cart. The village took on a gentler feel.

Mattei and Julia turned into another smaller street. The houses were all similar, mainly one storey with tinned roofs. Pylons supporting a criss-cross of electric cables and telephone wires linked the houses together like random washing lines.

Julia paused outside a metal gate, painted in emerald green with a gravel path leading to a matching front door. The small garden was planted generously with vegetables and flowers. It was so bright and colourful. He could have been walking the yellow brick road from Munchkin land in the Wizard of Oz.

'My children bought this house for me after my husband died so that I would be closer to them,' she said proudly. 'We used to live closer to Bucharest but it was so busy. My husband was a taxi driver for many years, always working and no time to look after a garden! Now I have time but not the same energy.' She looked at him, smiling.

There was virtually no room to pass either side of the house and so she led him through a narrow hall to the back of the house. A small concrete yard boasted an assortment of herb pots filling the air with the scents Mattei was very familiar with in the kitchen at Casa Flori. There was an old wooden table with three mismatched chairs and she beckoned for him to take a seat. He did as he was asked, just wanting to come straight to the point and ask her where Christine was but he realised that Julia was in no hurry. She disappeared to the kitchen and he sat in silence, feeling uncomfortable. He could hear the rattling of cups and plates until finally, she returned with a tray of chai and a pandispan cu fructe, a traditional cake with berries.

'I know you are a chef so I hope my cake is good enough for you! My three boys love their cake and this is one of their favourites. I must make three or four each week!' she laughed quietly.

'Thank you for making me so welcome' Mattei replied. 'My mother also used to make this cake and she taught me the recipe. My mother, I mean, being my adoptive mother but then you know I was adopted.'

He was hoping she would turn the subject round to the purpose of his visit but she seemed to be more interested in him. He was starting to think she might be a little mad but he didn´t want to seem rude.

'Now let me have a look at some of the pictures you brought with you!' she said, putting on a pair of reading glasses.

Mattei opened the envelope and dropped the photographs he had brought on to the table. He chose a picture of when he was about five years old standing between his adoptive parents, their hands placed proudly on his young shoulders, all of them beaming at the camera. It was one of his favourites. One by one he selected pictures which he passed to Julia who studied each as he told her of his years growing up in the countryside, graduating from school and training as a chef in London.

At last, Julia seemed ready to move on the conversation.

'My son is mainly responsible for this meeting. He works for a charity to help young people. He showed me your advert with your picture because it mentioned the home where I used to work. He is passionate about what he does and he knows there is always a chance I might come across someone through my past work and here you are! I thought I recognised who you were looking for and now I am sure.'

She paused, looking into his eyes and continued.

You look so alike,' she ventured finally. You have the same face and eyes, though Christine is not as tall as you are.'

Mattei's heart skipped several beats at her mentioning their likeness. He was suddenly full of questions but Julia motioned for him to listen. She spread her hands across the pile of photographs, staring at the life in pictures before her as if looking for somewhere to begin. Mattei waited patiently. After a few moments of silence, she spoke again.

'Yes, of course, you were one of the lucky ones to find a home with loving parents. I sense you are impatient to learn what I know of your sister but I want you to hear more before you decide what you will do next. I hope what I can tell you will help you understand how differently life turned out for you and Christine. We cannot turn the clock back but we can use time and history to help us move forward in a better way,' she said and she began her story, unravelling the missing years.

17

Legacy of a Dictator

'Do you remember anything of the orphanage?' she asked. 'You would be about three years old. Your sister was about six years old. I was one of the care workers in that place. I remember you both arriving. You were separated. They did that depending on your ages, or to split boys from girls. Christine wanted to keep you with her. She screamed and kicked out horribly. She scratched my face and drew blood! I don´t think you would remember.'

'I don´t remember much,' said Mattei, 'I know I wasn´t there for very long, that it was a bad place. Cold! I remember it was cold all of the time, even with many children in the same room. We were in beds together but I cannot, or maybe choose not to remember anything more. I have, of course, looked at these places from media postings and news stories over the years but never really associated myself as part of it. I had a happy childhood. I know I was lucky.'

Julia agreed, patting Mattei's hand.

'You were indeed, lucky. When Ceausescu's reign came to an end, not long after you arrived, the world found out what went on behind those walls, a few like you made it out. Before this, the state thought they could do a much better job when it came to looking after children. There was even a policy to encourage parents to give up their children to these institutions in the name of communism. Women were expected to have at least five children, a duty to procreate, with little means to look after them. Some parents had no choice but to abandon their children.'

Mattei looked confused. 'So, would my real parents have left us there simply because they could not afford to keep us?' he asked.

'Possibly,' Julia answered. 'There were many reasons children were turned over to these places. Sometimes they were handicapped. Sometimes, the parents did not want them or could not cope with them. Many believed the propaganda that they would be better off there. Ceausescu wanted to increase the population and with the help of his wife Elena, they forced a way of life upon us. They banned abortion and contraception and made divorce virtually impossible. They taxed childless couples but also paid money for women to go out to work, if you were lucky to find any. You could get married at the age of fifteen and were even awarded medals for the number of children you had. I lived through that time and I had my three lovely boys. I also had two stillbirths, both girls. After this, I suffered the humiliation with the 'menstrual police' as we called them, gynecologists that came even to schools or to your workplace to investigate non-pregnant women or women who had miscarriages. Nobody cared that your babies died, they just wanted you to keep going regardless, like cows!'

Julia apologised to Mattei for being so personal but even after so many years, his generation should not forget what went on in those days. They say history repeats itself but that was a time she hoped would never come back.

'We needed money badly and so I got a job as a care worker in 1986, even though I had no training. Nothing could prepare you for the conditions in there. The outside world assumed we were heartless and cruel but I can tell you we did care, very much. We were as handicapped as some of the children, with no money or skills. I alone had thirty-two children in my care. We were allowed only one hour of hot water each week to bathe them all. There was no choice but to wash them in cold water and some even were hosed with cold water to be quick. We did not have proper supplies. No money came, sometimes we did not get paid but we tried hard. Sometimes I brought soap from home to at least make them clean. The children would often pee in their beds. You would see the steam rising in the morning because they tried to keep themselves warm. We had to shave their heads to stop the lice. They had few clothes. There was one set of clothes given per year which they put on when a government official came to visit. Otherwise, they were virtually naked much of the time. I would go to work dressed in my ski jacket in winter and those poor souls had nothing. Some of them died, mostly from pneumonia. That was the worst thing, sitting with a child in an isolation room knowing they were going to die. Imagine digging the graves yourself! We would put wooden crosses where the graves were but sometimes that was a waste of time as the people came from the nearby town and stole the crosses for firewood.'

Mattei kept quiet, listening to Julia. He could not imagine what it must have been like to go to work every day like that and then go home to your family. She offered him more tea which he accepted, allowing her a break from the story. He was still unsure where this was leading to in terms of his sister´s whereabouts but patiently waited until Julia returned with fresh tea.

She poured him another cup and sensing his mood, explained again why she needed to tell him the background. He should not blame his birth parents for abandoning them, nor was the orphanage responsible for the appalling conditions. The man accountable was Ceausescu and thankfully he and his wife got what was coming to them in the end but it left a terrible legacy, an entire young generation without any real chance to succeed in life.

Mattei told her about how he found out he was adopted, how his new parents could not have children of their own. With Ceausescu gone and the plight of so many children revealed they were desperate to do something when they had a chance. They had wanted to adopt a baby but were told they should try for an older child.

'They found me and they loved me very much,' he said.

Julia cut another slice of cake and passed it to Mattei.

'It must have taken some persuasion for you to be released to them as it was complicated for Romanians to adopt in those days. I don´t know exactly how they managed it but it was your salvation. At that time, suddenly everyone was interested in the plight of Romanian orphans. Some were lucky, many were not and some remained forgotten forever, God rest their souls,' she said, making the sign of the cross.

'Christine stayed in that place for another year, still held like animals, without any learning or stimulation. There were children there that would never be able to relate to the real world. They had no idea how to behave and no real contact with the outside. They did not know how to love or be loved. Many were always just silent, rocking themselves for some comfort. We didn´t have the resources or the time for so many. Things slowly began to improve after Ceausescu. Before that, not even the locals had access to the orphanages and were just as horrified at the conditions as the rest of the world. Gradually help came from charities and sponsors inside and outside of Romania. The government changed to a democracy but the attitudes of some people were often still influenced by old ways, things took time to change.'

The big place was eventually closed down and all the children were moved to smaller orphanages, mostly closer to Bucharest. I was able to change jobs. I even began to receive training. I worked another 15 years as a care worker and I worked in the home your sister finally grew up in.'

Mattei was trying to take in as much as possible but with so many questions, he did not know where to start. He was feeling guilt and anger that so many others seemed to have no chance to enjoy even the simplest of childhood experiences. He had so much freedom, growing up on his parents' farm, climbing the mountains, swimming in the lakes, good food and education. It seemed incredible to him that he had a sister who would have known none of these things.

'Christine must have remembered she had a brother,' he said, 'why did she not try to find me? I had no real recollection she even existed except some vague dreams I couldn´t make sense of at the time. It was only when my mama and papa died in the car crash that I found out the truth.'

Julia answered him. 'You have to understand that years growing up in the way she did makes you seem only a distant memory, she was isolated from much of the world as you know it. Christine would not even have had the means to come looking for you and by the time she became an adult, probably thought it best not even to try. Mattei, this is why I wanted to meet you, to be sure it was you but also to explain something of the life she had growing up. As I told you, things did get better. She went to a different kind of home, with only twenty-four young people of mixed ages. It had a garden where we grew vegetables. We shared household chores, so they learned to mop floors, wash dishes, to do more everyday things. It was more like home and she seemed to like helping to make it one. Perhaps that came from her very early childhood, before the institution. Some days we would try to teach writing or play games but they still didn´t mix much with the outside community. They had so little. As they got older, they were allowed to go out but some just started to steal or get into trouble. Some even ran away. Volunteers started to come and help and it was one of these people that made a difference to your sister. Christine was one of few who learned to read and write and they got her interested in drawing. Your sister seemed to have a natural gift. She was always asking for crayons and paper. She would draw everything she saw, even us!'

Julia reached in her apron pocket and took out a carefully folded paper. On opening it, Mattei saw a likeness of a younger Julia. His sister had captured all the features which made her recognisable, even as an older woman now.

'She drew this when she was about fourteen. I have more if you would like them,' she said. 'I don´t know why but I always kept them. Christine left them behind. I somehow thought she might come back one day and be interested in having them but perhaps you should take them.' She went back into the house, returning with a brown leather bag. Together they went through the drawings.

'Some are sketches of the darker times, hard for even me to understand. My favourites are the ones she did of the other children, so simple and yet you could reach into their souls and imagine what they were feeling. She drew other things too, flowers, animals. I guess it was her way to escape as no one would bother her while she was drawing. If they tried, she would wave them away like annoying rats!'

Mattei could see what she meant even though some pictures were simplistic and childlike. He felt more positive as Julia continued to describe his sister, passing on stories and watching her grow to a woman of eighteen. She told him she was kind and well-meaning.

'She could be tough. I liked her. She stuck up for the little ones if they got bullied. Maybe a deep part of her did remember you. Your sister made a best friend in the home; a boy called Dorin. He had been brought to the home when he was about eight years old, the same age as Christine. I believe his father was an alcoholic and a violent man. Such an unhappy childhood if you can call it that,' said Julia, shaking her head sadly.

'He arrived covered in bruises and Christine was one of the first to befriend him. He was very lively, always playing jokes on the others, laughing, despite his troubled background. Perhaps it was an armour. He looked out for her and she looked out for him, like brother and sister. I could see she needed to protect what was hers, including Dorin. I suppose we knew when they reached a certain age, their feelings for each other would mature into something else. It wasn´t encouraged, of course but it was going to happen. They would talk about leaving. Dorin was always restless. Maybe it was the Roma in him. He was full of stories about how their lives would be once they left. He filled her head with all kinds of crazy dreams. When they both reached eighteen, they left together. That would be in summer 2001. That´s the last time I saw her when she hugged me and gave me the drawings as they were leaving. She was not sorry to go. It was like she was proud to be going, just a last wave as they turned the corner of the street.'

Mattei was disappointed that the connection stopped there. He was grateful for what she had been able to tell him but at the same time it left him feeling empty. He was back to his puzzle with only part of the dots joined up and he still could not imagine what the picture would turn out to be. What had happened to her after she left? He looked at his watch and realised he would have to get back to Casa Flori. But just as he got up to go Julia cast him another ray of hope.

'It is my son you need to speak to now. I will ask him to call you. I will tell him I am positive you are Christine´s brother.

She then passed Mattei a photograph. It was of a group of six children together taken in the garden of the home. It wasn´t difficult for Mattei to pick out his sister amongst the faces, it was like he was staring at himself, at the age of fifteen. They looked so alike. He was elated to see her there, shocked to be looking at his own flesh and blood.

'You can keep it. My son has a copy and now I believe this to be your sister he can add it to the information you already sent out. I don´t want to make you so hopeful, she would be twenty-five years old now but it is a start. My son will help you, I am sure but he will want to talk with you first.'

She offered to walk with him back to his car but he politely refused, shaking her hand warmly as he said goodbye. Julia gave him the leather satchel that contained the pictures Christine had drawn. He was glad at least someone seemed to have cared about his sister. He had nothing but admiration for Julia. No matter what life had thrown at her, she remained compassionate, despite the years of despotism. Her family and her children meant everything to her and maybe this is what he should be thinking about now.

However, doubts began to creep into his mind as he made his way back. If he found Christine now what should he expect from her after what Julia had described to him and what had become of her? He was curious and if he didn´t pursue this, he wondered if he would have regrets. He needed closure, to know he had real family out there. Julia had said Christine had grown up very differently to him and would not necessarily see the world in the same way he did. He understood that but surely if they were blood brother and sister, it opened up possibilities to have some relationship. Julia had given him hope.

He had a sister and he wanted to know more.

Part Two

Christine

18

New Beginnings - Summer 2001

'Wake up Dorin, wake up!' hissed Christine. She was shaking Dorin by the shoulders, trying to rouse him from his drunken stupor. She felt groggy, having pulled herself out of bed too quickly, wriggling into a pair of tight jeans and throwing on an old wool sweater as the hammering on the tin door of the caravan grew more intense.

'I know you are in there you lazy low lifes!' a voice hollered.

Christine recognised the foreman's voice. She looked at the small alarm clock by the bedside. It was one o'clock in the afternoon and it was Monday. The temperature inside the caravan was almost the same as the cold mid-November day outside.

Empty bottles and beer cans littered their cramped living space. Pots, pans and dirty dishes lay piled up in the kitchen sink. There was condensation dripping down the windows from the small amount of heat generated by their two bodies and the place smelled of stale laundry and alcohol. Christine was having little success with Dorin and she began to punch him randomly.

'You have to get up and answer the door Dorin!' she growled impatiently.

He waved his arms about wildly trying to defend himself from the blows she was raining down on him, his eyes still closed. Eventually, when he couldn't stand it any longer, he rolled out of bed. He stood naked and blinking in the daylight that crept in from the sorry pieces of rag that acted as curtains. He pulled on his jeans and groped his way over the debris to the door. It wasn't the first time the foreman had come knocking. Dorin stood with his hands either side of the doorway blocking the way.

Christine was pushing as much of the clutter as possible under the bed and into the small toilet, anywhere that helped look like there was a real floor in the space. She could hear the exchange going on between the two men. The foreman was furious that they had failed to show up for work. Dorin's pleas for understanding that he and Christine were both sick with a stomach bug and full of diarrhoea were useless. The foreman replied they were indeed full of shit and their days numbered. They should report to the boss's office.

The pair had been living on the outskirts of Ploesti

for six months having left behind their institutional way of life for a new one together. They had taken the few possessions they owned and caught a bus to the city outskirts. With newly issued government ID's, they started work on a construction site which also provided them with a roof over their heads.

They were luckier than most that when they turned eighteen were pushed out with nowhere to go, as adults, no longer the responsibility of the state. There were few social structures in place at that time that cared apart from a few charities and people like their new employer who felt obliged to do some good for such outcasts. He also gained cheap labour to carry out menial work on the site.

Poleisti was one of several cities in Romania that was now enjoying a property boom. It had been attracting investment since the post-war years with its proximity to Bucharest sixty kilometres away. It continued to expand its industry, focused around oil refineries with pipelines running to Bucharest, the Black Sea and the Danube.

Following the ousting of the Soviets and formation of the Socialist Republic of Romania, Ceausescu rose to power on a mission to industrialise the country. He courted western leaders and like many Eastern bloc countries signed up to massive borrowings regulated by the IMF. They imposed harsh measures of austerity. By the end of the 1970's with the USA's decision to reverse its monetary policy, it pushed Romania further into recession. Behind certain western political doors, the intent was to establish a new ideology, to defeat socialism and communism.

By the end of the 1980's when Romania had finally

paid off its international debt, it was too late for Ceausescu. A tide of revolution swept the country by the people who blamed him for years of deprivation, sweeping corruption and an increased disparity between rich and poor. Following his downfall, the new government signed up to free-market reforms, lifting foreign exchange restrictions and allowing the flow of foreign investment once again without the interference of a dictator.

New types of businesses, including big retailers and textile manufacturers, were bringing money and jobs into the area. There was a demand for new housing to cater for the new educated middle classes, thirsty for higher standards of living. From all their years raised in poverty, Christine and Dorin emerged into this new market world ill-equipped, uneducated but full of optimism.

When they first arrived from the home, they could hardly believe their good fortune as they stepped off the bus and made their way over to a series of portacabins that acted as temporary offices. The site was quiet. The workers had finished for the day. They met their new boss, who quickly laid down the ground rules. They should turn up on time, work hard and do as asked by the foreman. They would be living in a caravan just to the side of the site alongside two other workers caravans and everyone was expected to keep an eye out for trespassers or thieves. In return, they would receive a small salary. Their rent would be taken out automatically and paid to the landlord who was a good friend of his. He introduced them to the foreman, a weather-beaten statue of a man that ran a tight ship and without question would throw them overboard without references if they didn´t follow the rules. The boss handed them a key to their living quarters and instructed them to turn up at six o´clock the following morning.

Dorin and Christine took the path that circled the perimeter of the site. An assortment of machinery and earthmoving equipment sat behind locked gates. Towers of cement bags and bricks lay stacked around concrete pads prepared for the new apartments that would be rising from the ground in the coming months. It was early summer. A breeze swirled the dust around them by the bucketful. By the time they reached the door of their new home, their nostrils were full of powdery earth and their eyes were dry and stinging but they hardly noticed. They were just so excited to be free!

Christine put the key in the door and stepped up into what felt like a palace. To one end, a neat kitchen offered a two-ring gas cooker, small sink, fridge and a few cupboards. In the middle was a toilet and shower and at the far end was a table with bench seats that could convert into a bed. She pulled back the thin floral curtains that did little to keep out the sun´s heat or the light. She continued to explore every cupboard and nook crammed into the space. They had never had a key to a place before or a room to themselves. She would be able to cook. She was so excited.

Dorin took the bench seats up and started to fit the double-spaced bed together. There were blankets and sheets stored that smelled new and pillows that were soft and feathery. They threw themselves down onto the sponge mattress and wrapped their arms around each other before tearing their clothes off and making love. As adolescents, they had taught themselves about their bodies, exploring and experimenting but usually only in short bursts behind buildings or rough ground close to the home. They laughed, not caring how much noise they made. Now they could do whatever they wanted. It wasn't to last.

19

Dust and Mud

Over the next few months through summer, they both worked hard, turning up even before six o´clock in the morning, six days a week and staying on site until the last person called it a day. Dorin would load cement bags, barrow bricks and clean down machinery and working to keep the building site tidy. Christine kept the offices clean, made tea for the men and helped Dorin. They would return to their little palace in the evenings where she would prepare simple stews and bread she had learned to make herself. Christine was very content and feeling very grown-up.

They had little spare money. Christine and Dorin would take a bus into the city centre on their one day off and meander along the streets looking enviably in the shop windows, imagining one day they would be able to afford to buy things.

There were few green areas in Poleisti but they enjoyed exploring some of the grand old buildings and churches. Christine took to sketching the places they visited like the Nicolae Simache Clock Museum and the St. John Baptist Cathedral, capturing the passers-by she observed until Dorin would get bored and demand her attention. He would tease her and steal her pencils before running off, pretending to throw them away. He couldn´t understand why she was happy to sit and seemingly ignore him. Sometimes he would wander off and leave her to catch the bus back on her own.

As the nights drew in and summer faded, their routine began to change. The novelty of keeping house in the little caravan was wearing thin for Dorin. Instead of coming back home in the evenings he would disappear for hours, returning drunk on the homemade plum brandy distilled in the back gardens of the houses of his new friends. Or he would be drinking with Sasu who lived in the caravan next to theirs. Sasu worked onsite as a digger driver. Christine would fight into the small hours with Dorin who would go to work the next day still drunk, resulting in more and more friction with the foreman.

She did her best to cover for him but she too was losing interest in keeping house for someone who no longer seemed to care if the bed was put away or the dishes cleaned. He chose to pass his spare time in the company of others. It took a lot of effort to keep a small space organised and she was tired of nagging Dorin. She was worn out from taking over some of his workload on-site just to keep the foreman off their backs. Dorin´s answer was to encourage her to come with him. On the occasions she did and they were both drunk the rows they had would become physical, each hitting out at the other, before they made up, promising always to look after each other.

It was after a night like this that brought the hammering to the door on the November afternoon in 2001. They quickly showered, putting on their work clothes hurriedly in between gulping down lukewarm coffee and mouthfuls of bread. As they trudged across to the office, Christine´s muddy work boots felt full of lead in anticipation of what was to come, blaming Dorin for everything on their way.

When they reached the office portacabin, they were not the only ones there. The foreman had taken up position standing behind the boss, arms folded. The boss was seated at his desk with papers and architectural plans covering the surface and before him stood Sasu, Dorin's favourite drinking buddy looking unimpressed.

The boss began with Sasu saying he should know better, a man in his mid-forties with a skill as a digger operator throwing away his life on drink. He was always hung-over and could no longer be trusted to operate machinery without risking an accident to himself or those he worked alongside.

'How would you feel about that, if one day you killed someone? You are fired, with immediate effect,' he barked.

He then turned to Dorin and Christine. He had hired too many people like this and seen them waste his time. He had hoped these two would turn out differently as they had started so well but he was disappointed once again. He couldn't lay all the blame at Sasu's feet. They were young and easily influenced. He offered to give them one more chance but they had to promise to clean up their living quarters back to the way it was when they first arrived. The foreman had told him of the stinking shambles it had become.

'I cannot guarantee the landlord won't throw you out and if you do not have a place to live, you do not have a job,' he said, shaking his finger at them and then dismissing them with a toss of his hand.

'You have one afternoon to get it straight, or you are out!'

Christine was feeling humiliated. Why had she not made more effort? How could she forgive Dorin for landing them in it like this? She made her thoughts known to him as they made their way back to the caravan. But he was ignoring her cutting remarks walking ahead of her and listening to Sasu instead. Sasu was bitter.

'That foreman is a bastard. He's nothing but an ass creeping snitch. I'm one of the best workers here,' he protested loudly. 'I'm not the only one who enjoys a drink! He should sack all of them if that's what he thinks. We work hard for lousy money. Where is the harm in having some pleasure? I'll bet he's just the same when he goes home and yet he comes here in the morning and thinks he's God, a cut above the rest of us with never a good word to say to anyone! I was sick of taking orders from him anyway!'

Sasu put his arm around Dorin.

'We should leave together,' he said 'We can get other work easily for better money than here and with a place to live. It's only a matter of time before you get fired. I'm sure that foreman has it in for you, going on about the bloody caravan like it's any of his business how we live! Listen to me, my friend, I have been doing this job for many years and I know the difference between a good boss and a bad one!'

Christine couldn't believe what she was hearing. Surely if they took more care and kept the place clean, there would be no reason to be fired but she could see Dorin was listening to Sasu's every word. She knew he also hated the foreman who treated him like some slave dog and he wasn't much kinder to her either but what was the alternative? They couldn't just walk out. If they left, what about the wages they were due or their papers? She had to think.

Dorin headed straight for Sasu's caravan. She opened the door to theirs and began to empty it of bottles and rubbish. For two hours she worked cleaning the kitchen, putting the bed away, mopping the floors and toilet. Apart from the ragged curtains, it began once again to resemble their original little palace. She felt pleased with herself, a feeling which quickly evaporated when Dorin finally appeared. He was drunk, casting his body onto the benches and demanding to know where the bed was because he had to sleep.

She slapped him, just wanting to kick him back out.

'Go and sleep with your sad friend!' she screamed at him. I don't want you in here when you are like this. You are just ruining everything. What am I to do? You promised to take care of us, we promised each other and now you are making a fool of me.'

'You crazy bitch,' was Dorin's reply 'you need to wake up yourself and smell the coffee. Sasu is right. We don´t have any guarantee we can carry on here. He says he can get me a better job. I could take care of you. We don´t have to stay in this place. I´m bored with it. It´s time to go!'

They argued further and at last, reached an agreement. Christine had to be sure Sasu could be trusted to find them another place to live and work. They would stay for another couple of weeks and behave. If Sasu did as he promised, they could tell the boss they had a better offer and leave with their monies and papers. Sasu had said there was a job for Dorin on another building site. They could live with him in an apartment that his brother owned. They would be moving to Bucharest.

Two weeks later, Sasu was as good as his word. Dorin and Christine packed up their things and caught the train to Bucharest, leaving their reputation intact and a clean caravan. Another new beginning, she hoped!

20

Bucharest

Christine and Dorin stepped onto the platform at the busy Gard De Nord station making their way through the main concourse, following the exit signs. It wasn´t the friendliest place Christine observed, as they navigated their way through crowds of fellow travellers. The station had other users sheltering there, the drunks, the chancers and the groups of homeless young people. Outside and invisible to most, were the homeless who disappeared into maintenance holes, living in the labyrinth of tunnels that carried the dream central heating system for Ceausescu's palace.

The temperature was about ten degrees outside. A dreary rain fell, making their hands numb with cold as they carried the assortment of plastic bags and one battered holdall containing their belongings. Sasu had told them to look for the bus stop that would take them towards the district of Pantelimon, east of the city centre.

The journey took almost an hour despite being only seven kilometres from the city centre. The bus weaved its way along the busy main road with its triple lanes of traffic. The broad thoroughfare was lined with endless rows of identical drab apartment blocks, stretching away from the city centre. They stood ten and twelve-stories high, monuments to the communist days of state-owned properties and cheap housing solutions for the city workforce.

They were to get off just before Parcul Florilor and make their way back to a café on the corner of Soseaua Funden. They had to ask another passenger which stop was theirs, finding it difficult to identify any landmarks along the unchanging landscape.

Sasu seemed genuinely pleased to see them as they finally arrived at the café. It felt good to step inside the warm space with the promising smell of hot food. They clinked their shot glasses of Tsuica together, raising a toast to their renewed friendship.

'Noroc' they chorused, downing another before food arrived.

After a homemade thin broth of supa followed by sarmale and polenta, Christine and Dorin felt like they had landed in luxury. Sasu even paid the bill boasting of how well he was doing and how much Dorin was going to enjoy the new job.

'No more trekking across muddy fields, my friend, we are building beautiful city apartments, working mostly inside making the brickwork and building rooms.'

'Is it far?' asked Dorin.

'It is the other side of the city but guess what?' Sasu grinned. 'We have a ride every day with a good friend of mine who drives a van for the building company delivering supplies. We will leave early, at seven and you will be doing odd jobs like before but the pay is better than in Ploiesti.'

He pulled on his thick coat and slapping Dorin on the back motioned for them to leave.

'So, shall we show the little woman where home is?' He nodded towards the door.

It was a short walk only two streets behind to another tall grey building, with layers of concrete balconies spilling over the car parking area below. Odd air conditioning units and washing lines littered the small outside spaces. Once through the entrance, they waited for the elevator, something Christine thought twice about, reluctant to enter such an enclosed space. Sasu pressed the button for the fourth floor.

'Don´t worry, it's kept clean and it hasn't broken down since I´ve been here. You can take the stairs but it's dark and a long climb. I´d risk this any day but if you get stuck just bang on the door, someone will hear you,' he said cheerily.

He told them how his brother had bought the apartment when the state was selling them off.

'The government didn´t want the burden of maintaining them or caring for future generations who might have carried on living here. My brother got it so cheap! He´s working in Ireland now, says he´s not coming back, so I have responsibility for it. I have made a friend of the administrator of the block and I told him you were moving in. You have to pay

'Intretinere,' and if you don't, there is a shame list. Neighbours will inform and make your life miserable, so always greet them if you pass even if you don't know them. It's customary and they will know you are not using more than your share of water and electric. Some have metres but we don't.'

He opened the door to the apartment. He was proud that they had two rooms, unlike others, that only had one open space.

'I have the bedroom and you two can sleep here,' he said, pulling back a rough curtain made from a blanket that hung across one side. Behind was a bed smaller than the one Christine and Dorin had shared in the caravan.

A basic kitchen filled the remaining space with a washing machine plugged in next to a small table with four plastic chairs. There was a free-standing cupboard supporting a TV and off to one side a bathroom with a shower and toilet but no door, just another curtain. Outside the balcony was filled with rubbish, empty plastic flowerpots and bags of tools. It faced onto the block opposite, making the whole place feel dark.

Maybe if they could save enough they could rent a place of their own thought Christine taking in the untidiness but for now, she was just glad to have four concrete walls instead of tinned ones to get through the winter. She thanked Sasu for his generosity to which he added, 'Now that brings me to the subject of rent. You must pay me without fail each month. You take care of your share and I will take care of you, that's how it works.'

Christine wanted to know how much they would

be paying but Sasu dismissed her saying he would work it out with Dorin It was he who was in charge of earnings, not her. A man didn't need to be answerable to a woman.

'He thinks I'm stupid.' she thought to herself, believing that Dorin would tell her anyway and he might not like to think so but when it came to planning their future Christine was sure she had the last say.

Sasu suggested she go out to get some supplies.

'I don't need much he said but maybe you should get some things for yourselves and you can get your bearings. Dorin and I are going to watch the football. Petrolul Ploiesti are playing Dinamo so it could get noisy!'

Christine felt it was an excuse to get rid of her but she didn't mind so much. Let the men enjoy their Saturday football. She noted there was plenty of beer in the fridge if very little else. She changed her socks and put on some dry boots, pushing their bags underneath the bed. She would look for some boxes to store their things.

It was mid-afternoon and getting dark but she found her way to a small supermarket and a bread shop buying enough to last them a few days with the small amount of money she had kept back from their last pay packet. She found a couple of cardboard boxes that would fit under the bed and made her way back to the apartment.

As she struggled out of the elevator with her boxes and shopping a little dog came bounding along the corridor, a bright blue bow tying up its fringe and revealing soft brown eyes. It sniffed around excitedly.

Christine was bending down to fuss the cute dog as it licked her hands, enjoying the attention when a door at the end of the corridor opened. The face of a woman appeared with a matching blue bow pinned to the side of her hair, calling the dog to her. Christine barely managed to say hello before the dog returned to its owner and the door closed. So much for being courteous to the neighbours, she thought.

Back in the apartment, the men were celebrating a four to one victory for Dinamo. They had drawn their chairs up as close as possible to the television and she had to squeeze past, neither of them making any effort to make room for her. She started to organise some space for the things she had bought, pushing aside several empty beer bottles and trying to clean some of the accumulated grease off the counters.

'Do you have to do that now? You will have all day to yourself tomorrow. We can´t hear the television!' complained Dorin.

She retreated behind the bed curtain, deciding to unpack some of their belongings into the boxes. She organised a box of clothes for Dorin and one for herself, sliding them under the bed and leaving the rest in the plastic bags. She would give the whole place a going over tomorrow and try to make more room. If there were going to be three of them, it needed to be tidy, or it would be worse than the caravan. She didn´t want to live in a man pit.

The men were absorbed in their after-match analysis. The only conversation she managed was to ask about the lady with the dog.

Sasu grunted. 'That crazy hippy? She dresses that dog in clothes like herself. She´s not right in the head, the nosey cow poking her face out of the door all the time. That rat of hers growls and yaps at me all the time. I want to give it a good kick! I told you to watch out for snitching neighbours.'

'It's not a rat. It's a Yorkshire Terrier,' stated Christine, finally settling on a chair in the kitchen and thumbing through a glossy magazine someone had left behind on the train. If this was a sign of things to come, it was going to be a long winter.

It was still dark when Dorin and Sasu had left for work the following morning. Christine was glad to sleep a little longer pulling the blankets over her and enjoying the peace. Dorin had siphoned the covers off her all through the night and she had felt cold despite lying so close to him.

As daylight appeared, she got up, pulling her socks over cold feet and heading for the kitchen to make herself a coffee. All around her was a mess, with dirty dishes piled in the sink and lines of empty bottles and rubbish left open. She looked into the bathroom and nearly wretched, having heard Sasu emptying his bowels earlier like a bad symphony for the ears of the whole neighbourhood. Broken hinges were evidence of a door, once upon a time. She would ask Dorin to fix it. Tying two plastic bags over her hands and arms, she started to clean the whole place from top to bottom.

It was on her second trip back from the municipal garbage bins that she met the little dog once again. It scampered over to greet her, turning in circles and lying on its back begging for more fuss. There had never been pets at the orphanage but over the years Christine had befriended various stray cats and dogs which would come for any scraps. She liked to draw them, capturing their play on paper. She loved animals and this little dog was undoubtedly pretty, today wearing a yellow ribbon and floral jacket.

The woman was standing in the corridor watching, 'Papusica, here, here! I´m sorry if she bothers you, we were going out for a walk! My name is Lucia,' she said.

Christine stared at the retro outfit the woman was wearing, flared flowery trousers and a long multi-coloured knitted coat. Her plaited hair hung like a grey rope almost down to her waist and on top of her head was a woollen hat with a huge yellow flower on it. Christine hesitated, fascinated by the woman's eccentricity and colour.

Lucia broke the pause, 'I noticed you had moved in and I am pleased to see you have been working so hard to clean the place. That Sasu has some filthy habits,' she added, gathering up her little dog in her arms. Her smile was infectious and Christine smiled back.

'My name is Christine. I moved here with my boyfriend from Ploiesti. He has a new job here,' she said proudly and then impulsively she added, 'Your dog is beautiful, maybe I could draw her sometime?'

She wasn´t usually so forward but when it came to subjects for her drawing, she forgot about what anyone else might think. She had missed her pencils and paper as they had been so busy moving.

'A portrait of Papusica, how wonderful! You are an artist?' exclaimed Lucia.

'No! It´s just a hobby, something I do in my spare time. Sorry, I didn´t mean to intrude,' said Christine wondering what on earth had prompted her to make such an impulsive suggestion when she didn´t know the woman. She could turn out to be as loopy as Sasu had described.

'You may come for ceai, perhaps tomorrow afternoon and show me some of your drawings. If you would like to draw my darling Papusica you will be welcome but we must go now!' said Lucia disappearing like some apparition into the elevator and leaving Christine nodding in acceptance as the doors closed to her.

For the rest of the afternoon, with everything in its place and looking decidedly better organised she prepared a thick vegetable stew, a warm celebration meal for Dorin and Sasu. She was looking forward to hearing all about Dorin's first day.

As it turned out, they didn´t arrive back until the late evening. Christine sat watching the TV, beginning to worry where they were. When they finally returned, she was furious to learn they had stayed out with the van driver, stopping off for something to eat on their way home. They both reeked of alcohol. She took herself off to bed, followed by Dorin.

'It was my first day,' he whispered, 'I couldn´t say no when they invited me, especially as it was the driver's idea. I´m sorry, Christine. I see how you have fixed the place.' He cuddled up to her, pulling the blankets around them both. He had a point. She would let it go this time. She had just been disappointed after all her efforts.

It didn´t matter to her that she didn´t see Sasu the next morning. She decided that she would go out for a walk, get some fresh air and explore the neighborhood. She still had Lucia's invitation to look forward to in the afternoon.

The winter sky blended into the concrete surround, making her walk gloomy. A flurry of snow began to dance around her and soon she began to feel cold but passing by a row of offices, she was distracted. She stopped by the garbage bins lined up outside. She rifled through the contents picking out paper, coloured cardboard and strips of coloured plastic. She found some foil and polystyrene. There was even a discarded red cushion. She began to form ideas to prepare their home for Christmas and hurried back to the apartment.

She spent the rest of the morning and early afternoon fashioning silhouettes of nativity figures, stars and angels and Christmas baubles made from the variety of materials. Lanterns now hung from the balcony shaped from the coloured plastic and inside collages of Christmas scenes decorated the walls. She was feeling very pleased with herself, totally absorbed in what she had been doing when there was a knock at the door. She opened it cautiously to find Lucia standing there peering past her, obviously curious to see inside. Christine opened the door wider.

'My my, you have been busy. You did this all yourself? How clever of you. What an incredible difference!' marvelled Lucia, taking in the Christmas theme.

Christine wasn´t accustomed to praise. She suddenly felt foolish, maybe Lucia was mocking her and her decorations were ridiculous. She shouldn´t have allowed her in. Butinstead Lucia took her by the hand, like some mystic creature, with a warmth and enthusiasm that quickly evaporated any of Christine's misgivings.

'Papusica and I are waiting for you to come and have ceai. I thought you might have forgotten,' said Lucia.

'No, of course not, it's very kind of you!' answered Christine, gathering her keys and following Lucia to her apartment like a child that had accepted candy from a stranger. She was not sure what to expect but there was something about Lucia she couldn't resist. She would soon find out if curiosity got the better of her.

21

Lucia- A Coat of Many Colours

'Come in, come in! Don´t worry my dear, we don´t normally invite people we don´t know for tea but my Papusica likes you and she´s sensitive about people. I can see there is something special about you! It is a change to have company, isn´t that right, my dolly?' she beamed, picking up the excited dog.

Christine looked about her. It was a two-roomed apartment just like theirs but it may as well have been a grand house. It was bright and homely. There were no plastic seats or makeshift tables. The furniture was traditional and all hand-carved. There was a vase of flowers on the kitchen table, a display cabinet filled with china and figurines and a standing light with a hand-painted shade next to a comfortable looking small sofa. A colourful rug made the floor warm. Pale rose walls decorated with paintings of birds and flowers hung in white frames, their plumage and petals full of textures. Christine wanted to touch them.

'My husband was an art teacher in a school,' said Lucia, seeing Christine admiring the paintings. 'In his spare time, he would paint for me. I have always loved birds and flowers but he did other works too. He died of cancer a few years ago. I miss him every day but I have these to remind me. Isn´t it strange that you told me you liked to draw and here you are having tea with us? He was always interested in what other people could create and would bring work home from some of his students to show me. He would have liked you!'

The two women sat together over tea, Lucia reminiscing about her husband and how they loved to spend time in the parks or visiting the old city together. She told Christine they both shared a love of art. Lucia would also paint but nothing as good as her husband though he tried on many occasions to teach her. She took more pleasure in other people's work. She didn´t ask Christine too much about herself, as if sensing her reluctance to talk about her previous life. She could see it was difficult for her to trust people.

Christine did tell her that she loved drawing from an early age. It moved her into a different place, brought her alive inside, by what she could put onto paper. It was a strange conversation to be having but Lucia seemed to understand her feelings. She could never talk to Dorin like this. When Lucia asked her if she could see some of the things she had drawn, she did not hesitate to go back into the apartment. She retrieved the collection she had hidden under the bed, choosing the ones she thought were best.

'These are very good, like moving stories. I cannot believe you have taught yourself so well. You are naturally talented, truly!' exclaimed Lucia holding up a sketch Christine liked. It was of a man doing up his shoelace on a park bench, surveying a pretty girl as she walked by. His expression showed a hint of flirtation with the girl looking over her shoulder at him, seeming to be flattered.'

'I know it makes me happy to do this,' said Christine, 'especially when I draw people. I try to guess what they might be feeling or thinking. Dorin thinks it is a waste of time, so I hide all of this from him. It costs money to buy the paper and things. When we were moving, he wanted to throw them away but I kept them. I don´t have real paints, just pencils and charcoal. I need to find some work then maybe I could buy paints,' she confided.

'I might be able to help you there!' Lucia announced, jumping up from the sofa. Papusica added to her excitement by barking and wagging her tail. 'You see, she knows!' said Lucia. She brought Christine over to a polished wooden bureau, dropping down the lid that made a desk. Inside its shelves were full of pots and tubes of paint, different artists brushes, pastels, pencils and underneath stacked in drawers were different types of paper and canvas.

'I never had the heart to throw any of this away when my husband passed away but I think you are a sign. It could be put to good use again and I can help you. It will be our little studio, our secret, you don´t have to say anything to Dorin, just come when you like!'

Lucia was giggling like a schoolgirl at Christine as she looked into what must have seemed an Aladdin's cave, full of treasure.

'As for money, I can see you are capable and a hard worker. I might be able to help you there too! I have a job as a cleaner in offices nearby. It's night-time cleaning but I don´t like to leave Papusica on her own for so many hours. They should have two people. It is too much for me. I would be happy to share with you. I have worked there for many years. Why don´t I put in a word for you? In the day we can paint!'

Christine couldn´t believe what she was hearing. What had she done to deserve this woman's kindness or was she just crazy? She stared at Lucia, dressed in her bright colours like the birds painted on the walls, her long hair clipped back in yet another ribbon matching the one the Papusica wore. She hesitated. What would Dorin think? He might tell her to run a mile. He might be angry to find out she would spend her days learning to paint, yet here was a chance, an escape from the black and grey world next door! She made up her mind not to tell him. Let her enjoy her secret and see how it went. It could work, she would be earning some money. The men wouldn´t care less what she did in the day. Lucia was already shaking her head enthusiastically to prompt her to say yes.

'I will call on you tomorrow afternoon and we can start!'

Christine agreed. She would know tomorrow if she

was joining Lucia in fairyland and it would all come true. She returned to the apartment just as Sasu and Dorin arrived back.

Sasu, threw his coat over a chair and kicked off his dirty boots. 'I can´t smell any dinner,' he grumbled.

'How am I supposed to know when you are coming home after what happened last night?' retorted Christine.

'We work hard all day. The least you can do is have some food ready and what have you done to the walls?' he moaned, suddenly noticing the decorations she had put up earlier.

Dorin came to her defence. 'She is trying Sasu. It looks nice ready for Christmas, you think? She makes stuff all the time. You know she took care of our last place, she just wants to do the same.'

'She should find some real work, not just play all day. A woman's place is not just in the kitchen. Dorin, you need to teach her how to be useful and don´t let her talk to me like that!' He grabbed a beer from the fridge and parked himself in front of the TV. Dorin shrugged his shoulders, taking off his boots by the front door and hanging up his coat. Christine began to reheat the stew she had prepared the previous day. She ignored Sasu's remarks, her head still full of the prospects Lucia had planted.

Once Sasu was fed, the mood settled and he was even complimentary about Christine´s cooking. They shared their workday with her, joking about the van driver who was having an affair with the foreman's wife behind his back. 'The foreman is as soft as a puppy's arse, not like the last one,' commented Sasu.

At last, they went to bed. Christine lay as still as

she could, curled up beside Dorin but she couldn't sleep. Sasu snored loudly and her thoughts were with Lucia and the painting she would be doing.

She started work cleaning at the offices with Lucia two days later. Dorin was pleased she had found work even though the contact had come from the weird neighbour. She did not elaborate more on her friendship with Lucia. Dorin was like his old self, full of dreams and optimism.

It was on the last Saturday leading up to Christmas that they had gone into the city together, just the two of them. They had been to the Christmas market in University Square spending the evening under the canopy of bright lights, enjoying the music and the traditional colinda sung by the children in their national dress. Christine noticed how Dorin kept looking at her. She wondered why until he suddenly took her hand.

'Why don´t we get married Christine, then we will always have each other, won´t we? What do you think?'

His romanticism surprised her. It was true they had always been together. It was what she wanted, to be married, to have a place of their own and one day maybe a family. She didn´t hesitate to say yes. They celebrated late into the evening, catching the last bus home and falling into bed giddy on love and alcohol. Fortunately, Sasu was already snoring.

Christine couldn´t wait to share her news with Lucia when she knocked on her door the following morning. Dorin was still asleep. She blurted out the news before she had even stepped inside. Lucia was pleased for her if it made her happy, though she secretly hoped her being married wouldn´t change Christine in any way. She had quickly grown fond of her and looked forward to the time they spent together. 'How will you celebrate?' Lucia had asked her excitedly. She lapsed into a dreamy world, remembering her wedding celebrations, which she insisted on sharing with Christine. She brought out some faded photographs to show her.

'My wedding day was the most special day of my life! We got married near Băneasa, where I was born. Back then, we were still in the communist era but this did not stop us from having a very traditional village wedding. After the civil ceremony, I had time to prepare myself for the real party. I wore a lace dress my mother had given me and the prettiest veil! We went to the church and although it was beautiful and I tried to listen to every word the priest said I thought at one point I would fall asleep. He went on so long! Our Nasi (godparents), our parents, my bridesmaids, the best man all came to the church ceremony. Then it was home to our evening wedding party. It seemed everyone from the area came. Maybe there were a hundred people. So much food to prepare! Days before, we were cooking at my parents' house and in friends' houses too! We had beer and homemade wines overflowing the place and the music and dancing went on all night. I was kidnapped, as is the tradition and taken to another house for a few hours with my girlfriends. My dear husband had to pay the ransom in whiskey! I traded my veil for a scarf, quite a game as you must refuse it at first then accept it and then my husband had to remove my garter with his mouth, it was so funny. My best friend, God rest her soul, caught my bouquet of roses. I made it myself from the roses in our garden. We were lucky to have such generous friends who came with their envelopes of money. It was such a happy time!'

Christine knew she would not have the kind of wedding Lucia did but this would not deter her. Getting married was something she had always wanted. It would mean she was somebody and belonged to somebody and she was sure she would love Dorin forever.

'It must have been wonderful, Lucia,' said Christine. 'But we are new to the city. We don't really know anyone. There wouldn't be much point to a big wedding and it would be so expensive! I am just happy to become Dorin's wife. I don't need a party. Provided we are legally married at City Hall, that's good enough for me,' said Christine, a little too dismissively for Lucia. What girl didn't dream of her wedding day? Lucia decided to take matters into her own hands.

The following day, when Christine left for the offices to clean, she kept an eye on the elevator door waiting for Dorin to appear on his way back from work. She had never really spoken to him before but she was determined. Her directness made him uncomfortable. She told him that Christine deserved a real wedding and asked him what he was planning. He was irritated.

'What do you expect me to do? We're not going to waste money on people we hardly know, feeding them and filling them with beer and neither of us is religious so forget church!' he scoffed. Was this Christine's idea? She never mentioned any special arrangements. He knew Christine had made a friend of this crazy bird but the last thing he wanted was her interfering in their lives. It was their wedding, after all. Lucia gave up and retreated into her apartment.

Dorin hadn´t even thought about a wedding party, nor considered Christine might expect one but he decided maybe they should do something. She did deserve more but he had neither the imagination nor the means. He grumbled to Sasu about it, accusing Lucia of putting ideas in Christine´s head.

Sasu agreed it was impractical for Dorin to even think about what was involved in a traditional Romanian wedding. 'The last wedding I went to I hardly knew the people but they spent crazy money on flowers, dresses, bridesmaids, did the whole church thing and had a big party and for what? I had to give them money to help pay for that? The bride looked like a horse! Come to mention it, I think she was!' he roared laughing. 'Look, your Christine is no horse and you know spending money on women isn´t one of my priorities but I do like a party. I'll tell you what I can do. I will have a word with my friends who run the café, the one where we first met when you came here. It might be rent a crowd but maybe we can come to some arrangement on how to pay! People expect to give money to the bride and groom.'

Dorin was pleased with the idea and taking all the credit when he told Christine. She hadn´t expected anything and it made her happy. It would make a promising start to their married life.

Lucia was excited there was to be a celebration and immediately offered a dress for the occasion. 'I was not always as round as this 'she said, chuckling in her girlish way. She went to her wardrobe and lifted out a cream embroidered peasant dress that looked like it dated back to the 1970´s. 'With a little adjustment, this would be perfect for the occasion and I will help you with your hair!' Christine felt sure she would end up with a bow in it. She wasn´t used to wearing dresses and thought she would feel overdressed in what Lucia had planned. Lucia just radiated her usual warm powers of persuasion.

'My dear, you must do something special for your wedding party! People need to know you are the bride! I promise we will make this perfect for you and you will feel special. Dorin is lucky to have you!'

The marriage took place at the Second District City Hall on the morning of the 7th of January 2001. The celebration was held at the café the next evening. Lucia helped transform Christine into a princess for the occasion. She tamed her curls and added a little makeup. Lucia had removed the long sleeves from the dress and fitted the bodice top to her petite figure. She finished it tying an ivory ribbon to her waist, leaving the long skirt trailing in soft waves to the floor. Christine carried a bouquet of silk flowers they had made together to save the expense of real flowers and added a delicate one for her hair. She looked as radiant as any bride.

Sasu singularly carried out the tradition of shaving Dorin. Usually this initiation was done by the best man and groomsmen, in keeping with the ritual to signify the transition of the groom from boy to man. Dorin had borrowed a suit and as they made their way to the café, Christine felt very proud of how he looked. She had never seen him in a suit before! Lucia snapped as many photographs as she could. The owners of the café had made it known there was a wedding party and attracted various onlookers as well as their regulars. They had set up a table in the centre with coloured balloons. The wedding party included Sasu, Lucia and two of the people from Dorin's work, with their wives, so Christine did not have all-male company. There was a modest selection of food, including the traditional samarles but no cake. A friend of Sasu played the accordion with almost everyone in the café joining in, forming a circle to dance the customary Hora. Lucia left first to go home to Papusica, the rest of the celebrations continued into the early hours with everyone, including Christine the worse for wear.

It might not have been a wedding as grand as Lucia's but it was more than she could have imagined and people gave money. It managed to cover the costs of the party and all the extra drink Dorin seemed to order for his new friends. Most importantly, she was now Mrs. Christina Marie Daniela Haluška. Life couldn´t get any better!

22

The Ugly, the Bad and the Blessing

Life took on new promise for Christine. She would spend her days in the company of Lucia learning to paint, with visits to the city and parks to find subjects for her new projects. In the evenings she went to clean at the offices nearby. She would prepare a meal for the men before she went and by the time she got home, they were usually fast asleep. Lucia was happy to cut her hours of cleaning in half, enjoying the friendship that was developing with Christine.

At the weekend, Dorin and Christine would go out and explore the city together. It was the only time they had together as there was very little privacy if they stayed in the apartment. She gave Dorin the money she earned, keeping back just a small amount for herself. It annoyed her that he insisted she do that and she knew that Sasu was behind it, controlling their money. He would openly tell Dorin he should keep her under control and not let her dictate to him, even that he should slap her sometimes and put her in her place, that she was lucky to have him. She had begun to resent Sasu and his influence over Dorin. She knew they were both drinking heavily and through the winter, she argued more and more with Dorin, especially about how they were ever going to get a place of their own. Dorin complained about being treated like a donkey at work and henpecked at home, almost jealous of the free time she had during the day and therefore she never mentioned her painting.

One day in late January she made a more extended trip than usual to Cismigiu Park on the opposite side of Bucharest. Its frozen lake was full of movement with a mix of expert and novice skaters she sketched quickly, trying to catch their expressions. She was so absorbed in what she was doing; she didn´t notice a man observing her drawing. It startled her. She hugged her work to her defensively.

'No please, carry on,' he had insisted,' you are very talented! May I see some of your other drawings?'

She had been reluctant at first, shy but she allowed him to see three she had decided were complete.

'How much do you want for them?' he asked.

'They are just charcoal, what do you want them for?' she said, suspiciously.

'I can see it's the park and I love the expressions you have captured with the skaters. I always come here to walk, even in winter. These remind me of my visits. I will hang them in my house.'

She wasn't sure if he was serious or not. She asked for fifty lei. He counter-offered thirty and so she met him in the middle at forty, holding out the sketches and her hand for the money. He thanked her, tucking the drawings under his warm coat and pressing one hundred and twenty lei into her hand.

When she told Lucia she had thought forty was the price for all three they had laughed until tears ran down their cheeks, Christine had never felt so proud. She gave the money to Lucia for safekeeping. Lucia encouraged her to continue offering to sell her pictures but Christine was shy, saying they weren't good enough but from time to time she would sketch caricatures of people passing by in the nearby parks and sell them for a few lei. She hung on to her savings, unwilling to tell Dorin should he mention any additional earnings to Sasu during one of their drunken stupors. She would take back control when the time was right. Unfortunately, that time never came. In a matter of months, dictated to by the actions of others, her life capsized into a whirlpool of change.

The freezing temperatures of winter were disappearing but the March weather remained characteristically cloudy. Christine had returned from the offices, glad to be back to the relative warm after her late-night walk home. When she entered the apartment, she was greeted yet again by the smell of alcohol. The kitchen was littered with empty bottles and dried up plates of uneaten food. The toilet smelled of urine. Dorin was completely passed out on their bed, still fully clothed and Sasu sat in front of the

TV downing another beer. He was drunker than she had ever seen him, even for a regular Friday night when they spent most of the paycheck.

She was furious. Unable to stir Dorin, she turned her disgust towards Sasu, even swiping at him, accusing him of getting Dorin into such a state. Sasu reared up, knocking the chair over and coming at her like a bull. He pinned her by the throat against the kitchen wall, her feet barely touching the floor, unable to make any noise in protest. His face contorted as he spat at her.

'You ungrateful fucking bitch! I´m sick of you sticking your nose in my business. You think because you make a few meals and do some laundry you own this fucking place? It´s my place and you should think yourself lucky I took you in. It´s time you knew who the boss is. That sap Dorin doesn´t seem to do the job! You are going to learn once and for all!'

Before she could even gather her breath, he slammed her head sideways down on the kitchen table, covering her face with his workman's hand. She was powerless to stop him, prevented by the sheer weight of his body against hers, as he wrenched down her trousers and forced himself on her from behind. She could see Dorin, still unconscious on their bed, oblivious to the scene but she was unable to call out. It was all over in minutes as Sasu staggered back away from her, feeling his way precariously to his bedroom and slamming the door behind him.

She dropped to the floor, weakened and shocked, the silence around her was deafening. Had she asked for that? What just happened? She should kill him, go after him with a knife or something, or should she get help, bang on Lucia's door, what could she do? She felt sick crawling to the bathroom and emptying her stomach contents into the filthy toilet bowl. She pulled herself up, slowly turning on the shower, stripping off her clothes under the water and scrubbing herself until her skin nearly bled. Dorin never moved. She put on clean clothes and pouring herself a brandy, sat in the darkness of the kitchen, hugging her knees, rocking to and fro, as silent tears fell from her cheeks.

She stayed like that until first light, before slipping out of the apartment to walk the streets and feel the fresh air around her. Her head was in turmoil. She told herself she was tough. When she returned, she knew the men would be nursing sore heads. Dorin would be ignorant of anything, possibly Sasu too. She couldn't tell Dorin. He would never believe her, especially as he had been there! Maybe he would say it was her fault! If she said anything, Sasu could threaten her again, or he could lose Dorin his job if he wanted too. She had to stay quiet, erase it from her mind somehow. She was good at burying her emotions, blanking things out like she used to when she was in the orphanage. It had happened and there was nothing she could do about it. They were not in a position to leave. She would have to continue living through it, even though she hated Sasu with every fibre of her body. She was determined to plan their exit from his clutches.

Over the next two months, she carried on as normal, avoiding time in the apartment with Sasu and absorbing herself in her painting. Lucia noticed a subtle change in her. Christine seemed subdued and her paintings contained darker subjects, pictures of street children gathered in groups, their faces full of mistrust or fear.

Christine justified this, explaining to Lucia that she was exploring different things and that art was all about expression, not just pretty birds and flowers. Lucia accepted her explanation and continued to encourage her but she sensed something had gone from Christine and she was right.

Two missed periods and the realisation that she was pregnant brought Christine to Lucia's door one afternoon, unable to hold back her tears.

Lucia put her arms around her but Christine pulled back in frustration.

'I cannot keep this baby!' she exclaimed.

'Christine, you are talking about a child growing inside you. It is a gift, whatever you may think. What about Dorin, have you told him?' It was easy for Lucia to say, she had never been able to have children. Christine had become the closest thing she had to a daughter.

'You don´t understand, Lucia! It´s worse, so much worse! I am afraid. I don't think the baby is Dorin's. I didn´t choose this!'

Lucia was silent for a few minutes. 'Christine, tell me what happened? Are you saying this was against your will?' Christine nodded, yes.

'It happened, just once, he came at me, I couldn´t stop him!'

Lucia was horrified, she guessed it was Sasu. She hated him as much as Christine, even more so now. Christine wiped her tears, trying to regain her composure.

'I cannot tell Dorin what happened. He would not believe me and the thought I might be carrying a child that is not his makes it worse! We have always been so careful. He still dreams of a better life. I can´t burden him with this!'

'You cannot be sure about that, Christine, some men can think differently, maybe he will believe you and just because of one bad encounter you cannot be sure it's not Dorin´s child.'

'You are talking crazy Lucia! Dorin will think I planned it, that it was my fault to get pregnant. I will have to live with a lie, with the possibility he´s not the father. Look how we live. I am not ready to bring a child into this world that will have nothing, no future. It´s hard enough for us! When Sasu finds out he will throw us out for sure and we don´t have anywhere to go!' Christine snapped.

'Sasu is happy for you to pay more than your fair share, he´s not going to throw you out in the streets immediately and lose money. You will have time to sort out something but you need to tell Dorin. It could be good for you both, he´s doing okay, isn´t he? He has a job, you are saving money and your art is so good, you can sell more!'

'Selling a few silly pictures isn´t enough and with a baby to think of, it will be even harder. I give nearly all my cleaning money to Dorin because he says Sasu needs it. The truth is Sasu takes it and they spend it on drink, Sasu's way of controlling things. It´s not fair!'

'So, you see, Christine, you would be better off without Sasu. How can he say Dorin is like a brother to him when he has no respect for you? He´s just a conniving, manipulative man, full of bullshit! Please, Christine, don´t think of throwing away a life because of one ignorant man.'

Christine had listened to Lucia. She couldn´t face terminating the pregnancy, nor could she ever tell Dorin the truth. She announced she was pregnant a month later when it was getting harder to hide and she was beyond the possibility of an abortion. Dorin had not taken the news well, accusing her of carelessness, of putting him under pressure. What would happen when she couldn´t work anymore? Sasu often complained to him there was barely space for the three of them but to announce there was a baby on the way? She should keep out of the way of him, for now. They wouldn´t be able to stay there anymore, how could she have let this happen?

Several more weeks drifted by until one warm Saturday morning in early July, Dorin went out early without telling her where he was going. She had dressed in readiness to disappear to Lucia's when Sasu emerged from his bedroom.

'I hope you are packing!' he growled.

'What are you talking about?' She looked at him in surprise. Dorin had told her not to say anything about the baby. Had Sasu guessed for himself despite her efforts to conceal the pregnancy? She was sure he would have confronted them earlier had he known. He tried to ignore her.

'I am going out. I will give you one hour to move all your shit out and leave the keys behind.'

'Please Sasu, we have nowhere to go! What about the baby?'

He looked at her incredulously. 'Baby, baby, what

are you talking about? You´re pregnant?' and then he began to laugh. 'Even better you are leaving bitch, pack fast, he deserves everything he gets!'

Christine didn´t understand. She demanded an explanation fighting back the urge to scream at him. After all, it could be his child and he was the cause of all their problems, with Dorin's attachment to drink and his attack on her. Why, yet again, when she worked so hard and seemed to try to do the right thing was there always someone that wanted to punish her?

Sasu stood over her threateningly, pointing his finger in her face.

'You should ask that idiot husband of yours, not me! But since you ask, he almost cost me my job, the thieving bastard, stealing from the building site and after everything I have done for both of you!'

He told her how over the last months, Dorin hadn´t always come to work. He´d covered for him, thinking he was just hung-over. He never told him where he went, probably out drinking somewhere. Then things started to disappear from the site, like tools and small machinery until one day Dorin was caught redhanded. The boss questioned them both and Sasu was forced to beg to keep his job, while the boss sacked Dorin on the spot.

Sasu finished his rant. He never wanted to see either of them ever again. He left, slamming the door behind him. Christine was shocked and angry. She didn´t know who she was most mad at, Dorin or Sasu. She began to gather their things, not knowing what to do. She didn´t even know where Dorin was now. What if he didn´t come back? Lucia was out. She would have to wait and hope Dorin came back soon. She placed all their belongings outside the apartment door and was about to close it for the final time when the elevator opened and Dorin stepped out.

'What are you doing?' he asked her, surprised to see all their possessions stuffed into various bags in the dim corridor. She stared at him. Her face was pink with the effort packing in such a hurry, her voice as she challenged him.

'Is it true, what you did? You should have told me! Why have you been lying to me all this time about your job?'

'What are you talking about?' asked Dorin.

'Sasu has thrown us out! He told me everything and now he knows about the baby. What are we going to do now?' she shouted at him.

'I'm truly sorry, Christine, it wasn't meant to happen this way but Sasu lies, you know that! You know he was going to throw us out sooner or later. I have been busy doing my best to make things right for us, trust me. I was going to tell you I swear but I needed to sort some things out and I didn't want to worry you until I had.'

'All this is happening and you don't tell me anything? I'm worried now!'

Dorin began gathering up their bags. 'We have a place to go. I promise you things are going to be different now! Let's go!'

She felt betrayed. There was no time to explain to Lucia. Closing the apartment door, she hastily began scribbling a note and slid it under Lucia's door. Dorin was pushing the elevator button impatiently.

'Why are you doing that? We're not coming back

here. I don´t want to see this place ever again!' he snapped.

But Christine knew she would come back. Her savings were in safe hands with Lucia and she was sure she would need them once the baby came. Lucia had promised to help her. She wouldn´t let her down. Their possessions were piled into the elevator and she reluctantly followed Dorin, wondering where they could be going.

23

Backwards not Forwards

When they left Sasu's apartment that July Saturday morning Dorin would not say where they were going, he just kept telling her it would be alright. Christine's shock at their rapid departure had eased and she wanted to believe Dorin. They caught the bus to Unirii Square in the centre of the city. She still had no idea where they were going. It was all a game to Dorin, who helped her by carrying as many bags as he could, encouraging her through the crowded streets and onto a tram. Line 32 took them towards District 5, known for its' ghettos and bad areas. She became concerned, though her immediate surrounds were full of the usual busy traffic and streets lined with high rise buildings. This area was unfamiliar to Christine, far from their previous home on the Southeast of the city. They stepped off the tram near

Rahova produce market and began walking. After ten minutes, Dorin stopped.

'We are here, our new home!' he said proudly.

Rows of apartments, grey and blackened with damp stood in front of Christine, like ugly teeth with their three floors degraded and dirty looking. Heaps of garbage lay in the street and she had to dodge a bag being tossed from a window adding to the pile. She could see empty syringes lying openly in the rot. There were makeshift extensions on some of the ground floors made up of corrugated sheets and boarding. She could barely see how to enter the building. The only bright thing was the graffiti on the side walls. Groups of inhabitants lingered, staring at them as they passed. One or two nodded to Dorin. There were nineteen buildings in total, of three and five floors, some in better condition than others. This was the Amurgului Ghetto. Although it was not as bad as the notorious Ferentari neighbourhood that bordered it, it was home to the marginalised, its living ghosts inhabiting the concrete cocoons that once housed the labourers servicing Ceausescu´s grand palace. Now the apartments were a monument to neglect and despair.

A young boy ignored them, as if they were invisible as they entered a dark stairwell. He was injecting himself, concentrating on getting the needle into his thin pale arm. Christine was horrified but said nothing as they climbed the stairs to the second floor. Dorin unlocked a door and they stepped inside. She accustomed her eyes to the dark space, about seventeen squalid square meters with a small bathroom and a walk-in larder. There was hardly any furniture, just a filthy brown sofa speckled with cigarette burns, a red plastic table with two chairs advertising coca-cola and a stained mattress. The kitchen consisted of a greasy old stove and a sink under a window. A bare light bulb dangled loosely from the ceiling centre. She put down the bags she was carrying and burst into tears. How was she to have a baby and live in this place? The caravan had been a palace, even Sasu's apartment had cleaned up nicely with its elevator and small balcony.

In the oppressive heat of the summer, the smell of abandonment made her retch. She tried to open the window which was caked in grime obscuring the daylight. Dorin went to help her.

'Don´t cry, Christine, it will be okay. It´s ours. Just you and me, we don´t have to put up with Sasu anymore!'

'It´s not just you and me Dorin, we have to think about the baby now, there is so much to do and nothing in here clean enough to sit on, let alone sleep!' she sobbed thinking of the place they had left and her refuge with Lucia now so much further away.

'I wanted to start clearing it up before I brought you here, Christine but that bastard Sasu spoiled everything. At least we are rid of him, the lying shit.

Dorin was so pleased with himself for finding them somewhere; he was annoyed at her reaction. It was not like she was in a fit state to complain. He had done his best and he was lucky to find something, even if it was an illegal rental. He had not gone back for his identity papers at the building site once he had been caught stealing and he needed to avoid any further trouble.

He happened by chance to meet a new friend in a bar shortly after the sacking. Dorin was drowning his sorrows, openly complaining that he was hard done by for taking a few tools no one would miss. His sympathetic companion told him he knew of someone looking for workers just like him. He would put in a word for him, for which Dorin was grateful. He said nothing to Christine, the work turned out to be burglary, something he was good at but of which she would not approve.

His new boss was a man he never saw, the legitimate owner of a taxi company which fronted the real business of theft to order. Some of the taxi drivers were innocently casing properties on their customer runs, memorising codes punched into entrances, noting when people were out. They passed the information to the likes of Dorin, paid to gain entry for quick theft, high-value items that could be carried easily to agreed collection points.

The money was a poor percentage from his employer but worth the extra protection it gave in the staking out of property and handling of the stolen goods. Dorin would pocket a few items for himself, selling them to the same pawnbroker he used to dispose of the stolen tools.

Ever since the sacking from the building site, he had only himself to think about, no more kowtowing to people who just treated him like something they wiped off the bottom of their shoe. He was enjoying the camaraderie of new friends and it was through this network he found a place for him and Christine to live. It wasn't much, he knew that but at least it had electricity and running water through an illegal tap into the mains supply. The rent was cheap and provided that was paid; they could exist just fine. He was sure Christine would find work again.

'I know you can fix this place up. You always do. I will help you I promise! Look how nicely you fixed Sasu's place and how ungrateful he was. At least this is ours!' he said, trying to console her with as much patience as he could muster.

Christine felt the fluttering of her baby inside her. She slowly nodded her head, pressing her hand protectively over her bump and looking around at the paint peeling walls and mould growing on the ceiling. She would make something of it; she had too.

24

A Baby Changes Everything

Light began to filter through the cracked windowpane, creating reflections like a kaleidoscope on the wall opposite. Christine thought how pretty they were, a welcome brightness amid their cramped space. Dorin was still fast asleep beside her. Nothing was going to wake him from the drunken state he had arrived home in the previous night. She pulled herself out of bed and tiptoed over to the cot. She looked at the angelic face of her six-month-old daughter Rosa, fast asleep, perfect in every way, she would soon be awake for her feed. Looking out of the window Christine looked forward to getting out into the June sunshine. She knew just where she would go for the afternoon, packing her sketchbook into the pushchair along with a change of nappy and feeds for Rosa.

When they moved in during the cold winter, Dorin

had kept his promise to help her make it a home. He painted the walls and appeared with items of furniture, so they now had a bed, a new table and chairs, kitchen cupboards and shelves in the pantry. She didn´t ask how he afforded these things. He told her not to worry as he had a good job cleaning the cars at a big taxi firm. She was content adding homely touches, with bright cushions and curtains to hang at the window and some of her paintings on the walls. She occupied herself preparing for the baby with Lucia's help. Dorin questioned how she afforded all the nappies, pushchair and baby clothes that began to invade the space but Christine said it was all through Lucia. He didn't care Crazy Bird was interfering, at least he wasn't paying.

Once the baby arrived, Dorin stopped being so helpful. She couldn´t blame him. The baby cried and the nappies smelled. It took all of her time to keep their home organised and tidy, along with the demands of her daughter. Together with the noise from the neighbours and the cold that penetrated through the thin walls, Dorin spent more time out. That left her time to work on the hand-painted cards and labels that one of the stallholders at Rahova's flower market offered to sell for her. She loved the flower market. Even in the winter months, it was full of colour and scents keeping the wholesalers and shops of Bucharest supplied.

Dorin badgered her to get a real job, painting cards was nothing more than a hobby but Christine argued it was hard to go back to work. Who would care for Rosa? Ask your best friend, Crazy Bird, he had said but it was too far to travel to Pantemelion every day and expect Lucia to babysit. When she did visit, Lucia was determined she keep painting. She made extra money painting portraits of pets from photographs supplied by friends of Lucia and saved half the money for Rosa with half towards the housekeeping, telling Dorin she was cleaning again. He moaned it wasn´t enough and then they would argue because she knew any spare he had went on beer. Somehow, they managed to get through the winter.

On a Sunday afternoon in June, everyone seemed to be on the streets. Christine had settled herself down on a bench in the shade of a small park. It divided the dismal housing blocks from the single-story houses that continued along the grid-patterned streets, devoid of anything culturally and yet on a day like today alive with people. She began making quick sketches of the women dressed up, the men in large-sized suits with their wide-brimmed hats, the pigeon cages atop wooden posts and the children playing in the dust. There was a lady selling sunflower seeds, her face etched in deep lines, her bony hands pushing a broom to sweep up the discarded shells. There was a barbeque stand with a queue of hungry customers waiting to buy mici, the beef and pork spiced sausages dished onto bread buns and dripping with mustard.

She had been sitting for some time absorbed in her mission to capture as much as possible when a woman joined her, sitting at the far end of the bench but leaning curiously in the direction of her sketchbook. Christine put down her pencils and stood up to check Rosa.

'I´m sorry,' said the woman. 'I didn´t mean to

disturb you.'

'It's okay,' said Christine, picking up Rosa and sitting back down, bouncing her gently on her knee.

'She is a beautiful baby, how old? About six months?' asked the woman, admiring the little girl in her rainbow dress and ribbon added to her dark curly hair.

Christine nodded. The woman introduced herself as Katerina and told her she had a boy of the same age. Christine hadn't met many new mothers and was enjoying someone to share stories of sleep interrupted nights and the move on to solid foods. Katerina went on to explain her husband was taking care of her baby, Marcus, while she was working. She passed Christine a leaflet detailing the symptoms of Tuberculosis and the name of a charity with the contact details for people to seek help.

'I am a social worker', she explained. We are trying to campaign to get people more aware of this terrible disease.'

Christine knew something about TB. Lucia had made sure she registered with the medical centre near her and used her address. Fortunately, Christine still had her identity papers, although Dorin had lost his. Rosa was vaccinated and Christine also tested. She had no idea of the extent of the disease in the area she lived until Katerina told her more.

'Many people try to hide it from their friends and family because it is considered a disgraceful disease that affects only poor and miserable people. Or simply through ignorance, they don't recognise what a cough can mean. The lack of medical centres and access to health care means people go untreated and it just continues to spread. Anyway that´s enough of that, I'm taking my break now,' she smiled opening a Tupperware box and offering Christine one of the neat cut sandwiches her husband had made for her. Christine accepted the kind gesture whilst trying to stop Rosa´s hand reaching for the bread. She placed her back in her pushchair, peeling a small piece of banana for her.

'I was admiring your work. It would seem you are an artist,' continued Katerina, nodding towards the sketchbook.

'No not really, it´s more of a hobby although I do sell some of my pictures and I make hand-painted cards,' replied Christine. She showed Katerina the sketches she was doing. Katerina could almost smell the women's cheap perfume, hear the manele music playing in the background and taste the mici, from the detailed pictures. Christine told her she planned to paint them as a series and put them in a multi-frame which she could display among the cards she sold. 'If I keep them simple, I can copy the same scenes onto my cards. People seem to like nostalgia,' she laughed.

'Well, I would certainly be interested to see more of what you do and to buy something. Do you have a studio nearby I could visit, or where do you live?'

Christine suddenly felt shy and embarrassed, not wanting this educated new friend to know she lived in a dilapidated block among the so-called poor and miserable.

'I have most of my work at a friend's house,' she replied, meaning Lucia, 'but I also sell at one of the stalls in Rahova flower market if you were looking for cards and I have a few pictures on display. I live not far from there and usually, go twice a week to see what has sold.'

'Well, I will come and find you then, do you have a card or something?' asked Katerina.

'No but look for Camelia's Bloomers. It's the name of the stall and you can´t miss the lady who runs it, she sits on an old stool waving a walking stick and shouts at everyone to buy!'

'Sounds interesting, I´ll look forward to going and I hope you will be there too. It has been fascinating meeting you. Perhaps we can have coffee sometime if you are around?'

As Katerina walked away, briefly turning to wave, Christine felt pleased she had met not only a potential customer but a new friend with a baby too. She hoped that Katerina wasn't just being polite. She packed her drawing away and focused her attention on Rosa who squirmed uncomfortably, as she wiped her face and hair now smeared in banana. They headed home, with Christine keen to start on her latest project. She had a good feeling Katerina would come back and they would have coffee, perhaps the first of many together.

Part Three

Mattei and Christine

25

Opening the Possibilities - Summer 2008

When he returned home from his meeting with Julia, the first thing Mattei did was find Ana. He recounted everything Julia had told him and handing Ana the photograph he asked her if she could pick out his sister from the group of children. He was thrilled how easy it was for her to pick out Christine.

'It is amazing! To think what it must have been like for her growing up, compared to me. I want to meet her if we can find her. At least now we have a photograph. Maybe I could put out some more ads, maybe in some of the newspapers or the internet,' Mattei said enthusiastically. Ana looked at him, questioningly.

'What and attract every crazy person out there who says they have seen her, or know her? Do you know how many people might bombard you with false hopes?'

'What do you mean? What is the harm in widening the search?' asked Mattei, 'With a photograph of her it should be much easier!'

Because when David helped you put the information together in the beginning, he kept the search confined to registered sites, charities, groups specialising in this kind of thing that would respect some confidentiality. If you start throwing out ads randomly, you might get people claiming rewards or even pretending to be her for all you know! Putting all this personal information out and pictures, it´s sensitive stuff! Why don´t you wait for Julia´s son to call you? I´m sure he has more experience in this kind of thing than any of us, it´s his job. Let's see if something can come of it. It is the first real lead you´ve had, so find out what he can do before you go off on a tangent just because you have one photograph.' Ana was talking sense. He needed to calm down.

'Ok. It´s just that I didn´t know what to expect from Julia and it was more than I could have hoped for. It has been six years since Christine left that home. I guess she could be anywhere but you can´t blame me for feeling excited! By the way, I haven´t said anything to anyone else so far. I wanted to see how the meeting with Julia went.'

Mattei had kept everything to himself, confiding only in Ana, who seemed to understand him completely.

She appreciated what he was saying but thought it was wrong to keep it from the others. 'I think you should let Maria and David know and Alex too. They are the closest you have to family and they will only be thinking of you. I know you worry Maria and David have enough to think about and that Alex isn't on your side but I'm sure they would want to support you. You wouldn't even have got this far if David hadn't put the advertisements out for you.'

What she was saying was right but he was still reluctant to involve Alex. He didn't want any negatives put in his way at this stage, or to be discouraged.

'You are probably right again,' he smiled, 'but let's wait until I speak with Julia's son, maybe get a little further ahead before I go bothering everyone else, okay?'

Ana agreed with him, feeling a little satisfied with herself that Mattei had chosen to confide in her. She was intrigued to know what would come of it.

He didn't have long to wait for the phone call from Julia's son. He had finished service in the restaurant and started to clean the kitchen when his mobile rang. He took it out of his pocket and looked at the number. He didn't recognise it but knew it must be him. He went out to the garden so he could take the call alone.

The voice was warm and friendly. At first, they chatted about the meeting with Julia with Mattei telling him how welcome she made him, stuffing him full of cake. He thought how kind she was and she gave him hope. Alexandru was equally full of praise for his mother.

'She is the one who inspired me to start working

with the charities that help bring families back together. She cares a great deal about what became of all those young people who spent time in those care homes. Sometimes, I have good stories to tell her, sometimes not, which brings me to the question of your sister, Christine. I cannot promise you anything but with your permission, I can try to find out more. My mother told me Christine and Dorin got jobs in Poleisti when they left that home. I have access to certain information through the charity and should be able to check this out as a starting point. If it's okay with you, Mattei, it would be helpful if you can send me an email agreeing that you have given me consent, for our records.'

It was positive news for Mattei and he was happy for Alexandru to find out more.

'Of course, whatever you need,' said Mattei, full of optimism. Alexandru was cautious.

'Please, be prepared. It isn't always as easy or straightforward as we would like. Sometimes it comes to a dead-end. Sometimes we are lucky in locating someone. Sometimes it doesn't work out and we find things we wish we hadn't.'

'What do you mean by finding out things you wish you hadn't?' asked Mattei, suddenly aware he could be opening Pandora's box.

Alexandru explained to him there were often obstacles in finding those that had left the state institutions. There were runaways or those that left when they became adults, disappearing with nowhere to go and little chance of being found. Sometimes people preferred to stay hidden.

'In this case, it is different. Luckily, we have a good

start because we know Christine and Dorin had jobs. I will make some enquiries. Be patient and I will let you know if I can find out more.'

Mattei thanked him. He would write the email straight away, giving Alexandru permission to keep searching. For a change, his mind was not on his kitchen, the anticipation of what might come was gripping his imagination. By the time he got home, he was feeling tired. He didn´t even stop to have a beer with Alex, taking himself off to bed and leaving his friend wondering if he was feeling okay. Mattei was not ready to tell the story so far. It had been a long day and he felt strange linking the present with the truth of the past as if they were not connected, as if he was part of something else. Ana was neutral. It seemed natural to speak to her. He would find the right time to include everyone once he understood more himself.

The hotel was at full occupancy and a week flew by with everyone putting in long hours. Mattei was forced to take his mind off the search for Christine. Ana felt she had been at the hotel forever and at times wished she was idling in a bikini on Marbella´s beaches. She missed that part of her life, stranded here in the mountains with little to entertain her. Although there were no more trips to clubs in Brasov in the evenings, there were shopping trips with Maria. Maria admired her taste in clothes and wondered how she could afford some of the things she chose but Ana reminded her she wasn´t at Casa Flori for the wages, she had savings and when it came to fashion, she didn't cut corners on quality. They had fun and Maria often insisted on paying for lunch. 'I don´t know how we would have managed without you,' she said.

Ana surprised herself in how capable she was. She enjoyed the fact that others would search her out if there was a problem to solve. She had taken to wearing the fake reading glasses she had bought in Brasov when working behind reception. She felt it made her look smart and efficient.

It was during a short break one afternoon when she was sitting with Mattei on the picnic table outside the kitchen that he took a call from Alexandru. He motioned for Ana to stay and listen to their conversation.

'Hi, Mattei! I hope I haven´t caught you at a bad time. I know you must be busy. It was to let you know that I managed to find out more and I wanted to keep you up to date.'

'I appreciate that. Thank you,' said Mattei, 'Have you found her?'

'Not that quickly!' answered Alexandru, 'but I did check their work record in Poleisti and it seemed they stayed there for about six months. They were working on a building site. These tend not to be long term jobs but I managed to speak to the original manager of the site who is still with the same company. He was able to dig up employment records off his computer. He said they had been good workers overall and left with their paperwork intact. He thinks they may have gone to Bucharest as he received a request from another building site asking for a reference and verification of Dorin´s papers. He gave me the name of the company but when I tried to contact them, they were less helpful. It was too many years ago and too many staff changes.

'That doesn't sound too promising,' Mattei, replied, a little deflated. He was wondering about ignoring Ana's advice and setting up his own search again but Alexandru sounded determined.

'I know this sounds disappointing but I do have more contacts I can follow up, so I am continuing and I will circulate what I have so far amongst colleagues in the city. As I said before be patient, we haven't exhausted all sources yet.'

'Thank you Alexandru, I hope we speak again soon,' replied Mattei, hanging up and looking across to Ana. 'I guess you got the gist of that. It doesn't seem much. There must be more I can do.'

'Mattei, you hardly have time to do this kind of search right now. We are so busy and like I said before, Alexandru seems to have a better idea how to trace someone. All you can do is play pin the tail on the donkey and hope you get lucky. Let him keep going. It's not as if you are desperate, like it's a matter of life and death and you need a kidney transplant or something!'

She made him laugh. She put everything into perspective for him. She made him feel a lot of things he realised.

'Do you mind if I ask you something?' he ventured shyly, looking down at his shoes. 'Sorry if it's an awkward question and you don't have to answer but is there a boyfriend or was there somebody before you came here?'

She froze for a moment before regaining her Ana business-like composure. 'Well, of course, there were boyfriends! But no one special since you ask. I don't have time and being here is temporary for me, to gain more experience so I don't need to worry about trying to keep a relationship going elsewhere. I´ll be moving on soon.'

Mattei felt good that she did not have a boyfriend but also disappointed she intended to leave.

'Pity, we´ve got used to having you around. It won´t be the same if you go. You would miss us!' Mattei looked at Ana enquiringly.

It was an uncomfortable moment for Ana, sensing where the conversation might go if she let it continue. Maybe she should have told him she had a boyfriend. It would have been more straightforward but then perhaps she was enjoying the fact that Mattei was attracted to her in a way other men weren´t. She did have feelings for him and she would miss them all but in truth, the glamour of the bright lights and the desire to return to her true identity meant more to her. She felt safe at Casa Flori but it wasn't enough. Nothing was going on between Mattei and her and she would be leaving, she wouldn't hurt him. He had a sister to find and she was sure that would take his mind off any intentions on her.

'Don´t you think we have enough on our plates to deal with right now?' Ana answered, giving him a playful slap.

'Yes, Ma'am, we do! Right, back to work then! I have dinner for thirty to prepare for tonight and you need to get your apron on!' he laughed.

As Ana headed back to work, she thought about how much she wanted her life back. At least Mattei had a choice in what he was doing. Patience was never her strong point and although most of the time being Ana was easy, it wasn´t real, she just wanted to be herself, back with her parents and brothers, who would solve all her problems. Razvan had stopped her like a schoolgirl expelled for bad behaviour. She hoped things would move quickly for her and Mattei. It turned out to be much sooner for Mattei.

26

Lost and Found

It was little more than a week later when Mattei took another call from Alexandru who came straight to the point.

'Mattei, we have found your sister!'

'How?' asked Mattei, his blood suddenly pulsing, making him dizzy. He was out walking Baloo and even the dog stood still staring up at him as Mattei began pacing in small circles. 'Are you sure it´s her? I wasn´t expecting anything, so soon!'

Alexandru sounded excited. 'I know! It took me by surprise but I´m sure we are right. I told you that I was sending out information to contacts I have in the city. I started with a friend who works in social security, trying to find any registration for Christine, that she might also have been working. They aren´t allowed to give out any information but she pointed me in a different direction to someone she said might know her, based on something that was in the records. It was a wild card but I made contact with a different social services office and emailed the file of what we had so far. A lady called Katerina got back to me to say she recognised Christine from the photo attached. Katerina is a social worker. We spoke on the phone for quite a while. She wanted to know as much as I could tell her and says she has known Christine for several years.'

Mattei's reaction was immediately to bombard Alexandru with questions, where was his sister, could he meet her? What was she doing, was she married, why was she known to a social worker? He had so many questions all at once!

'Firstly, I cannot tell you anything about Christine. Katerina respects that there should be confidentiality and therefore, it´s not with me she should be sharing details. I know this is great news to you Mattei but now we have to make sure we follow this up the right way. Katerina knows Christine personally and understandably she doesn´t want to drop her into something like this without warning. She is sure it would come as a shock to her. Katerina has asked if it would be okay to contact you directly. She says she would like to write to you first. I also feel it´s the right way to do this. Please let me know what happens. I wish you luck!'

'Of course, said Mattei and thank you for all your efforts.' He was in shock himself. He believed he was going to meet the sister he hadn´t seen since he was three years old!

Mattei headed home, feeling stunned. He couldn't

help, smiling, taking in big breaths and whistling out sighs in an attempt to calm himself. Alex was sitting on the veranda as he approached, enjoying a beer.

'You look like the cat that got the cream, what's up?' asked Alex.

'You got time? I'll grab a beer too. I've got some news,' said Mattei, as he leapt up the steps two at a time past his friend, to the kitchen where he took out two beers. He certainly had Alex's attention. Returning to sit beside him, Mattei started at the beginning.

Do you remember David putting together all those ads for me to look for my sister?'

'Yeh, don't tell me you've found something?' asked Alex.

'More than that, I've found her!' Mattei beamed. He told Alex the full story, about meeting Julia, his contact with Alexandru and the call he had just received. It was a lot for Alex to take in.

'Wow, are you sure this is for real? It didn't take long, did it? Why didn't you tell me about this before? I would have come with you to meet this woman, Julia.'

'I didn't want to drag anyone in on what might have been a wild goose chase and it was something I needed to do for myself,' Mattei lied, knowing he had asked Ana to go with him. Alex felt hurt at being kept in the dark. He and Mattei shared everything.

'It all sounds a bit too quick, how suddenly in the space of a few months you managed to find her, after all these years. I know it seems pretty certain this is your sister but you can't make any assumptions.'

'What do you mean?' asked Mattei.

'You cannot just assume to drop back into somebody´s life unannounced is what I mean. She might not want to meet you.'

'Why wouldn´t she want to meet me?' asked Mattei taken aback by Alex's first impression.

'Just because you have this need to find your family, it might not be the same for her. You have a nice life and a good future but you don´t know anything about her, except what this Julia could tell you. You don´t know this person Mattei! Why do you need to complicate things? Your family is here. They always have been!'

Mattei knew Alex would react with a negative.

'How can you say that?' he exclaimed, 'I have a chance to know her again. I´m not going to let this pass. I don´t believe she wouldn´t want to meet me. You´re just saying that because your mother doesn´t contact you, it doesn´t have to be the same for me!'

Mattei regretted the words as soon as he said them. He had thrown a low punch regarding Alex´s mother and how she walked out on his father and Alex. How insensitive could he be about Alex´s feelings but it was too late. Alex stormed off the veranda back towards Casa Flori.

Alex was angry. Why couldn´t Mattei see he was trying to be realistic. His comments touched a nerve. He had no desire to contact his mother. His father never even mentioned her, the woman who had just upped and left him for somebody else. How hurt would Andrei be if Alex decided to track her down out of the blue? He thought Mattei was selfish by not including him. He was only trying to help. He ignored Mattei's shouts to come back.

Mattei stared after his friend, bending down to clear up the beer bottles. Baloo hovered at his feet, sensing the upset, his tail wagging in sympathy. Mattei gave him a reassuring hug. He felt terrible about the way he had handled things so far, upsetting Alex like that. Ana had told him he should have said something, maybe he should have but something in him had stopped him. He needed to let her know he had told Alex.

He couldn´t find her in the hotel so he went through the garden to her room and knocked on the door. She was back in her room after her usual afternoon run and taking a shower. She wasn't expecting any visitors and her hair was still wet when she opened the door to Mattei. He looked quite pale and lost, running his hand through his hair in agitation.

'Do you have time to talk? I have more news,' he said.

'Yes, of course. Is it good news?' Ana said, inviting Mattei to sit down on the one chair there was in the room. She sat opposite him on the edge of her bed.

First, he told her the good news, that he now had a contact in Katerina, who confirmed his sister was living in Bucharest.

'That´s amazing, what a brilliant piece of detective work by Alexandru! You don´t seem as pleased as you should be, what´s up?'

'I was so excited. I saw Alex at the house and he sensed something was up, so I told him the whole story but he didn´t share my reaction to finding Christine. I said some things I shouldn´t have and now I´ve upset him,' confessed Mattei.

'What were you expecting?' she asked, shrugging her shoulders.

'I wasn't thinking, I have to apologise to him,' said Mattei. Ana was sympathetic.

'Of course, you must apologise to him but. Alex will understand. It happens. Sometimes we avoid telling things to those closest to us, believing they might say what we don't want to hear.'

'You don't tell me what I don't want to hear. So far, everything we have talked about has just made practical sense. I'm still not sure if I could make Alex understand.'

'Well, you know you can talk to me, anytime but you need to make it up with Alex. Come on, I'll walk up with you and help start things for the evening,' said Ana quickly running a brush through her hair.

They emerged together from her room just as Alex appeared on the terrace. He looked surprised to see them together, Ana with her hair damp and Mattei following like a puppy. It suddenly dawned on him that Ana probably knew everything, even before he did and it made him angry again. Mattei looked up, overtaking Ana and bounding up the stone steps.

'We need to talk Alex, I said things I shouldn't have and I'm truly sorry. See you at home later?'

Alex shrugged his shoulders 'Sure, just us, eh?'

Mattei nodded, taking his hand from Alex's shoulder and heading into the kitchen.

Ana followed on behind, looking quite pleased with herself but seeing Alex's expression she realised what was formulating in his head 'It's not what you think,' she said, looking him straight in the eye. He shrugged his shoulders again, in indifference.

'It's none of my business who you invite back to your room, though I wonder if you have any other secrets, things you two aren't telling me that you'd like to share?' he asked with a hint of sarcasm. Ana gave him a stubborn stare.

'No, I don't think so. Like you told me I was a good friend, nothing more. Now I have work to do, maybe see you later.' She turned her back to him and Alex watched her saunter towards the kitchen, tossing her hair as she went.

Later that night, when it was just the two of them, Alex let Mattei do most of the talking. Alex wanted to challenge him over Ana and how she was worming her way into his affections but he kept silent, not wanting to fall out again with the friend that was truly a brother to him. He could only hope that Mattei wasn't heading for a double fall caused either by a long-lost sister or a woman he was sure was hiding something.

Mattei was determined to keep going. He received an email from Katarina. It was fairly short. It told him nothing about Christine. Instead, it requested he tell her more about himself. He had expected something different but decided at this stage to answer her questions as Alexandru advised. He wrote an honest account of himself and Katerina promised she would speak to Christine. He could hardly wait for the response knowing she would be talking to his sister.

27

Cities to Cross and Mountains to Climb

Christine´s memories of her family roots lay buried in a box to which she had long thrown away the key. As she absorbed what Katerina was telling her the scene in the park became unreal, the children on the swings froze in midair, the rowers on the lake floated above the water. All the colours of a summer afternoon merged and everything moved slowly in a circle around her. Katerina was reaching for her hand.

'Christine, Christine,' she was calling to her, gently.

It was Katerina's idea they meet in Cisumigui Park for a picnic. It was one of Christine´s favourite places and they agreed to get together with their children. Rosa and Marcus had been occasional playmates for most of their lives. Christine looked forward to being out in the open air and was unprepared for what Katerina was telling her.

'It happened by chance. You know I wouldn't deliberately pry into other people´s business, it came through work. I wasn´t expecting your picture to flash up on my computer but there you were and a brother I never knew you had, was asking to find you.'

'You know more about me than anyone, apart from Lucia. What did you tell him about me? You have no right to have told him anything!' protested Christine, unravelled by the revelation.

'I didn't tell him anything about you, not before I talked with you first. I wouldn´t do that. I wanted you to read his letter and then if you want, I can make a response,' Katerina replied.

The letter spoke of a successful young man, trained as a chef, who had travelled and now settled in the countryside in his own house. He was a stranger to her, light years away from her own life. How could he have suffered from the sense of loss and rejection that she had to be left by your parents? His life seemed to have been a bed of roses compared to hers. She couldn´t reconcile the baby-faced boy she had last seen with the grown handsome man in the photograph that accompanied the letter, though she could see how they resembled each other. Why would he come looking for her now? She had Dorin, Rosa, Lucia, her friends including Katerina. Why would she need to complicate her life with a long-lost brother trying to satisfy his curiosity?

'I don´t have anything in common with this person,' Christine started to say, 'Anyway, what would he think of us, where we live, how we live. He comes along out of the blue and expects some happy reunion?'

Katerina was expecting her to react like this. 'He seems genuine and I don´t believe he is asking to meet you out of curiosity. I have known you for long enough. Over the last five and a half years I have seen the struggles you have made it through. The Christine I know is one of the most caring people I am proud to call my friend, a tireless worker and talented artist! From what I have learned about your brother so far, I think these are things you have in common and getting to know each other could bring more to your life and Rosa´s.'

Christine felt overwhelmed. She called for Rosa to come to her. 'Time to go!' and she began to gather up the remains of their picnic. Katerina folded the picnic blanket and looked across to where the children were playing. She appreciated how unexpected her news was to Christine and before the children reached them, she spoke again.

'What happened all those years ago was not of your choosing, not for either of you but now you have a chance to put things right, not to remain angry or think your brother was to blame any more than you for being separated. I understand this is something you need to think about but maybe there is more to gain than to lose. How do you know if you don´t try? Please, I know I can help you with this. I can meet him first, if you like, to make sure, before we go any further, put my professional hat on,' Katerina said, smiling.

It wasn´t the first time Katerina had persuaded

Christine to do something she had initially shied away from and she owed her a great deal for the support she had always given her. 'Okay, meet him. I trust you will know if it is the right thing.' She hugged her goodbye and set off across the park with Rosa, towards the tram stop that would take them home, back to her daily battles.

Katerina returned to her home and set her fingers to her computer, tapping out a reply to Mattei.

Dear Mattei,

Thank you for sending the email telling me more about yourself. I do appreciate how you came to be looking for your sister and what it must mean to you.

I can tell you is she is well and she has a husband and a daughter, Rosa, nearly six years old. Her daughter looks just like her and I can see the family resemblance with you from the photographs you sent.

Although we have been friends for several years, she has never opened up about her years growing up, nor mentioned anything of the family she was forced to separate from so many years ago, so it came as a surprise to me also that she had a brother who wanted to make contact.

I met with her yesterday and spoke to her about how you have been looking for her. I showed her the email you wrote to me. You will understand it came as a shock to her and this has released many emotions in her, especially when I tell you things have not been easy for her. Life in parts of this city, for too many, is very much about day to day survival. She has had more than her fair share of setbacks but she is one of the strongest people I know.

We have agreed that I meet you first, as in my

experience in this kind of situation; you need to go slowly to have any chance to move forward. There is no step by step manual on how to handle any reunion. Meeting a biological family member after a separation is a step into the unknown and there are always two halves to every story. You may share the same DNA but you are strangers and like any relationship it begins with finding common ground, it isn´t easy and sometimes it doesn´t work, like in any relationship.

I believe Christine is at a point in her life that could benefit from having you part of it once again and I am happy to act as an intermediary. She agreed that I could make some introduction and prepare you better for any meeting.

I can travel to you if you can suggest a day and time we can meet.

I look forward to hearing from you.

Yours sincerely, Katerina

Mattei read the email several times over and then printed it out. He was excited but confused at the same time. He was pleased the letter suggested Christine wanted to meet him but he was not expecting it to be so complicated. He needed to speak to his intermediary and he went to find Ana.

Ana read the email several times. He waited for her to finish and then let his thoughts tumble out.

'I wasn´t thinking that I would be going through a social worker to find out about my sister and I don´t know what to think about her comments about problems Christine may have. What does she mean exactly? I don´t know this Katerina woman and yet she says she wants to meet me first. It makes me nervous like she is vetting me. I just want to meet my sister and what kind of talk is that, saying it might not work out? It seems so formal!'

'Whoa, slow down, Mattei! She certainly knows your sister better than you do and you do want to meet Christine, don´t you? It seems good advice to me to take it step by step. You have an image in your mind of how Christine will appear. You know the old expression, rose-coloured spectacles?'

'I don´t have rose-coloured spectacles!' Mattei said defensively.

'Katerina is just saying to be better prepared. She sounds like she wants to help Christine, whatever that might mean and she is experienced in this kind of thing. What is it that´s bothering you? You have already decided you needed to do this, isn´t it better to have someone like her to help you both? By the way, congratulations, it sounds like you are also an Uncle!' Ana teased, trying to release some of the tension she could see in Mattei.

'I hadn´t thought about that, pretty amazing really, I´m an Uncle!' Mattei grinned. 'You know, when I first read this, I felt like it was interfering. Who is this person going on about my DNA and talking about relationships?' He got up from the chair, putting the letter back in his pocket and seeming more resolved. 'It must be better to do it this way and I have to accept it could be a bumpy ride, it isn´t only about me. If the shoe was on the other foot and Christine was looking for me, I would have been just as shocked. I will arrange the meeting with Katerina.

28

Meeting Katerina

Several days after he had spoken to her, Katerina arrived at Casa Flori. She stepped out of her car, admiring the carpets of bright flowers spilling over the balconies on the warm August day. Mattei came out to greet her, approaching with a broad smile and an outstretched hand. He was relieved to see her relaxed, dressed casually in a soft skirt and tee shirt. He had been nervous about meeting her thinking she would turn up in a suit with a clipboard ready for an interview.

She laughed when he told her. 'No nothing like that. I was glad you invited me to come here. It gave me a good reason to escape from the city. It has been so hot lately. I´m a little early, I was expecting more traffic and not sure how easily I would find my way,' she said to him, returning his handshake.

Katerina's first impression of Mattei was of a charismatic young man, welcoming and friendly. It was a promising start to know how at ease he was.

He led her through to the terrace seating her comfortably in the shade of the sun umbrellas and leaving her a few moments to take in the rolling countryside views, while he fetched a tray of coffee and slices of blueberry cheesecake he had prepared earlier.

'It is beautiful and thank you for the welcome,' she said, looking at the mouth-watering desert he had put before her.

While they took their coffee, Katerina told him she had visited Brasov, Bran and Poiana, skiing in the winter, all the usual tourist things but had never heard of Casa Flori. They talked about the hotel and what plans Mattei had for the restaurant which broke the ice but he was anxious to bring the conversation round to his sister.

'How exactly did you meet?' he asked her.

'It was by chance, about five years ago. I was working with an American charity called Doctors of the World, to raise awareness about the spread of tuberculosis and other health issues related to poverty. At that time, our country had the highest record of the disease in Europe but the government wasn't doing much about it and it fell to outside help to reach those most vulnerable. I had been canvassing a particular neighbourhood, in Rahova, handing out leaflets. It was a Sunday; many people were out on the streets. It was a good time for me to be there. I sat down on a park bench to take a break and was fascinated by a young woman next to me, with a pretty baby in a pushchair about the same age as my son. She was sketching and I couldn´t help but be nosey! She showed me what she was drawing, the street scenes in front of us, really good! She was unusual, not the kind of person you come across in those neighbourhoods. She told me she sold some of her work and of course, I was interested to see more, perhaps to buy something. She told me she was often around the flower market where one of the stallholders displayed her artwork and I ended up buying several of her paintings and hand-made cards! After that, we became friends.

'Julia told me she always loved drawing. She showed me some of the pictures she did before she left the home. Where does she live now?'

From Katerina's description Mattei, was imagining Christine lived in a colourful artisan neighbourhood but this was the opposite to what Katerina was about to explain to him.

'She lives in the Amurgului ghetto, with her husband, Dorin and her daughter. They have always been in the same place, not the nicest of areas, although things are improving. If you were to go there, you would probably be quite shocked, especially the neighbouring district Ferentari. It is where I do a lot of my work, as a social worker.'

Mattei was familiar with reports from this district. 'I have seen things written about conditions there, how gangs rule the place, how people live. There was news recently of the arrest of Vasile Balint, one of the Camataru brothers. It said how they lived in luxury and used the terrible conditions as a barricade and they even kept a private zoo with lions in the middle of all that! Some of the scenes are shocking!' he said frowning.

Katerina could see Mattei's concern his sister was living close to that. 'Well, all of that is true but not everyone who lives there is tarred with the brush of criminality. Much of the population is Roma and there is huge discrimination. It's tough to change things, the local authorities try to ignore the problems but we need to improve schools and health care. Many of the people who live there don´t have identity papers. Many live in illegal buildings and basic services aren´t even connected. However, you do find pockets of good community spirit, especially among women. Last year, a new community centre opened, the Centre for Creative Education and Active Art, set up by a theatre group to highlight problems in the neighbourhood. They did something similar in Harlem, in New York, again all outside help. It gives people a voice and brings more dialogue with the authorities. There are all kinds of workshops and training groups and they organise speakers to come, including me. The debates can get quite heated. They have done tree planting, cleaned up garbage, many different things. Christine volunteers, helping to run drawing workshops and Rosa joins in dance classes. She is a perfect example of why we should never give up on people, who given half a chance, can make their lives better.'

'It sounds as if she has a busy life,' said Mattei.

'She does,' replied Katerina, 'but it hasn't always been busy in a good way.'

Katerina asked if she could have some water, it was warm sitting on the terrace and when Mattei returned with a pitcher of icy water and two glasses, she continued.

'Not long after we met, I persuaded her to join the TB campaign by training through the Roma Centre for Interventions and Social Surveys as a health and sanitary mediator. The pay wasn´t much, about four hundred lei a month but she was glad to earn extra money and not worry who would take care of Rosa. The hours were flexible, distributing leaflets and persuading people to come to a mobile unit we set up to offer diagnosis. She was good at it and she helped people get registered with a doctor if they didn´t have a stable residence to get access to help. She might have gone on to train further.'

'Might have? Does she not do that anymore?' asked Mattei.

'No. Things happened that made it hard for her to continue.' said Katerina, hesitating. She wasn´t sure she was doing the right thing telling Mattei so much but she wanted this to work and decided the more he knew, the easier it would be. She felt she could trust him and he persisted.

'You said in your letter that she had setbacks in her life. What happened?'

She told him how Dorin became ill following a bad experience with the police, after which he was never quite the same, that he had problems with alcohol and more recently, a heroin addiction.

Mattei was unsure of what to say. So far, he hadn´t pictured Christine this way, married to a drug addict and an alcoholic. He let Katerina continue.

'Christine has been battling with it for some time but it has taken its toll on her. I help where I can but people like Dorin don´t appreciate interference from civil servants like me, it has caused problems for her in the past. Alcohol and heroin is a recipe for anxiety and depression and she has to deal with that. Christine is very loyal to him, they have known each other since they were children but, how can I put this, with his condition he can be difficult, sometimes resentful. It's hard for her to keep up her art and such a pity with all her talent, she could do so much more. Her friend Lucia, an elderly lady who has been a huge influence in her life, tries to encourage her. Christine doesn´t realise how good she is and she is struggling. She cannot rely on Dorin when he isn´t well. We managed to get him on a treatment scheme and he´s been clean for about three months but the period of post-acute withdrawal symptoms can go on for months. She is determined to get him well again.'

Mattei did not like what he was hearing. Drug users repulsed him. 'How did he get like that and how does this affect Rosa?' he asked.

'Dorin doesn´t have much of a relationship with Rosa sadly but you cannot judge why some people can end up like that. All walks of life, rich and poor, you cannot discriminate. A lot of Dorin´s problems stem from the environment they live in and the people he mixes with. When things started to go badly for him, I think he found it harder to accept what Christine was achieving, her involvement in community work and her passion for art.

Mattei was struggling to understand. 'Christine doesn´t sound anything remotely like him. How can she be married to someone like that?'

Katerina nodded. 'Perhaps that is something you

will understand better if you meet. You don´t know her yet. Like I said, she is very loyal and you wouldn´t give up on someone just because they went through a bad time, would you?'

'No! Of course not!' Mattei exclaimed, not wanting Katerina to think badly of him.

He was curious to know if Dorin had worked but Katerina skirted round the question suggesting as she had been sitting a long time perhaps Mattei could show her around. He was ready for a distraction with so much to take in and decided to show Katerina where he lived.

As they approached the gate to the farmhouse, they met Ana, returning from her run, with Baloo. He introduced her to Katerina but Ana didn't linger. He guessed she was heading for a shower, which was right but Ana was also trying to keep a low profile, still wary of meeting anyone from her home city.

Mattei showed Katerina around the farmhouse and she admired the furniture his father had made and the textiles his mother had crafted. She wondered what Christine would make of it, a home she could only dream of and that her brother was lucky to have. How would she feel?

Katerina suggested to Mattei that if Christine agreed to meet, he should come to Bucharest for the first meeting, rather than bring her to Casa Flori. Better on neutral ground, she told him, at a cafe or a restaurant in the old city.

They meandered around the garden with Mattei asking more questions about what Christine was like and Rosa too. His gut feeling was that she was a nice person, caring and a good mother to her daughter but a person denied so many opportunities. Her husband seemed to be a root cause. Katerina agreed.

'Sadly, it is and one of the reasons I wanted her to make contact with you is a result of what he has been through and how it affects her. You might bring a different perspective to her life, to help her stay strong. Dorin isn´t in good health and Lucia is getting on in years. They are the only family she has along with Rosa. I think in the long term she will be glad you found her.'

Mattei hoped so but he was concerned at Christine's reaction. 'You told me it´s taking some persuasion for her to agree to meet me and I must admit I was a bit baffled by all the stuff you wrote about DNA and everything. I appreciate you coming and now we have met, do you think there will be any difficulty arranging a meeting? After all, I´m a nice person!' he grinned, with Katerina capturing a quick reflection of Christine in his smile. She assured him she would do her best.

'I´m just saying keep your expectations reasonable. With Christine, I think she chose to forget so much of her childhood. It wasn't a happy one, being brought up in an institution. She concentrates on the present, juggling everything to get by, day by day. That is why I wanted to meet you, so you would understand what might be sensitive for her. You are a reincarnation from her past! If you meet her, you can´t go wading in, full of promise, especially when you have so much compared to her. She has her own life and has worked hard. She won´t appreciate it if you come across the wrong way and I don´t mean that unkindly.'

Mattei understood his need to reconnect was very

different to the way Christine might be feeling but from what he learned, he was even more determined to be part of her life. As they walked back to Katerina´s car, he urged her to speak to Christine and arrange a meeting as soon as possible. Katerina waved back at Mattei as she drove away. She liked him and was confident it would be good for Christine.

Once she returned to Bucharest, Katerina didn't waste time in setting up a meeting. She was full of encouragement, telling Christine how much she liked Mattei, how he determined he was to meet her and for all the right reasons.

'Speaking as your friend, I truly believe this to be something positive for you, Christine. Let's try.'

In her mind, Katerina was sure it would be the start of something life-changing for Christine but she could have no idea just how complicated it would become, not only for Christine but for everyone.

29

Building Bridges

Katerina reserved a table in an open-air restaurant overlooking Parc Florilor. It was close to Lucia's and convenient for Christine to leave Rosa with Lucia. She chose to sit to one side under the shade of trees with an open view across the park. It gave them some privacy but at the same time, the openness made it a less daunting environment. She knew Christine would be nervous and made sure they arrived ahead of Mattei. She did her best to help her relax, taking up a middle seat and ordering a coffee for herself and a coke for Christine.

Christine was scanning the crowd to see if she could recognise her brother, hardly hearing what Katerina was saying but she wasn´t the first to spot Mattei walking across the park towards them. It was Katerina who stood and waved him across, holding her hand out in greeting as he approached. Christine remained frozen to her seat.

'Hi Mattei. I'm glad you managed to find us ok.' said Katerina, turning to Mattei so that it was less obvious Christine was studying him.

Christine's mind was searching, trying to reconcile the handsome young man in front of her with the little brother she remembered feeling so protective towards as a baby. He had the same thick dark hair as hers which tended to curl but his teeth were white and straight, unlike hers which were crooked. He was much taller than her and his frame was strong, suntanned and healthy. In contrast, her shoulders were bony and her skin pale by comparison. His eyes were bright and did not carry the dark circles beneath them as hers did. It was hard for her to understand how everyone else seemed to see their likeness yet shockingly she saw something of her mother in Mattei, a smile, a flash of familiarity from years ago, of a mother she had loved and who had once loved her.

Mattei was polite, conscious of Christine's silent appraising.

'I'm not so familiar with this side of the city and the traffic was a bit of a nightmare but I managed to be on time at least. I used to visit more often when my friend Alex was at University but I was away in England for a time and now living Brasov I don't tend to get to Bucharest much. It seems to change every time I come, with new buildings and roads.'

'It's true, I get lost myself sometimes and I live here!' smiled Katerina.

A waiter came across, handing each of them a

menu and asked Mattei what he would like to drink. He ordered a coke, like Christine.

Katerina was doing her best to bridge any awkwardness though Mattei seemed to be entirely at ease, allowing her to guide the conversation. 'Christine knows the city like the back of her hand, don´t you?' said Katerina in an attempt to encourage Christine to say something.

They ordered food and Katerina and Mattei slipped into conversation that left Christine feeling more of a spectator than a participant as if these two were already best friends. It was mainly Katerina's fault. She had plenty of opinions about Romania being the newest member of the European Union and hoped the upcoming elections would bring change, the present government failing to tackle high-level corruption or implement reforms in the judicial system, or health care.

Christine felt detached. She looked again at her brother. Why had their lives turned out so differently? It didn´t matter what government was in charge, it would do little for her existing at the other end of life´s spectrum.

Why had he such good fortune to find a home and a life, to be educated, to travel? She had agreed to see him and then wanted to see him but now felt almost resentful he had come looking for her, to know things about her and the kind of life she led, so clearly removed from his.

Mattei desperately wanted to change the subject despite Katerina's intention to keep to fewer personal questions on their first meeting. He could sense Christine was becoming uncomfortable but he was glad when Katerina excused herself to go to the bathroom and he could speak to Christine alone.

'I have things I have been longing to ask you, Christine, of what you remember before we were separated. I did some research to find the place we used to live, a small house with some land but now it has new houses built on it. I found out our parents sold everything they had to con men who promised them a better life in a different country. As far as I could find out they went to Italy, with our two older brothers but I couldn´t find out any more, it was like they just disappeared. I believe they intended to come back for us one day but they never could.' Mattei hoped that some news of their parents' whereabouts might be helpful to Christine but the effect was the opposite. She sat back in the chair, folding her arms in self-defence against the words that tried to justify their parents' actions.

'What kind of people could ever consider leaving their children in a place like that, an institution for the abandoned? They were never going to come back for us and anyway, it was too late once you were adopted.'

Mattei shook his head.

'I don´t believe our parents left us because they did not love us. Things were very different back then and they probably believed all the propaganda about state care, people were so poor. I cannot blame them for trying to make a better life.'

Mattei's interpretation of things did not match hers. 'What would you know about being poor, about having nothing? It´s fine for you to say! How would you know what it was like to stay in that terrible place for so long? I didn´t know what happened to you, I could barely survive myself and I had no one, locked away with bars on the windows for two years, the constant noise of children having to fight every day for basic attention. I was just forgotten and then shuffled into another home. I had to forget about you and everyone else because there was nothing I could do. Look at you with your new life, why do you want to go back to the past? Why look for me now?'

'Because I didn´t forget you, Christine, even if I have few memories of that time. It´s true, I was one of the lucky ones but I didn´t know any different. I can´t change the past and it´s not why I am here. I can´t explain it very well but maybe sometimes you felt it too, that there was a part of you that was missing? Isn´t that why you agreed to meet me today?'

But Christine wasn't ready to step back into a portal. Katerina returned and could sense how Christine was struggling. She caught the attention of the waiter and motioned him to bring more cold drinks over. She had seen it before when people were reunited. It was like riding an emotional rollercoaster where each party suffered guilt, anger, joy, everything you could imagine. She needed to apply some brakes and did her best to diffuse things.

Little by little they all relaxed again until Christine said she needed to get back for Rosa. Mattei wanted to see her again and to meet Rosa. He apologised if he made things sound difficult and asked her to give him a chance. 'Please come and visit me. I would love to meet Rosa. I have plenty of room and you would have more time to get used to me. Worst case it could be a holiday for you. If you haven´t been to that part of our country before, it is beautiful!' Mattei stood and went to embrace her.

Christine didn´t know how to respond, she still felt some bitterness but she was polite and put out her hand, wishing Mattei a safe journey back to Brasov.

She walked away from the meeting with the wounds of the past, burning into her soul. Every emotion she had managed to bury was surfacing, the bewilderment that her parents could have given up their children so readily. She would never do that to Rosa. She had worked hard to build a life, why couldn´t they have done the same without abandoning part of their family? She was better off than many others who had failed to come out of the remnants of Ceausescu's childcare policy unscathed but that was down to her determination. She knew how easy it was to have something one day and then lose it the next, someone or something always seem to come along and tug at the carpet beneath her feet but she kept going. She didn´t blame Mattei but she didn´t believe that getting to know him again would bring anything else other than an opportunity to be let down again. She had Rosa and Dorin to consider. To involve this new person in their lives was complicated. She needed some stability in her life.

She arrived at Lucia´s ready to pick up Rosa.

'So how did it go?' enquired Lucia brightly, her expression of optimism masking her concern over Christine´s weary posture.

'Where is Rosa?' asked Christine, almost rudely.

'I put her in the bedroom for a nap. We went for a walk and I think the heat made her tired. I´ll make some chai.'

Lucia's answer to everything thought Christine, though she noted Lucia looked tired, her face was more pallid than usual considering they had been out in the sun and walking. Perhaps she took too much for granted relying on Lucia to look after her boisterous child. Her lovely daughter could wear out the most energetic of people with her constant chatter and curiosity but Lucia always said this was to be encouraged and she considered herself lucky to have her.

As Lucia prepared tea, Christine rested on the sofa casting her eyes over the collection of drawings and paintings that seemed to fill every available space. Lucia insisted Rosa showed the same talent as her mother for artwork and they shared many happy hours through colour and crayons. Pride of place was a large canvas Christine had painted in oils of Papusica, wrapped in an abstract of colour, Lucia's coat of many colours. Papusica had been put to sleep two years before and both Christine and Rosa missed her almost as much as Lucia but life goes on Lucia had reminded her.

Christine peered in at her slumbering daughter, curled fast asleep on the bed, dressed in a pink princess tutu, her hair tied in multicoloured ribbons. 'What little girl doesn´t like to play dressing up?' Lucia had argued when Christine complained she stood out in the street and might get picked on.

'So, tell me, what you thought of Mattei.' said Lucia settling down next to Christine and handing her a cup.

Christine spoke truthfully that her brother seemed a charming man. She told Lucia more of how he discovered his adoption after the death of his stepparents. She agreed there was a resemblance but apart from looks, she did not feel any connection.

'Well, it is only the first time you have met. It will get easier, I´m sure. When will you see Mattei again?'

Christine sipped her tea and closed her eyes. 'I don´t want to,' she stated. Lucia was disappointed.

'Christine, why so? You agreed to meet him this time, so how can you dismiss him so soon with such certainty?'

'He´s just a reminder of what might have been for me, supposing I was the one that was adopted? I have had so many things unplanned thrown against me, having Rosa, caring for Dorin, not knowing what our future holds. What good can come of this now? He seems to feel sympathy for what our parents did. I do not.'

'It means he has found forgiveness and you have not,' said Lucia.

'Well, isn't it easier for him? He grew up with a real family.'

'But you have family now, Christine, so you should understand how important that feels and don´t forget he has lost people he loved most tragically. I can understand his reasons to bring something back to replace what he has lost.'

'Oh yes, very convenient for him now!'

'That is bitter Christine. He didn´t know he was adopted. You seem so angry. I feel you are punishing yourself! Does he want to meet with you again?' Lucia asked her, pouring more tea.

'More than that. He wants me to go to stay with him, at his home and bring Rosa. He suggests we make it a holiday where we can all get to know each other better.'

'What a wonderful idea! When was the last time you had a holiday?' exclaimed Lucia.

'Never! Lucia, it´s a crazy idea and I cannot leave Dorin alone, even for one night.'

'Take him with you! It might do him good, get him away from temptation and what a wonderful chance for Rosa to spend time in the countryside!' said Lucia enthusiastically.

Christine laughed at the thought. 'Can you imagine Dorin with all his problems following us to the countryside for picnics, he won´t even come to the park!'

Lucia persisted but Christine shook her head. 'How could it work? Sometimes, Lucia, you see the world in too many colours, you never see the shades of grey like I do but they are there and we have to deal with them.'

'I know they are there. Every day I think of my dear husband, my beautiful Papusica but I choose to remember them in the light, not the dark as you do. You carry these demons too deeply Christine, not wanting to remember your past but I urge you to confront them, to find forgiveness like your brother has. I feel he is another sign, like the way you and I found each other.'

'Now you are talking about signs? How could someone tracking me down be a sign?' asked Christine, used to Lucia´s belief that everything in life happened for a reason.

Lucia slowly stood up, hearing Rosa stirring. She checked she was still asleep and closed the bedroom door gently, taking her seat again next to Christine.

'I didn´t know how or when to tell you but now would seem appropriate,' said Lucia speaking softly. Christine felt a sense of unease as Lucia took her hand.

'It would seem I am going to go the same way as my dear husband and I don´t have long. I have felt it for some time now, my body feeling weary, telling me something wasn´t right. The doctor has confirmed I have cancer. There is nothing they can do. It´s too far gone and anyway I would rather meet my husband at the pearly gates with a full head of hair and in my best dress than go through any treatments!'

Christine covered her face in her hands to stifle the shocking sobs that came and challenged Lucia that it must be a mistake. How could she speak so calmly? She didn´t believe it. Of course, there would be treatment! Lucia had never said anything and she didn´t even know she had been seeing a doctor. Lucia took a big breath, almost with relief that she had finally told Christine.

'Everyone´s time is up sooner or later, that is why we have to make the most of what we have while we are on this earth and I am happy that I have been able to teach you things. You know you have been like the daughter I never had and I am grateful. Now I want you to do something for me, promise to know your brother. I will be able to leave you knowing there is someone there for you. Your future and Rosa´s could be so much brighter knowing you have other family. Think about Rosa, please. Without this chance who will she know? I worry for Dorin´s health and that you will end up carrying a burden. You are always laughing at me with my superstitious ways and signs but I sense these auras and I feel that positivity coming now, I think it is in Mattei, your brother. You need to let go of the anger you feel about your parents leaving you. I lived through those years when Ceausescu programmed our lives and I cannot find it in my heart to judge your parents so cruelly. Will you promise me this? Say yes to Mattei, make a bold step into the light and I will be happy!' she said in her fairy tale language.

The thought of losing Lucia was too much for Christine to bare. She had always been there for her and Rosa.

As she sat on the bus with her arm around Rosa on their way home, she thought again about Lucia, what a difference she had made to her life. She knew Lucia wouldn't be there forever but this was too soon, so cruel! If only Dorin could get better. She wondered if she had always done the right thing, pursuing her love of painting, spending time with her friends and she always focused on what was best for Rosa. They had grown apart. Perhaps she had been selfish in pursuing the things that she believed would make their lives better. Maybe she should have tried harder to involve him.

She thought about their life together back to the time when Rosa was about three years old when things began to change. On a winter's day when snow covered most of the city, the gas bottle connected to the stove in the kitchen ran out of gas. It provided their only source of heat, so Dorin went out to get a replacement. She knew he could often get waylaid and she was upset when he didn't return home quickly. It was so cold. She and Rosa made a tent on the bed with the blankets and climbed inside to keep warm, pretending they were hiding from bears that would smell the deep bowls of tasty soup she had prepared before the fuel ran out. Dorin didn´t come back. She began to worry as the night went on, unable to sleep, not knowing what to do when someone banged on the door alerting her there was trouble. Dorin had been arrested.

The Romanian police motto is "Safety and Trust" but for many vulnerable groups; the sex workers, drug addicts, homeless people and Roma, there is another saying, "Leave your rights at the door if you visit a Romanian Police station".

Dorin was Roma, an easy target on a day when few people were around, arrested on his way to get the gas bottle, under suspicion of selling contraband cigarettes. He happened to have two cartons of cigarettes on him. It was a sideline to supplement his other work and he had intended to drop them off to a regular, avoiding the streets the police would typically patrol but he was unlucky that day. The police knew him. They always suspected he did more than sell illegal cigarettes.

Under the rules for 'administrative escorting', he was taken to the police station and held in a windowless room, with no access even to a toilet. The only proof he was ever there was a form dropped into a box, signed by the policeman who had put him in handcuffs. Unfortunately, the documents relating to the particular individual's rights were not as analytically laid out as the police officers. Dorin underwent an interrogation that amounted to little more than abuse and an attempt to get him to confess to crimes he hadn´t committed. They were always careful to hit the soft spots on the body, careful not to break any bones. By the time it was all over, he had a ruptured spleen, a hematoma on his left eye and a wound on his neck. A friend found him struggling to reach home and went in search of Christine. She had called Katerina out of desperation, to help with Rosa while she went to the hospital.

Katerina had been appalled, determined to raise a complaint but the bureaucracy of this for someone like Dorin was a cost Christine wasn´t prepared to go through and Dorin had no fight in him for such a process. Katerina used her influence as best as she could to bring attention to the authorities and police that this kind of practice could not go on. It must have had some impact as they seemed to leave Dorin alone.

For Dorin, it was bad enough he was no longer fit to work at the so-called taxi firm. They had no use for him over the months it took him to recover and no wish to risk keeping him on. He constantly complained. Rosa irritated him with her chatter, making his head hurt and he would tell Christine to take her out of the way. Christine stopped working as a mediator. They were struggling for money, many of the bills went unpaid but he still managed to get to a bar when her back was turned and find solace in beer in exchange for the cigarettes he continued to sell.

Dorin became depressed and Christine was forced to retreat to her other life spending as much time as she could with Lucia to keep Rosa away.

Dorin improved as winter turned to spring. He was tired of living on handouts from his wife and needed to make money, deciding to work for himself. His skill was in thieving and so he would travel to different parts of the city mainly in search of tourists that could be relieved of wallets, phones and any other valuables in exchange for cash at the pawnshop. He was patient enough to follow people and cheeky enough to approach them offering to carry their bags for them at the train station then running off with their suitcases. Sometimes he used the street kids as a decoy. He would make out he was helping those who were being harassed by beggars by scaring them away and urging the people to avoid them, picking their pockets as he did so. The unsuspecting tourists would think it was the street people who had lifted their possessions.

There were plenty of opportunities and he began to feel better, back in charge of his finances. When Christine questioned him about his whereabouts, he shouted at her to mind her own business. She shouldn´t complain if it meant there was money coming in, he was no different to Robin Hood, only taking from those better off. He resented her 'do-gooder' attitude, nagging him to get a real job. He argued that people like Katerina were parasites, paying lip service to the likes of them with their social centres and community bullshit taking home fat paychecks to their pristine houses. 'They are all corrupt, the worst kind of thieves. It´s the politicians and the police that should be in prison but instead, they waste their time chasing the likes of me,' he would go on at her.

Trying to persuade him otherwise was futile. Instead Christine would try to convince him they should spend more time together, to go to the city like they used to but Dorin still seemed to prefer the company of others to her. Their lives continued in this way, with Dorin becoming increasingly secretive about where he had been and what he had been doing. She noticed his eyes were often bloodshot. He was drowsy, nodding off in front of the television and lost weight despite the tasty meals she provided for him. She wanted him to see a doctor but he refused.

The problem became apparent when she arrived home one day with Rosa unexpectedly to find him snorting two lines of a synthetic drug laced with heroin. 'I´m not an addict!' he protested. 'I don´t inject. It´s just a little something a friend gave to me. It makes me feel good and everybody does it,' he whined.

It was the first time Christine had ever lost her temper in front of Rosa. The little girl was frightened, crying hysterically. She tried to pull her mother away as Christine knocked Dorin off the chair and swept the powder off the table with her hand as fast as she could. Dorin stood up unsteadily, angry to be robbed of the high he was expecting. He tried to leave but Christine barred the way. Rosa watched cowering in the corner as they grappled. The rowing continued as Christine scrubbed the floors and furniture where the white dust had scattered. She threatened to go to the bar he frequented and announce to all the scum there to leave her husband alone. Eventually, Dorin gave up the fight and promised he wouldn´t do it again.

She battled over the next weeks to get him clean, following him regularly, making sure she was home to take care of him, relying on Lucia yet again to take care of Rosa. He seemed to listen, although he carried on with his drinking. She began to trust him again and for a while, things calmed down, until the powder, pipe and burn stole Dorin from her once again. It became a vicious circle.

Her thoughts were interrupted by Rosa tugging at her arm as they arrived back in Rahova. Christine had made up her mind and Lucia was right. It was time to make significant changes, for all of their sakes. She would take up her brother's offer of a holiday and persuade Dorin to come with her and maybe it would lead to a change. He wasn´t the man she married. She missed the Dorin that was fun and laughing, always teasing her. He was a shadow of that person now, standing on the edge of a black hole waiting to be sucked into a never-ending downward spiral. She would keep her promise to Lucia to reconcile with her brother and at the same time, take care of Dorin, though he would prove to be a reluctant passenger.

30

A Soul Awakened

It was getting dark when Mattei parked in front of the station exit. He was confident he would recognise Christine amongst the crowd, there being only one exit which led on to the car park and taxi area. He was not sure what to expect meeting Dorin and wondered how this would affect his chances of getting to know Christine better. She had only agreed to come for two nights, saying they needed to be back in Bucharest to collect Rosa. He was disappointed she wasn't bringing his niece.

He saw her standing next to a man he assumed was Dorin. He was smaller than Christine, with rounded shoulders and a shaven head making him look even thinner and wirier, his eyes appeared sunken. He put out a cigarette as Mattei approached.

They exchanged polite greetings with Mattei

offering to carry Christine's small bag for her but she did not accept. When they got to the car, Christine and Dorin climbed into the back seat. He felt like a taxi driver, talking to them in his rear-view mirror, as they stared out of the side windows. He tried to make conversation about traffic, about their journey, how hot the weather had been, everything he could think of but there was a nervous tension in the air. The pair continued to look out of the windows even though there was nothing to see in the darkness leading to the countryside. After several minutes he noticed Dorin had closed his eyes. It was one of the most extended trips Mattei had ever made driving from Brasov to home.

The farmhouse was empty. Alex had decided to stay with his father for a few days and give Mattei some privacy. In truth, Alex preferred to avoid something he felt would be awkward. Baloo was tied up at the back of the house. Mattei lead the way into the house, cleaned the day before by Elena and Alina, who also prepared the spare room for them. No one had slept there since his parents died but Mattei felt it was time to close that chapter. He suggested Christine and Dorin make themselves at home and freshen up if they needed to and then join him in the kitchen where he had put out some food.

He could hear muffled voices coming from the bedroom as he took out a beer from the fridge. Eventually, Christine emerged apologising that Dorin wasn't feeling well and wouldn´t be joining them tonight. Mattei was relieved. His first impression of Dorin wasn't a good one.

'Oh, I'm sorry, look no worries. Perhaps Dorin will

feel better in the morning. Are you hungry, can I get you a tea or a beer or something else if you prefer?' asked Mattei.

'A beer, yes, thanks.' Christine smiled tensely, sitting herself down, taking in the homeliness of her surroundings with its crafted textiles and dried flowers that hung from the wood beams.

'It´s a nice house Mattei, how old is it?'

It was a start with Mattei only too pleased to tell her the history of the place. They ate together, with Christine describing some of her favourite places in old Bucharest. The conversation was not awkward. Christine shared her interest in history and the parts of Bucharest she liked to explore and draw.

Mattei asked about her drawings and paintings. 'Perhaps you might be inspired to do some while you are here. I will show you the best place from which to paint tomorrow!' He wasn´t sure if he had assumed too much, by Christine´s reaction.

'We are only staying two days. Dorin and I have to get back. Anyway, I don´t do so much these days,' she added rather sharply glancing to the bedroom door where she hoped Dorin was already asleep.

There was a moment of silence before Mattei decided to speak first.

'Don´t worry. I tend to be over-enthusiastic about things sometimes! Always chasing the butterflies and thinking the world will follow me!'

Christine suddenly laughed. 'You are right! I remember you doing just that one day and you fell into a stream. I thought you had drowned before I fished you out and had to take you back to mama soaking wet. She was furious with me for letting you out of my sight even for a moment!'

The recollection had come from nowhere and surprised her. She had just blurted it out. Mattei was immediately curious to know more but Christine was hesitant. She seemed more relaxed talking about the present and Rosa but when Mattei asked her why she hadn´t brought his niece, she replied, 'Another time, maybe.' They cleared away the plates and remains of the food.

Christine didn´t want to tell him Rosa was left behind because there was no guarantee this meeting would go any better than the last one and she didn´t want to confuse Rosa by introducing her so soon, it would be unsettling. Better to leave her behind with Lucia and it was a short trip anyway. Dorin was a different matter. She needed to keep an eye on him.

They said goodnight, Christine heading back to her room to find Dorin lying quiet in a dreamless sleep. The small cup he used to take his prescription of Suboxone was empty on the bedside table. The mix of Buprenorphine and Naltrexone relieved the pain and reduced the cravings for heroin. He was still suffering from post-acute withdrawal several months after he had started using again.

In the previous winter, she had recognised the signs and he couldn´t hide the needle marks. She tried on her own to coax him off but by spring she couldn´t cope anymore. She confided in Katerina who helped get him into a treatment centre. The first week of withdrawal was the hardest time of Christine´s life, watching the man she loved unable to sleep, writhing in agony as his muscles convulsed, followed by bouts of nausea and vomiting. She cleaned the toilet after constant diarrhoea and would soothe him when he lay curled in a ball in pain, sweating profusely. His moods altered. Sometimes, he cried, telling her he was sorry and she would cling to him, just wanting him to get better. At other times he pushed her away, angry and he would forget where he was. She didn´t blame him, she blamed the environment that surrounded them and she wanted to change that now, more than ever. She hoped he would rest in the short time they were here.

The early morning brought a soft mist that began to dissolve magically as the sun spread its warmth. Christine was standing on the porch fascinated by the changes of colours in the countryside around her as the sun continued to rise, so different to waking up in the dull concrete of their city apartment. Suddenly Mattei emerged from around the corner of the house, equally surprised to find her standing there.

'You're up early! Did you sleep well?' he asked, a little concerned. 'I was going to get some breakfast ready.'

'I tend to get up early, it´s normal for me and I wouldn´t have missed this for anything,' Christine said, taking a deep breath of the clean air.

She hadn´t slept well, dreaming and digging deep to remember a time before orphanages, a home she could picture that had chickens running about and a stream that had meandered through green banks at the back of the house. Perhaps it was this place that reminded her of the village where she had once lived.

She had dreamt of her father chopping wood for the winter and her mother washing clothes outside in a heated pot of water. Now she wanted to be able to remember more, for Rosa´s sake so she could explain her mother hadn´t always lived in the city.

'You mentioned a place you wanted me to see. Could we go there?'

'Sure, should we wait for Dorin?' Mattei replied, eager to go before she changed her mind. However, Christine was ready, knowing that Dorin would sleep longer. He needed that peace more than a walk in the country.

'Ok,' said Mattei, secretly pleased it would be just the two of them. 'Why don´t I grab some bread and cheese. I can leave some things on the table for Dorin if he wakes up hungry. Do you mind if I take the dog? He´s had his breakfast so he´ll be glad to have a run but I will need to introduce you first.'

Having put their breakfast in his small knapsack, he showed Christine to where Baloo was chained next to his kennel. He thought she would be nervous but Christine happily let the dog sniff her, talking to him and allowing him to accept her. She told Mattei she liked animals, that Lucia once had a little dog. Maybe one day Rosa would have a pet of her own too.

They headed up the track to the shepherd's hut.

'I´ll take you to the hotel later if you like and show you where I work.' said Mattei.

They reached the little wooden cabin and Christine stood in awe of the view.

'This makes Bucharest seem small. It´s always so crowded with people and traffic, even the parks I visit don´t feel like this!'

'I´m glad you came. What made you change your mind about meeting again?' asked Mattei.

'Lucia changed it for me. She told me I need to

think about Rosa, that it was not fair on her not to know she has blood relatives, a wider family.'

'Yet you didn´t bring Rosa with you,' said Mattei, disappointed that Christine seemed to have taken so much persuasion to come, with her daughter the only reason she was here.

'Rosa isn't the only reason I decided to come. I know how it sounds but it´s more complicated for me. I was afraid to risk anything and now you know more about me, perhaps you can understand why .I have had time to do some thinking since we last met. I realise I should get to know you better and do some mental housekeeping as Lucia put it, to throw out the things in my head I don´t need! You know, she likes you even though she has never met you! She´s like that, a bit crazy sometimes but she can sense things about people and I trust her.'

'Well, I´m glad, or we might not be sitting here today,' said Mattei smiling as he retrieved their breakfast from the knapsack. They sat on the same blanket with the same view as Mattei had shared with Ana, when he first talked about his past.

'I do remember you as a baby,' Christine began, speaking hesitantly at first. 'I had to watch over you. Mama and Tata were always busy. Sometimes you would wake in the night and mama would ask me to give you your milk, as we shared a bed. When you were old enough to walk, I used to take you with me to find sticks to light the fire. I remember we had chickens and we would collect eggs together. The house was small, just two rooms but mama taught me how to keep it neat.'

A picture came into her mind, like a postcard, of

her mother sitting in a fireside chair sewing while she told stories to her children, settled by her feet. Christine told Rosa stories but she had never really thought about where the stories came from, until now. Perhaps she was romanticising. After all, it made no sense to have gone from that to abandonment in a terrible place.

'Do you remember anything about our older brothers?' asked Mattei.

Christine was thoughtful, taking her time eating her bread and cheese and not speaking with her mouth full. 'Not much,' she said as she finished. 'They were quite a bit older and played together most of the time. They used to tease me and I don´t remember them having much to do with you. They spent more time with our father and weren´t always around. I think they went to school but they were always in trouble. Mama used to shout a lot at them and so I think that´s why Tata kept them out of her way. They must have been useful, being older, maybe that´s why they took them but left us behind.'

They continued to talk, breaking down barriers. Christine answered Mattei's questions about how she started painting. Mattei said he could appreciate what she felt, telling her about his passion for food, how he enjoyed creating art on a plate. 'You see? We both have the same talent. It´s just that you use paper and I use plates. I will show you later!'

Mattei was enjoying himself.

'Do you have to leave tomorrow? Can´t you stay, maybe bring Rosa here? She would love to see all the animals. I could introduce her to Maria's´ daughters, Sasha and Brigit. She would have children to play with the same age as her. You could do as much painting as you like. Katerina told me you could make money from your work. If you meant what you said about Rosa getting to know her uncle better, surely it would make sense?'

He was trying his best to be persuasive and he had found her Achilles heel with Rosa. As they headed back downhill, Christine's mind was racing like she was slalom skiing. Dorin wouldn't want to stay. He had come reluctantly and maybe suspected she would be persuaded to stay. He needed her and besides how would she manage for money, she couldn´t expect to stay here for free. She looked around her, the air was so clean and she would love to paint in this place. It didn´t seem fair but she would have to go back.

When they reached the house, Dorin was waiting on the front porch. He had been watching their approach down the track. He was sitting on the steps; a couple of beers lay empty beside him. Baloo charged towards him barking furiously at this trespasser on his ground. Mattei hollered after him, shouting to Dorin to stay still, Christine was sprinting forward. Dorin scrambled back up the steps just managing to escape inside, slamming the door behind him. Baloo was growling and scratching at the door with his giant paws. They heard Dorin screaming in between heavy bouts of coughing.

'Fucking what is that? Get it away!'

Mattei was apologising dragging Baloo by the collar back to his kennel out of earshot. Christine went into Dorin who was leaning over the kitchen sink spitting thick green phlegm. 'Are you okay?'

'No, I´m not okay! Crazy mother fucking dog. Why

doesn´t he have it on a leash?'

'We didn't think you would be outside like that. We were busy talking and the dog just came first. Sorry Dorin.'

'I´m not hanging around waiting for you, in a place I'm under attack by dogs,' he spat. 'There´s nothing here, just a bunch of peasants and wild animals, what do you expect me to do here? Why did you get up and leave me this morning?'

'We went for a walk that´s all, to a shepherd's hut up the hill, Mattei likes to go there. You should have seen it, Dorin. It's like a magic place.'

'I have no interest in going anywhere. The sooner we go home, the better. I don´t feel well.'

Christine snapped back, angry that Dorin was being so mean and spoiling what had been a lovely morning for her.

'Does the beer make you feel better? They told you to stay off the drink, yet you still do it, even here with a chance to get well!'

'Christine, we are here because you brought us here and not for the good of my health. I shouldn´t have listened to you. Now you are going to tell me that some miracle has happened and you are falling for all this pretend shit with your long-lost family. I´m telling you it will all end in disappointment.'

'You aren´t even trying!' she protested.

'Haven´t I always looked out for you? You are so selfish!' He raised his arm to her like he was going to slap her but held back as more bouts of ugly coughing ensued and Mattei entered the house.

'Do you need a Doctor?' asked Mattei.

Dorin attempted to put up his hand, as a no but his

whole body was shaking as he continued to cough.

'Let me help you!' Christine ventured.

'Quiet, for Christ's sake Christine! I wouldn't be in this state if you hadn't just got up and left me. I'm fine!' Dorin choked unkindly.

Mattei stood feeling helpless and embarrassed by the way Dorin was speaking to her.

'The dog is tied up now. You don´t have to worry. Why don´t we go to the hotel? I can show you where I work and cook for both of you.'

'He should rest first, take a shower if that´s okay,' said Christine.

Suddenly she was very conscious of the state Dorin was in, like a fish out of water, away from the streets he worked where he blended in so naturally.

'I am going to collect some eggs for the restaurant. Do you want to come with me Christine, like old times?' Mattei asked innocently.

Dorin grunted, with Christine giving him a look of defiance. 'Take a shower, I won´t be long,' she told him.

Dorin snarled at her when Mattei was out of earshot. 'Since when do you tell me to take a shower and don´t speak to me like I´m a child!' he said but Christine was already on her way out and not listening.

She followed Mattei out to the chicken coup behind the house. Most of the birds were grazing around the garden and the henhouse was empty as they went through the nest boxes, gathering the fresh eggs into a basket.

'I´m sorry about Dorin' Christine apologised.

Mattei was unsure what to say. He didn´t like what

he had seen of Dorin so far. The man was a mess, even taking into consideration everything Katerina had told him.

'It must be hard on you,' was all he could say.

It was Christine's turn to feel embarrassed. 'Katerina has told you things, hasn´t she? He wasn´t always like this, he used to be full of energy and full of fun but he is also stubborn. He´s not going to change, even though I can see it´s killing him. I´ve been thinking about what you said, about bringing Rosa here. Did you mean that?'

Mattei hesitated. Was this what he wanted? He had suggested it after all but what if it meant he was going to be taking on all Dorin's problems? Had he been selfish, wanting her to come here?

'I did mean it but maybe you could come just with Rosa, I don´t think Dorin is ready to be converted to the countryside.' He had to be honest with her putting it as diplomatically as he could.

Christine nodded. The acceptance of only part of her family would result in the very complications she wanted to avoid. Dorin would already be feeling unwelcome having been left that morning and scared by the dog. She hoped he would perk up.

They showered and changed and set off walking to the hotel in the late afternoon. Dorin waited outside to finish a cigarette as Mattei and Christine entered through the hotel lobby. Ana was sitting at the reception desk dressed in a pretty blouse and chic skirt, her hair fastened back in a chignon.

Mattei introduced his sister and Ana politely shook her hand, asking if they had enjoyed their day so far.

'Pleased to meet you, Christine. Mattei has been so

excited that you were coming.'

She thought how Christine could be much prettier, so like her brother and yet pale and tired, dressed in tight jeans with an oversized white tee shirt hiding her small frame. As Dorin followed them in, Christine introduced him but he just stood back silently, barely nodding his head in greeting. Mattei quickly sidestepped the stiff introduction.

'We went for a walk to the cabin this morning. I suggested it would be a great spot for Christine to do some painting one day.'

Ana nodded in agreement, smiling at Christine. 'Yes, it is beautiful up there. I pass by, most days. I like to go for a run in the afternoon. It´s like the place time forgot, so peaceful away from the madding crowd! It would be a perfect place for you to paint! I hear you are very talented!'

Christine blushed, studying Ana like a subject she could paint, with her unusual eyes, shiny hair and beautifully tailored clothes. She imagined Ana was more like the joggers in the city parks wearing their sporty outfits and expensive trainers than a country girl but she seemed nice. Ana seemed to know quite a lot about her.

'Is Maria around?' Mattei asked Ana.

'She won't be long. She took the girls out to Brasov today. David is in his office. It´s pretty quiet now. Everyone else is out for the day.'

Mattei said he was going to give Christine a tour and then start the prep for the evening meals. Once he got organised, they could sit on the terrace and have their dinner together.

'Maybe you could join us later, Ana?' Mattei asked

with Christine picking up eagerness to his invitation.

It was a tempting invitation for Ana as she was curious to know more about Christine but she felt uncomfortable with the Gollum-like creature Dorin in tow. She preferred to keep out of the way of him and hoped Mattei hadn´t mentioned she was also from Bucharest. She smiled briefly over the spectacles perched on her nose.

'I´m afraid I might be busy later, there are new arrivals due in and I´m sure you have a lot of catching up to do without extra company.' She wanted to be kind to Christine but wasn't sure what else to say. 'You will love the food Mattei prepares. He really does the hotel proud. We are all very spoiled.' she said. Fortuitously the telephone rang and she excused herself.

Dorin hovered momentarily staring at the pictures on the walls and glancing past Ana to the keys on the wall cabinet. She put down the telephone surprised to find him lingering there at which point he walked off with his hands in his pockets following Mattei and Christine into the lounge.

Christine commented quietly to Mattei.

'She is beautiful, isn´t she, with her blue eyes?'

Mattei blushed. 'Everyone notices those eyes and no, before you ask, she is not my girlfriend! She came to work here at the beginning of summer. I don´t know how long she will stay but it´s good to have company the same age besides Alex. She has been a good friend to me and I confess my sounding board, encouraging me how to contact you.'

'You like her, a lot, I can tell' said Christine smiling shyly.

'She works hard, she has to. At this time of year no one has time for much else,' he replied. Christine sensed the change in his voice when he said they were just good friends, that hint that he would have been happy to say she was his girlfriend.

Dorin feigned interest as Mattei guided them around the hotel and gardens, introducing David on their way. Christine thought she had never been in such a pretty place, much to Dorin's disgust. He wasn´t liking the fact that she was enjoying herself. The people were pretentious, thinking they were a cut above the likes of him. He didn´t care much for the girl in reception, peering down her nose at him through her glasses, with her smart clothes and expensive jewellery. He felt the same way about Maria and her pristine children when he met them briefly.

Mattei lead Dorin and Christine to the terrace just outside the kitchen where they sat together in the sunshine. Just far enough away from their hotel clientele that he wouldn´t be embarrassed by us, thought Dorin.

It should have been a holiday for both of them Christine thought but all she could sense was Dorin's growing resentment at being away from his familiar surroundings. He asked for a beer, while she drank tea, even though she tried to suggest he have something else. He was smoking a lot, complaining he was hungry, agitated and suddenly with an uncontrolled reflex knocked over his glass sending a shower of beer all over Christine's tee-shirt.

'Look what you´ve made me do, you stupid woman, always you cause me trouble!' He shouted, too loudly.

'It was just an accident, Dorin!' said Christine, embarrassed and trying not to draw attention as Dorin continued to make a fuss but Ana was passing on her way back to her room and immediately came up to them.

'These things happen, don´t worry. Christine, why not come with me? I can lend you a tee-shirt. Mattei will bring you another beer, Dorin,' and before Christine could object to another beer for him, Ana took Christine´s hand and led her away, wanting to separate them before Gollum made a scene.

Once inside her room, Ana gave Christine a clean tee-shirt, white, like the one she had been wearing, except it was Elle, not a baggy non-brand that had faded to off white.

'There is a bathroom to change and to wash off the beer,' she said kindly.

The bathroom door was slightly ajar and Ana caught site of Christine's reflection in the bathroom mirror. She looked away but she noticed bruises on her shoulders and upper arms.

'I'm glad Mattei finally found you,' said Ana as Christine emerged from the bathroom, 'It means the world to him. I hope you will feel the same.'

'You haven't known him for long, have you?' said Christine meaning to sound curious rather than rude. Ana just smiled.

'No, that's true but he is one of the most honest decent people I have ever met. I hope you see more of each other. You do look very alike!' She wanted to like Christine, for Mattei's sake. '.

Christine thanked her, worried about returning the

tee-shirt but Ana wanted her to have it. 'Keep it,' she said. It's the least I can do. I have plenty of others.'

When they went back to the table, Ana could see Dorin had already worked his way three quarters through a replacement beer. She quickly went back to her work.

Mattei finally set the table with a display of dishes that Christine could have painted. Dorin tackled them like a starving dog, the food hardly on the plates long enough to appreciate the effort, downing another two beers before announcing he was tired and he and Christine should get back to the house.

'We have an early start back to Bucharest in the morning,' he said, looking directly at Christine.

'It's a pity we didn´t have long together but there will be other times, I am sure,' Mattei replied politely, also looking to Christine hopefully. She rose from the chair reluctantly and followed Dorin out.

They started arguing as soon as they were in the lane heading for Mattei´s house. 'How can you be so rude, not even to thank Mattei for the food and you know you shouldn´t be drinking beer with your medication. I know you don´t feel well but you could have taken a little more interest, even for my sake,' she scolded him.

'I´m not going to pretend I am interested. I can´t sit around here, watching flowers grow while you ooh and ah over everything. What is wrong with you! Can´t you see these people are nothing like us? How long do you think it will last before they are bored with you hanging around? What is it you think you are achieving with all of this and you don´t seem to care about me, it´s like you are blind!'

'We could stay longer and Mattei says I could bring Rosa here, she would like it, Dorin, please!'

'You are fooling yourself, Christine! I told you it´s not going to work! Remember we said we would stick together, now you are tipping everything on its head. You are living in cloud cuckoo land!'

By the time they reached the house, Dorin was more than agitated. He pushed her up the steps and told her to start packing. It felt all wrong to Christine. She didn´t have to go back the next morning, just a few days even, she wasn´t ready. Dorin helped himself to a beer. She attempted to wrestle it out of his hand and continued to nag him until he finally lost patience, pushing her roughly against the wall.

'You make me do that, Christine! It´s not fair. I have had enough. Always the same with your poncy flowery curtains and walks in the park, thinking you are someone you´re not. You let people interfere with our lives, hanging around with that bitch Katerina who fills your head with voodoo. You think you´re better than me don´t you? Well, you´re not and if you think all of this is going to change your life, you are making a mistake. At least I know who I am and I´m not afraid to admit where I come from and the sooner I get back, the better!' He stomped off to the bedroom.

'You´re sick!' She screamed after him. 'It´s the drugs and drink that have made you like this. You didn´t used to be this way, Dorin. People are trying to help you. Here, take your dose.'

She offered him his medicine but he knocked it out of her hand.

'I´m trying to help you for god´s sake!' she pleaded.

'If you are trying to help me, then don´t even think about staying here. I´m sick of everyone interfering, leave me alone! I need to sleep. Do what the hell you like but I´m leaving first thing'!

He threw himself under the covers, shivering and sweating, curling up into a ball. He knew he had lost control and he had been trying hard over the last months to stay clean. He knew how determined Christine had been to meet her brother and he felt he was losing her. He didn´t want that. She was the one person who had stuck by him. He just resented the company she kept, people with whom he could never be on the same level, like Lucia, Katerina and now her brother.

Christine knew it was the side effects of coming off the heroin that made Dorin this bad. Maybe it was wrong to bring him but she couldn't leave him back in Bucharest, not even for one night. He had been improving and she wanted it to stay that way.

She closed the bedroom door quietly and retreated to the kitchen just as Mattei appeared. She wondered how much he had heard. She was ready to give up and go home.

'Let´s sit outside, Christine,' Mattei said gently. 'I meant what I said about coming back and with Rosa. I can see how hard it is for you but you have to think about yourself too. You told me you came here for Rosa, that Lucia persuaded you. Katerina supported you. It's only the second time we have met and I have enjoyed having you here. Please don´t leave tomorrow and think you can´t come back and soon!'

Sitting on the porch together, looking at the clear night sky, Christine wished she could stay. The whole feeling of being away from the city even for a short time was like a release from a pressure cooker and she strangely felt at home. Mattei was her brother and it had been a surprise to her to learn they did have a lot of similarities, beyond just looks. It would be nice but with everything else in her life right now it was too much. She thought about what Lucia was going to go through, what Dorin needed. She wasn't ready for this, not yet.

'It's easy for you to think we can hop in and out of each other's lives but it's different for me, bringing Rosa here, it's too soon. I will come back but Dorin is my husband, he needs me right now. Let's see how things go. We can keep in touch; I would like that.' she smiled.

They sat together for a while longer sticking to general topics and laughing, their sense of humour one of the things they shared. Christine promised if she came back, she would bring her paints.

The following day the weather had changed with a soft rain falling. The plan was to go with Mattei to the hotel while he made a start on breakfast duty and then Maria would take over while he took Christine and Dorin to the train station in Brasov.

Even before daylight, Dorin appeared in the farmhouse kitchen where Mattei was making coffee. Christine followed carrying their bags, ready to leave. She was subdued, whereas Dorin was upbeat knowing he was on his way out of this place and that she was coming with him. They drank their coffee in silence then headed for Casa Flori.

Mattei set to work in the kitchen, pleased that Christine was helping him and they could be alone again. Dorin went outside to have a cigarette. As he stood there, unobserved Ana left her room, making her way to the dining room to set out the guest tables for breakfast. Snooty cow, he was thinking, noticing she did not lock her door. It was too tempting. He was alone and everyone else occupied. He slipped into her room and in less than two minutes, being the professional that he was, emerged back out with some cash and a necklace he had removed from a blue box. He tucked them into his jeans pocket, beneath his shirt. He didn't have time to search the place for more and he did not take the full roll of notes from the rubber band. With any luck, he would be well away before the stuck-up bitch noticed anything. It was a hotel; people were susceptible to pickpockets and thieves all the time. He was sure he would get away with it. He went back inside, taking up a seat next to Christine.

Mattei poured out thick Turkish style coffee for each of them accompanied by his homemade tarapaine bread and jam. Dorin slurped his coffee refusing to eat and sat in deliberate silence, making the atmosphere strained. Once he finished, he gathered their things, heading for the car with a gruff thank you as Maria and Ana both hugged Christine.

Once again, there was minimal conversation on the journey. Dorin closed his eyes sitting in the back seat while Christine chose to sit in the front with Mattei. They arrived at the train station, Dorin exiting the car with their bags and Mattei and Christine following on behind. The train was already on the platform and Mattei waited while they boarded. He walked to the window where they had taken up their seats, his eyes still speaking to Christine through the glass. She put her hand up to the glass as the train pulled away. 'Bye little brother, speak soon!' she mouthed smiling. He lifted his hand towards her nodding, looking forward to the prospect, and full of optimism.

Dorin was lucky. Ana didn't notice anything was missing from her room until she arranged to go shopping with Maria over a week later. She had gone to get money from the roll of notes she kept in the drawer, picking it up and feeling it had somehow shrunken. She couldn't be mistaken, recounting the paper notes several times, sure that she had changed exactly five hundred Euros into lei the last time she had been to the bank. Now only a third of it was there. She tipped everything out in a frenzy, pulling the furniture back from the walls and searching desperately through everything she owned, including opening the little box that had contained her most precious family possession, shocked to discover her grandmother's locket was gone.

Finally, she sat on the end of her bed, and burst into tears, sitting amidst her self-ransacked room trying to make sense of the robbery. She ran her fingers through her hair, before making her way to the bathroom feeling sick. As far as she knew no one at the hotel had reported anything stolen. She went through everything again putting away her clothes, remaking the bed, even cleaning the bathroom.

Her first thought was to search out Maria but she hesitated. It could bring trouble, she would most certainly get the police in, there would be questions and it might expose her. She would have to tell Maria she wasn't feeling well and cancel the shopping. Who would have come into her room? Had she forgotten to lock it at some point? It had to be a quick opportunist. Nothing had been disturbed that she could recall. Then she remembered giving Christine the tee-shirt but then she had been with her all the time. Maybe Christine had said something to that shady husband of hers. That had to be it! She was angry. Mattei shouldn´t have brought them here touring them around the place not knowing enough about them. She had taken an instant dislike to Dorin the moment she clapped eyes on him. It had to be him with the help of Christine! She wasn´t going to let this go. She would phone her brother and ask him what to do. She decided not to say anything to Mattei for the same reason that others would get involved. She had no proof, only a suspicion and she was sure Mattei would defend his sister, even if he didn't know her fully yet or her pathetic husband. Mattei wasn´t the sort to leap to conclusions though he´d have to be blind she thought.

She called Razvan and told him of what had happened and her belief that it had something to do with Christine and Dorin. She told him everything she could about them. He was quietly concerned about her description of Dorin as a suspect, thinking if he had stolen the locket, he would be disposing of it through local contacts. It could spark attention if Dorin came into contact with anyone who might mention a girl with blue eyes on a wanted list for which Sergiu had offered a reward. He didn't share these thoughts with his sister, only promising he would try to find out what he could. The silver was probably liquid by now. Perhaps, it was time to reinvent Ana but it wasn't easy to find an alternative and he wanted to keep her as close to home as possible. Razvan couldn't know just how fast time was running out, nor how his sister's precious locket would be the cause of a deadly chain reaction.

Part Four

Collision Course

31

Cloud on the Horizon

Sergiu had been in Bucharest for the last three weeks of August. It was good to be away from the summer tourist invasion of Marbella and back in the city that was indeed home to him, though he chose not to live in his old neighbourhood. He had bought a luxury penthouse ten minutes north of the city centre, newly constructed and with open views towards to Herastrau Park, one of the most desirable areas of the city. He was ambitious and careful to invest his money wisely, buying two smaller apartments in the same complex and renting them out to ex-pats who paid premium rents to be close to schools, shopping and the city centre.

He had come a long way, disassociating himself from his roots and the communist tenement he grew up in with his parents and younger brothers crammed into two rooms. The noise and smell of poverty had disgusted him then and even now, when he visited certain parts of the city, it reminded him of the squalid conditions where they had lived. He looked on people that continued to exist in these places with contempt, unwilling to help themselves, with no idea how to work hard. Sergiu was satisfied that in exploiting the weak and lazy to service the wealthy, he was contributing to a better city. If he could afford to buy property like his, he was creating real jobs. He was a hero, an ambassador for success in a country once considered the poorest in Europe.

There were those in society that made noises about the level of corruption but few prosecutors. were brave enough to risk their own lives to tackle it. So far, for Sergiu, their interference just opened up more opportunities. There were many politicians and police that were corruptible and with the demise of some gangs and rival fighting for territory, it allowed him to use his talents. He would set one group off against another until they were weakened and had no choice but to merge into his expanding organisation, the ultimate take over.

Even in this shiny new neighbourhood, he had capitalised. The Camataru clan headed up by the Balint brothers operated an extensive prostitution ring. The prostitutes, many brought in from Moldavia, lived in slave-like conditions, packaged into flats all over Bucharest. They worked in many of the well-known entertainment venues such as the Hotel Intercontinental, the Athenee, and Hilton. The trendy discotheque Herastrau had become extremely popular with Romanians who were reaping the rewards of a new capitalist system and it became the hub of the Camataru clan´s prostitution operation.

Towards the end of the 1990´s gang warfare broke out and the brother's found themselves defending their position of power. They were one of the few clans to be successfully prosecuted. They were locked up and released several times with varied arrests starting in 2004. It was during this time of destabilisation that Sergiu was able to take advantage and expand the trafficking of Romanian and Moldavian women to countries such as Italy and Spain. But these days he spent less time on building the empire and more on trying to protect it with International forces putting increasing pressure on their activities.

Today he was meeting Ion, the owner of several pawn shops spread across the city and one of his most experienced information gatherers. Sergiu did not like the man. He thought his money had turned him into an over-indulged pig. Ion had no class but Sergiu tolerated him because he was eyes and ears to many things going on in the city that had proved useful over the years.

Ion opened his first pawnshop close to the old town in the 1990´s, selling anything from household goods, clothes and furniture. It was a legitimate business cashing in on people´s desperate need to sell whatever they could and those looking to buy cheap second hand goods. Many were still struggling to manage in the early post-communist years. By the time Ion opened his second shop he had branched into another market, one that took advantage of the lack of law enforcement, handling items that had no unique way to identify them and which the police had no resources to trace. He was the middleman, the fence, handling goods that were being stolen to order, mainly by gangs operating within the capital.

He was careful to front a harmless business from his shops. There were always plenty of petty criminals coming his way, shoplifters, pickpockets or purse-snatchers bringing him goods. He kept a balance between the things he would display and those he kept hidden. Sometimes he would deliberately inform on clients to the police, those he had no regard for, like drug addicts. It kept him in the good books of the police, so they didn´t bother him. He also ran a scrap metal business on land he owned near the railway tracks, breaking down everything from tools to bicycles which he could move on quickly with added value.

He opened another two shops but his success attracted the attention of protection racketeers and this was how he came in to contact with Sergiu. It hadn´t been a pleasant setup, he suffered two break-ins and they trashed his shops. On one occasion, he had been beaten with a baseball bat to within an inch of his life and finally had no choice but to pay for protection. He strongly suspected that Sergiu orchestrated the violence but lay the blame at someone else´s door, stepping in coincidently to offer him the protection he needed. However, it also turned out to be another business opportunity. They set up a refinement process removing impurities from melted down rings, necklaces and bracelets turning it into gold bars which Sergiu's contacts could move within twenty-four hours. Once sold, it was impossible to trace.

It cost Ion dearly but in return, he was able to run his business without risk from competitors or threats to his security but he never forgot the day of the beating and maintained an obedient respect for Sergiu.

Sergiu had arranged to meet at a lakeside cafe in Cismigiu Gardens close to the city hall. The meeting was to agree delivery times and collect any information Ion had gathered in recent weeks on police movements and other sources. The park was bustling with people out in the Saturday afternoon sunshine. There were families with their children playing on the swings, others enjoying boating on the artificial lake and those meandering through the tree-lined paths admiring the famous literary busts and sculptures that sat amongst the shady gardens.

As he passed over one of the little bridges that traversed the lake, he thought again of Mihaela. He remembered her posing there for a photo, one which he kept of her in the days she was innocent and carefree. Her blue eyes were laughing back at him, eyes that could seduce one minute and switch off the next, an asset in her trade. He had once admired her ability to do that and now it made him angry to think of it. He never loved her. There wasn´t room for any complication like that in his life but in the beginning, it was fun, like having a pet. When he first saw her in the café in Bucharest, he had thought her unusual, she had been cheeky, even flirtatious and he had seen potential in her and set himself a challenge. She would be his Eliza Doolittle, his protégée. He took satisfaction in educating her in everything, from sex to glamour girl, mingling with the rich and famous in Marbella. He taught her everything and yet she had dared to disappear. He had been too lenient with her, trusting her with information. The spoiled bitch had betrayed him. It had become personal.

He had exhausted all his usual sources trying to find her. He knew she had come back to the city. He had his spies out, posting someone outside both her parents and her brother's houses. The friends from her student days had no information to share and he was sure in his friendly questioning that none of them were lying. She was a loose end that continued to frustrate him. Her brother must be involved in hiding her but he couldn't risk going directly after him. There was too much at stake in taking out someone so incorruptible. His bosses would not appreciate any unwanted attention and yet it was not in their nature to leave business unfinished. So far, Sergiu's efforts had produced nothing. The threats from his bosses to clean up all dirt, even the tiniest spec still plagued him. Shit always rolls downhill and time was running out.

When Sergiu arrived at the cafe, Ion was already seated. He expected him to be alone but instead, he eyed an odious couple, greedily tucking into an enormous plate of the house specialty pancakes accompanied by two beers.

'I hope you don´t mind Sergiu, my wife wished to accompany me, it is such a pleasant afternoon,' said Ion, introducing his wife. The wife wore heavy makeup, her plump figure squashed into a low-cut orange dress and her fat ankles squeezed into a pair of bright pink Jimmy Choos and matching handbag that clashed with her dyed red hair. Ion wore a gaudy checked sports jacket over a mismatched designer shirt. A shiny medallion cushioned by a magpie's nest of greying chest hair puffed out from the quilt beneath it. Sergiu clamped his teeth in disgust, all the trappings of money, without any taste. He signalled the waiter to bring him an espresso.

He greeted Ion with a handshake and nodded courteously to his wife but as he took up a seat, Sergiu's eyes fastened on the woman´s neckline. An engraved antique silver Alpaca locket decorated with a pink enamel rose lay in her ample cleavage. He sat back in his chair, saying nothing more, his mind trying to work out how this woman came to be wearing a necklace identical to the sentimental family heirloom Mihaela coveted even above the Cartier he had chosen for her.

He patiently drank his coffee, waiting for the pair who practically licked their plates clean.

'I have private business to discuss with you Ion if your wife will excuse us for a few minutes.'

The wife duly obliged somewhat insulted that she was excess baggage. She sauntered off towards the lakeside where the swans and ducks gathered, jostling for crumbs thrown by passersby. When she was far enough away, Sergiu came straight to the point.

'That is an interesting piece of jewellery your wife is wearing about her neck. It is antique, German-made, 1920´s if I am correct,' said Sergiu.

The man was flattered by Sergiu's observation.

'You are correct, Sergiu. Yes, indeed a pretty piece. I gave it to my wife two weeks ago as a present for our twenty-eighth anniversary.'

Sergiu struggled to smile. 'Congratulations,' he said, wincing at the thought of anyone married to such an ogre for so many years.

'Thank you Sergiu. I did not appreciate you had an interest in antique pieces,' said Ion.

'Certain pieces interest me, yes and I see that it is engraved.'

'Well yes, as it happens, by coincidence, the 'A' is like Antonia, my wife´s name and the 'C' would be my middle name Costin, I could not resist it as a present and my wife loves roses. It is not so valuable but it was a romantic gift.'

Ion mopped the sweat from his brow with a handkerchief. He was no longer enjoying the conversation about his wife's jewellery. It was becoming too personal. However, he had just volunteered the most incredible information.

Sergiu was sure this was Mihaela's locket. How could it have ended up around that vulgar woman's neck? He would find out more but first, he would deal with their regular business. He ordered more coffee for himself and another beer for Ion with a whiskey chaser. He knew Ion was a drinker and he did not refuse. Another beer and chaser followed with Ion becoming more animated.

His wife returned to the table, concerned to see he was knocking back shots of whiskey. She leaned her bulging bosom in his face and hissed in his ear 'Ion, it is the middle of the afternoon and you are drinking like a fish, I think we should go now!'

She didn´t want their day spoiled and she did not appreciate being sidelined.

Sergiu discreetly motioned to Ion to get rid of her once more. How dare the woman interrupt, what a contemptible trout she was.

Ion could not be seen to cow-tow to his wife in front of Sergiu. He dismissed her as best he could.

'We have important things to discuss, nothing for your pretty ears my love, please enjoy the gardens a little longer then I will take you for dinner at our favourite place.' Reluctantly she made herself scarce. She would have words with her husband later for not obeying her wishes.

'You are very considerate to your wife, Ion, may I ask where you will be dining, perhaps I know the restaurant also?' asked Sergiu casually.

'We will be heading to Caru Cu Bere. It is a pleasant walk from here. The building is quite beautiful, with our favourite Romanian foods and excellent beer, of course!'

'An excellent place, I hope you enjoy yourselves. Ion, one more question, the gift to your wife, the locket, tell me, how did it come to be in your possession?' he said leaning forward tapping his finger on the table waiting for the answer.

Ion mopped his brow again. It was clear Sergiu knew something about this locket and he was obliged to answer.

'It came into one of my shops, I happened to be there and I thought how it would suit my wife. Sergiu, forgive my asking but why do you need to know?'

Sergiu had no further patience to play games. 'Do not ask why I need to know; rather tell me what I need to know. Who brought this to you?' Sergiu demanded. He was sure it was stolen but by whom and from where? Mihaela couldn't and wouldn't have parted with it.

When it came to business Ion knew which side his bread was buttered. The fact that he enjoyed an enviable lifestyle through his loyal cooperation he knew came at a cost. He was accustomed to giving up information. He had informed on various people over the years and never questioned the consequences of the information he divulged so long as he enjoyed Sergiu's protection but now it concerned a locket that adorned his wife's neck and that made him nervous.

'He is a regular of mine. His name is Dorin. He has been bringing me goods for many years, at first tools, then finer items. He used to steal to order, part of a larger gang but from time to time, he brought items I knew he had lifted himself. He became addicted to heroin, so these days he is a miserable specimen but I still take stuff from him, pay him less.'

'Where do I find him?' quizzed Sergiu.

'I don´t know exactly, he lives somewhere in the Amurgului district. He has a wife and child, he had mentioned them when he was trying for a better price but I had little sympathy for him.'

'I want you to get a message to him, tell him that you have a job for him and he should come to meet you. Set up a day and time as soon as you can and tell me exactly when he is coming and by the way, I must have that locket.'

Ion nodded but was becoming alarmed.

'Sergiu, it was a gift to my wife, I can hardly ask her to give it back!'

'I´m not asking you to, I can see that is impossible

for you. You set up the meeting and I will concentrate on getting back what is mine.' Sergiu could see who wore the trousers in Ion's household.

Ion was in shock. How was it possible that this locket had any connection to Sergiu? If his wife had not insisted on accompanying him or been wearing it on this particular day, it would never have become a problem. He had no choice but to agree as his wife was approaching, only a short distance away. He knew Sergiu's methods; he had a bad feeling.

'I will do as you ask of course but please do not bring any harm to my wife.'

'I have no intention to harm your wife, Ion and I am sure you will find some other trinket to satisfy her. You have been very helpful to me. Regrettably, there has to be some consequence but I am sure you will adjust and we can continue business as usual.'

He shook Ion's hand as if they were parting on the best of terms, a show for Ion´s wife as she tottered towards them. Sergiu turned to her. 'Please accept my apology for any inconvenience to your day, Madam. I hope you enjoy the remainder of the afternoon. Your husband has been most accommodating and his time is valuable to me.'

'Thank you, Sergiu, 'Ion´s wife nodded, plumping up her ample bosom in self-importance. 'My husband is indeed a clever businessman and well respected. He works hard but now I must insist we take our leave. He has also promised me some of his valuable time.'

She took her husband by the arm and together they headed off, like two film extras in a Bollywood movie. Sergiu watched them fade into the shady paths that led to the outside perimeter of the park. He took out his mobile and made a call.

It was a fifteen-minute walk from the park into the heart of the Lipscani district and the restaurant Ion and his wife were headed to but they were taking their time. Like so many visitors Ion and his wife enjoyed the charm of the pedestrianised cobbled streets with its backdrop of baroque, renaissance and neoclassical architecture. Many of the historic buildings elsewhere in the city had disappeared during Ceausescu´s destructive reign, making way for his modern visions, like the People´s Palace but this area remained a testament to time. The name Lipscani comes from the German town of Leipzig when medieval traders from that city would come to sell their wares to the locals and the Turks in the 1600s and 1700s. The streets thronged with people enjoying the open-air cafes, restaurants and trendy boutiques. Ion and his wife continued their walk past the Princely Court of Vlad Tepes, the Turk Impaler.

His wife was nagging him for keeping her waiting in the park so long, complaining her feet were hurting in her new shoes. She forced him into an expensive shoe shop where he sat contrite as she tried on a dozen pairs, finally emerging in more comfortable shoes. Two shops further on and she had added to the purchase with dresses to match, burdening Ion with designer shopping bags. At least his wife was in a better frame of mind. He was looking forward to a cold beer at Caru Cu Bere.

She was still babbling in his ear saying he did not appreciate her enough, especially as she went to so much effort to please him.

'You are not romantic like you used to be!' she

accused him. 'When was the last time you bought me flowers?' She poked him as they were passing one of the flower sellers found on nearly every street corner in the city. Ion could hardly get a word in edgeways as he juggled with the shopping, trying to get his wallet out once again as his wife leaned in to smell the bunches of red roses.

It happened so quickly, the pair of them distracted, Ion with his arms full, his wife still talking, the flower seller attending another customer. A man appeared from nowhere reaching to his wife's exposed throat with one hand and wrenching the silver locket from her while his other hand pushed her headfirst into the flower display. She screamed as she fell amongst the water buckets of blooms. The chain thief was long gone before she had any sense of what had occurred. Ion stood frozen in disbelief, with the shopping still in his hands. His wife was drenched in water and struggling to pick herself up, pulling loose stems and broken flowers from her hair. Other passersby had stopped to help her but she was hysterical screaming for her husband. Ion almost wanted to laugh! The locket was gone but his wife was unhurt. She would recover, though the repercussions of the event would probably prove to be expensive. All he had to do now was set up Dorin and then perhaps Sergiu would leave him to business as usual.

32

Beneath the Stone

The black SUV was circling the perimeter between Maria Rosetti, Caragiale and Icoanei towards the centre of the city. Sergiu looked out through the blacked-out windows, scanning the street that led to Ion´s pawnshop, waiting for Dorin to appear. He gave Ion instructions to make sure Dorin got into his car, alone. Dorin believed he was coming to the pawnshop to meet a contact who could make use of him and that he would be paid well for his trouble.

Sergiu drove the car slowly as Ion exited his shop with a thin, gaunt-looking man. Ion had his arm around Dorin's shoulder, patting him encouragingly on the back as he guided him along the street to where Sergiu was pulled over. The rear door of the car opened and Ion motioned for Dorin to get in. 'It´s fine this will not take long, trust me and it could be lucrative for you!' he told him as Dorin showed some hesitation. Ion did not follow him into the car and as the door closed, Dorin heard the clunk of locks. He sat directly behind the driver feeling distinctly ill at ease on the protective plastic sheets covering the luxurious white leather.

'Hello, Dorin,' said the driver. All Dorin could see was a pair of dark eyes in the rear-view mirror. He was locked in an expensive car where no one could see inside. What could this man want with from him?

Sergiu passed a photograph over his shoulder of a girl dressed in a yellow sundress, blonde and very beautiful, with blue eyes.

'Have you ever seen this girl?'

Dorin's hands were trembling. He had forgotten to take his meds that morning. Christine should have reminded him before she left. He scanned the photograph and handed it back, shrugging his shoulders.

'She looks like a film star. No, I haven´t seen her. What is this to do with me?'

'Have you ever seen her before?' repeated Sergiu more forcefully, turning towards him and staring him hard in the eyes.

'No,' repeated Dorin.

Sergiu put the photograph into the inside pocket of his black Armani jacket and then produced the locket recovered from Ion's wife. He dangled the pendant between his gold ringed fingers along with a fifty lei note. Dorin reached out his hand towards the money but Sergiu was faster, placing the money back into his pocket. He swung the chain hypnotically before Dorin.

'So, do you recognise the little trinket I recovered from Ion?' Sergiu asked.

Dorin shrugged his shoulders, trying to make out he didn't care and would not be intimidated.

'I bring lots of things to Ion, I don´t pay much attention to what they are.'

'I understand you were paid 50 lei for it. Cash for you, no questions asked, too generous in my opinion but that´s Ion for you. It is tough out there on the streets, isn´t it? I know quite a bit about you Dorin, that you are a good thief, with a wife and child to care for. Now try a little harder, how did you come by this little item?' Sergiu demanded. This skinny piece of shit was going to tell him what he wanted to know even if he had to beat it out of him.

Dorin wanted the money. 'It came from a hotel. I took it and some cash. It was on a table in one of the rooms, a cleaner left the door open.' he lied.

'What hotel, which one?'

Sergiu was confused. Why would Mihaela stay in a hotel? Was she working the hotels? Why had no one seen her around the city?

'I don´t know the name of it. I went there for a couple of days with someone to visit,' mumbled Dorin.

Sergiu was losing patience. He raised his voice. 'Why would you be going to a hotel? They would not let vermin like you within ten meters of the front door! You must be lying!'

'No, no, it´s true!' blurted out Dorin. 'My wife has a brother. He works in the kitchen. We travelled there on the train to Brasov. It was dark when he picked us up. We went somewhere in the mountains. I don´t know where we went or what the name was! I didn't pay much attention and I wasn't feeling well.'

'You mean you were off your head, don´t you Dorin?'

Dorin didn´t argue that he had been clean for several months. Let the man think he was still a user, he might hassle him less but Sergiu continued.

'So, this room you took the things from, do you know who was staying there? I will find out. Perhaps Christine will help me. I am sure she would cooperate better than you and maybe not even for money.'

Dorin was alarmed this man knew Christine by name. It was a threat and he didn´t want Christine mixed up in anything to do with this monster.

'I saw a girl coming out of one of the rooms. She was working there.

Sergiu asked him to describe her but Dorin insisted he hadn´t paid attention. Sergiu handed him another photograph, one of Mihaela standing on the bridge in Cismigiu Park when they first met.

'Is this her?' he demanded roughly. 'Look carefully and don´t lie or you won´t get your money.'

Dorin studied the photo. He told Sergiu he couldn´t be sure. The girl at the hotel wore glasses and had different hair. He was sweating in the back of the car partly from being confined with a human bull and partly from withdrawal symptoms causing him to fidget like a child.

Sergiu could see from his body language that he was not going to get much more out of Dorin and he was starting to hate the smell of him in the back of his car.

'Her name is Mihaela. Did you hear anyone call her

by her name? You said she was working there.'

Dorin couldn´t remember. He thought he could play dumb, get his money and leave.

Sergiu needed more information but the questions he continued to fire only served to make Dorin more agitated and his answers were vague and contradicting. He couldn´t seem to say precisely when they had been there only that it was about two weeks ago. The hotel looked like any other traditional Romanian style, stuck out in a field somewhere. Dorin seemed to have spent most of his time sleeping in his room, not caring where he was.

Sergiu was wasting his time with this half-wit. He would talk to the wife. He turned his back on Dorin, punched a text message into his phone and started up the car engine. As he pulled out, Dorin stiffened, his hands making fists kneading into the seat. 'Where are we going? I told you I couldn´t remember anything more!' The SUV turned into a dead-end alleyway behind Ion´s shop. The engine continued to hum and to Dorin´s relief, he heard the clunk for the doors to unlock.

'Get out you scum!' shouted Sergiu throwing the crumpled fifty lei note after him.

Dorin fell out in his hurriedness to escape as the car reversed at speed and disappeared. He gathered himself up, reaching down for the money. He needed a drink but as he started walking towards the street, he suddenly froze. Two giants stood before him, filling the width of the alleyway with their large gorilla frames. Dorin glanced behind him, retreating as they advanced. He rattled the handle of the rear door of the pawnshop then began to bang on the metal shield, calling out to Ion. He felt a hard punch smash into the side of his ribcage, sucking all the air out of his lungs. A vice-like hand gripped his throat, pushing him against the wall followed with a knuckled fist to his stomach. It sent him crumpling to his knees. As he lay in agony on the hard concrete, a kick caught him on the side of his jaw snapping his head back. He felt the taste of blood in his mouth and a stream of red flowed from his nose. He was dragged back up again in an arm lock, his head lolling sideways as he tried to focus on the face inches in front of him.

'The boss would like to speak with your wife. We will give you a ride home,' the torturer said.

'She´s not there,' Dorin attempted to say through a lip already swollen like a baboon's backside.

'No worries we can wait,' they laughed, bundling him into the back of a waiting delivery van. Dorin rolled around the floor, adding more bruising to his weak frame as they drove. They seemed to know where they were going. The van came to a stop and the door opened with Dorin blinking in the sunlight, confused. The two men supported him up the stairs to his apartment. No one was around and if anyone was, they were not about to interfere. Dorin was forced to hand over his key as a single heavy hand pinned him against the wall and the door was unlocked. Dorin stumbled over to the bed, like a drugged rag doll. One of the men took up a chair and lit a cigarette. The other one left, locking the door behind him.

Christine would have no idea of what she was entering. Monday was a day she could catch up on things as Rosa attended a summer class at the community centre which gave her a few free hours. She left Dorin sleeping. Things between them felt strained since their visit to Casa Flori. She didn't want any more arguments at that time in the morning. She gently woke up Rosa and got her ready for summer class.

She was out for a few hours, having dropped off Rosa and collected her earnings from the flower market. She stopped to buy bread and vegetables on her way home. As she arrived at the entrance to the apartment, one of the neighbours walked past her. 'I have seen someone helping your Dorin up the stairs. He didn´t look good, in trouble with the police again? Always the same your sort!' she shook her head in disgust. Christine never had much to do with her, an older woman who was tired of everything. The only thing she said she looked forward to was the day a coffin would come and release her from the ghetto.

Christine hurried up the stairs, sure that either Dorin was asleep or that he would have gone out. The neighbour must have imagined things.

She set her shopping bags down on the floor and fumbled for her key. Pushing the door open with her foot, she gathered the bags and stepped inside. The first thing she saw was a towering figure with his back to the window, the sun casting him into a silhouette. Her eyes then fell on Dorin whose moaning from the bed immediately caused her to drop her bags and rush over to him, leaving the door open. Blood was seeping into the sheets and his face swelled out of proportion to his body.

'Dorin, Dorin!' She turned to the figure in the room. 'You brought him here? Who are you? What is going on?' She was assuming that the man, who said nothing, was a friend who may have helped Dorin. Her assumption evaporated when the door closed and a second man entered the room, sitting himself down at her table.

'Good afternoon Christine. Your pretty daughter is not with you. Rosa is her name, yes?' asked Sergiu with a joker grin.

Christine was stunned. The ugly manner of these men suggested they were responsible for beating her husband but why?

Sergiu motioned to her like it was his house. 'Sit down, please. Nice artwork. I hear you are an artist and yet you live in this neighbourhood? That must be down to your husband, not much of a specimen is he and an awful memory too!'

'What do you want' asked Christine, ignoring his invitation. She went to a cupboard and brought out bandages and cotton wool, ready to help Dorin.

'I said, sit down!' Sergiu repeated as if he was talking to a dog. The figure at the window moved towards her and she was obliged to take up the chair opposite.

He took a cigarette out from a diamond-studded case, lighting up and blowing the smoke towards her. 'Your husband is a thief and it would seem incapable of telling me what I need to know. You see, he stole a particular item of jewellery, now safely back in my possession, which belongs to a friend of mine. She would not be too happy to lose it, I can assure you.'

'So return it, you seem to have punished Dorin enough. Why have you come here?' asked Christine, wafting away the annoying smoke.

'As I said, his memory is poor, must be the drugs. I need to know more. He told me you recently visited your brother, in a hotel near Brasov. That is where he removed the necklace and money.'

'I know nothing about any necklace or money. You must be mistaken. Dorin wouldn't steal from my brother!' Christine protested.

Perhaps not from your brother but I am sorry to inform you that your husband has been foolish. What is your brother's name?' asked Sergiu nonchalantly.

Christine hesitated. 'Simon,' she answered.

Sergiu could read a lie at fifty paces. 'I don´t think so.' He shook his head as if he already knew Mattei's name. He leaned back in the chair and folded his arms. The silhouette moved from the window towards Dorin.

'Mattei' said Christine quietly.

'That´s better. I suggest we start at the beginning' said Sergiu leaning forward with his gold fingered hands resting on the table before her.

She still had no idea of the purpose of the interrogation but was in no position to question it. She was forced to recount everything of her visit to Casa Flori, moment by moment, including every detail and most importantly, a description of Ana.

Sergiu knew for sure he had located Mihaela. He went over and over Christine's answers, the layout of the hotel, who else worked there and what Christine's connection was. How many people were staying there, how many staff? Which was Ana's room, did she go out? It got more interesting for him when he discovered Michaela went running, alone, past an isolated cabin.

'Are you done with us now?' Christine ventured bravely, concerned that Dorin was silent.

'No, I am not,' said Sergiu with a penetrating dark stare that kept Christine fixed to the chair. 'You will agree to help me further.'

He was already formulating a plan and Christine would prove very useful. By involving her, he wouldn't risk any alarm approaching Mihaela in the open. It wasn't difficult to persuade this weak little sparrow to do his bidding; otherwise, she would be joining the widow's club and her little girl would be entering the market in pretty underage girls.

Sergiu was coming after Mihaela. He would personally take back what was his and prove she had been nothing but an inconvenience to his bosses. He was looking forward to a pleasant expedition to Brasov. He began to put his plan in motion.

33

Teetering on the Brink

Sergiu instructed Christine to make two calls. The first was to Mattei. He was pleased to hear from her and even more surprised when she told him she was coming back to see him. Not only was she coming but she was bringing Rosa too and Dorin was staying home. She sounded different despite the good news she gave him. When they had last spoken only a few days before, she had been bubbly and talkative. He asked if anything was wrong. Sergiu, who was listening intently in the background, prompted her.

'I'm just fatigued. Dorin isn't well enough to travel and I think it would be good, as you suggested, to bring Rosa and we can enjoy a holiday together.' Mattei couldn't agree more.

The second call was to Katerina, explaining that Dorin had a stomach bug and she was worried Rosa would catch it. Would it be okay if Katerina picked up Rosa from the centre and keep her overnight? She would collect her the next day and then she was taking her up to meet her Uncle. Katerina was only too pleased to help, happy that Christine would have a break.

Once she finished both calls, Sergiu made Christine write a letter to be given to Ana. He gave her a mobile phone and left, threatening her again to follow his instructions. It was early evening and he was heading for the mountains.

Christine couldn't sleep, tending to Dorin who complained about pains in his stomach. He needed a doctor but the monster minder was impervious to her pleas. She lay awake, trying to work out how she could escape. The door was locked and she no longer had keys. Maybe she could phone the police but Dorin was a troublemaker to them, they wouldn't listen. What if she managed to call Katerina? But that could put Rosa and her friend in danger and besides, how could she use a mobile in such proximity to a guard? Even if she went to the toilet, he followed her, standing outside while she peed. It was hopeless.

Finally, when morning arrived she made Dorin as comfortable as she could, kissing him lightly on the forehead, before leaving with her captor and her suitcase to Katerina's.

Katerina offered to take Christine to the train station, concerned how pale and weary her friend was. 'You do need a rest. Let me know if there is anything else I can do. I will see you when you get back. Enjoy yourself, promise?'

Christine and Rosa stepped out of her car and went

to board the train to Brasov. She was aware of the man tailing them all the way. He sat on the train several seats away. She did her best to share Rosa's excitement who stared out of the window at the changing scenery; to Christine, the view was a nightmare.

Mattei met them at the station, delighted that Rosa ran straight to him giving him a big hug. He was alarmed how ill Christine looked but she assured him it was just tiredness. On the journey home, Rosa was bouncing with energy, asking Mattei all kinds of questions, so excited to have been on the train and wondering what they would be doing. Mattei was preoccupied with the road ahead and Rosa's chatter oblivious to the car following but Christine was aware, turning her head to see the driver was the same man that had been on the train. As they turned into the drive to Casa Flori the car carried on past them, she breathed a sigh of relief.

The driver was heading to a meeting point with his boss, at the base of one of the walking trails leading from Casa Flori to Bran.

Sergiu had arrived the night before, leaving his hire car a few miles away and picking up the path that lead to Casa Flori. Armed with route maps, a pair of binoculars and a flashlight he covered the distance under cover of darkness to the shepherd's hut Christine described. He made himself comfortable and waited until dawn, slipping back into the adjoining woodlands where he lay with his binoculars trained on the hotel.

He was wearing clothes he considered made him look like a camouflaged bird watcher, Khaki shorts, an army green tee-shirt, walking boots and a black baseball cap. The only difference was this 'twitcher' carried a Glock 19, a compact pistol concealed in the side pocket of his shorts and useful for shooting at close range. He was familiar with the whole geography of Casa Flori and from his vantage point focused in on a rotten apple with brown hair coming from her room and walking up the garden path to the kitchen.

He waited patiently until the sparrow and her little girl arrived in the late morning and satisfied everything so far was going according to plan, he climbed further up into the woodlands. On the other side of the ridge, a steep path led down to a rendezvous point with his driver. For now, he planned to get some well-earned rest in a hotel in Bran. His driver would take over the surveillance of the hotel from the same point and inform him of any changes of activity. Sergiu would return the following day, ready for the arrival of his prey.

Ana did not welcome the news that Christine was returning to Casa Flori. She learned from her brother that Dorin had taken her locket to a pawnshop. The owner kept it for his wife but then someone, who they never caught, snatched it from her neck in broad daylight. Razvan decided not to waste time talking to Dorin. He would put out feelers elsewhere to see if the locket turned up.

It wasn't good enough for Ana. She wanted to confront Christine. How brazen of her to even think of returning so soon! She would have to pick her moment. Her most prized possession was gone and she felt a massive resentment towards Christine, believing she must have known what Dorin was up to. She wasn´t sure she could even stand to set eyes on her again. Christine was in part a thief herself and Mattei didn´t know. What else was she capable of deceiving him of?

When Christine arrived, Ana kept busy. She offered to take over the prepping of evening meals to give Mattei more time to spend with Christine and Rosa at the farmhouse. He hadn´t argued, grateful that she was more than capable. They would return for dinner with all the extended family after the hotel guests had eaten. Ana was planning there would be enough distractions for her to speak to Christine alone.

Later, Maria, David, the girls and Alex were all seated together for the feast Mattei prepared. They made Christine and Rosa welcome but Mattei thought Christine seemed subdued. Perhaps she wasn't used to the level of banter that went on between them, or it was sheer exhaustion. He was very concerned for her.

Ana too seemed preoccupied. Over the last few days, he felt she had something on her mind but he couldn´t get her to open up. It would mean a lot to him if she and Christine could become friends.

What Ana knew was eating her from the inside and she couldn't say anything until she spoke to Christine. She deliberately sat as far away from Christine as she could waiting for an opportunity to approach her.

Christine was feeling an unbearable pressure. Her husband was a hostage and Rosa at risk. Somehow, she had to get the letter to Ana. A look of tension passed between them and when Ana got up to clear the table before the final course, Christine saw her chance. She offered to help and followed her into the kitchen where Ana had begun stacking plates into the dishwasher. Ana stood with two plates in each hand about to start speaking but before she could launch into her prepared speech Christine slipped the letter into Ana´s apron pocket, saying nothing and went out to the terrace where everyone gathered for coffee.

Ana was left alone in the kitchen. She opened the letter.

Dear Ana,

I am genuinely sorry that Dorin stole from you. I cannot defend him but I am hoping you will understand how unwell he is. I want to be able to return what is yours and to apologise in person. I have your locket and your money. I promise you I did not know until we returned home what he had done. I want to make amends but please, I would like to do this when we are alone and not to involve Mattei. I know you like running and you told me when I was last here you passed by the cabin in the afternoon. I will meet you there tomorrow and I hope we can put this behind us.

Christine

Ana stuffed the note into her apron pocket. How dare she assume she would be so forgiving? On the other hand, incredible though it seemed Christine seemed to indicate she had her locket and maybe even the money. Had the owner of the pawnshop lied to Razvan? She wanted to believe Christine because she wished to have her locket back. As she went to join them for coffee, she caught Christine´s eye and nodded in acceptance.

Christine went over to Mattei, who was doing card tricks for the girls. Desperately, she wished she didn't have to lie. She asked him if he minded she spend some time by herself the following day. 'I know I have come to see you and spend time with you but I want you to have time with Rosa too. Would that be okay? I might start painting,' she smiled, knowing Mattei would agree. She then excused herself to the bathroom and made a call on the mobile phone Sergiu had given her.

34

The Dog is Howling

At the hotel the following morning, Mattei completed the breakfast shift and prepped for the evening before returning to the farmhouse to collect Rosa. The two of them would be visiting Dracula´s castle in Bran. He teased her with stories and set her imagination running wild so the little girl couldn´t wait to explore. 'See you later this afternoon, Christine, plenty of time for you to relax and enjoy yourself. I can´t wait to see what you might paint!' he added enthusiastically.

'I was thinking to go back up to the cabin,' she said.

'That would be perfect, no one to disturb you. Take Baloo with you. He will be some company without interfering!' Mattei laughed.

She waved her set of paints at him and ushered

them out 'Go on enjoy yourselves!' she laughed as bravely as she could. She had no intention of taking Baloo. She had forgotten any mention of him in her descriptions to Sergiu. She couldn't complicate things now.

She waited in the quiet of the farmhouse, pacing the floors until it was time to set off up the track to the cabin. She just wanted to get this over. Ana would get her things back and Sergiu would leave them all alone. She was desperate and Sergiu was talented in using her, with a story of a lover´s tiff. She didn't know what she was stepping into, yet she sensed there was more to it than a necklace being returned to its rightful owner or a boyfriend needing to face a cheating girlfriend. Sergiu had gone to extreme measures and now there was no going back.

Sergiu trained his binoculars on Christine as she made her way up the cart track. He was satisfied she was alone and so he made his way from the cover of the dense woodland into the cabin ahead of her. Christine's legs were shaking as she climbed the few steps to the door. She was sweating, not from the heat of the sun but from fear. The door opened for her.

'Clean yourself up and get a grip,' he growled at her.

'How do I know Dorin is okay?' she pleaded.

'You don'tbut I don't intend to hang around here any longer than it takes, so keep doing what I ask and I will let that husband of yours go.' Then to secure her commitment, he sneered at her adding, 'I see pretty little Rosa has made some new friends.'

She waited on the steps for what seemed an eternity, pretending to sketch on a small pad in pencils she had brought, hoping Ana would come soon. After nearly an hour, she saw her approach with Baloo trailing after her, as she jogged up the path. It was customary for Ana to take the dog but Christine didn't know that. 'She's coming,' she said, quietly enough for Sergiu to hear her from inside. Ana stopped in front of the cabin steps, her hands on her hips, bending forward while she caught her breath as Christine stood up.

'Thank you for coming,' said Christine nervously.

'I told you I would pass by, now what is it you have to say?' said Ana with a razor edge to her voice.

'I wanted to tell you I'm sorry, sorry about what Dorin did. I wanted you to come by yourself, so I could return your locket and the money, without Mattei knowing,' she said, sticking to the script given to her.

'You've got a nerve! Why should I trust you? I thought he sold it and probably spent the money, though it's the locket that matters most. Do you have it?' Ana asked incredulously.

Christine nodded. 'It's inside. Why don't we go in out of the sun? I brought some cola with me,' motioning for Ana to follow her. Ana climbed the steps, leaving Baloo to lie down on the soft grass. Perhaps she had thought wrong of Christine after all.

Christine stood with her back to the small kitchen counter with her hands, gripping the edge and tears in her eyes. Ana was expecting a cold drink and a locket. Instead, the cabin door swung closed, pushed by someone standing behind. Ana turned as Sergiu slid the metal bar across, preventing any escape.

'Well, well, what have we here? Ana, is that what

you have decided to call yourself? I preferred you blonde, that colour makes you so ordinary,' he said sarcastically.

'Sergiu!' Mihaela exclaimed, the colour draining from her face as she looked from him to Christine. Christine shook her head, trying to communicate that she had no choice.

'You treacherous bitch, what made you think I would not find you?' snarled Sergiu.

He made straight for Mihaela shoving her roughly onto a wooden chair. She could see her locket fastened to his thick neck. She grabbed the sides of the chair, staring wildly at him. He brought up the back of his hand and slapped her across the face. Christine looked stunned. What had she done?

Sergiu continued his torment of Mihaela.

'You thought you could simply vanish. You betrayed me, after everything I have done for you! Most girls can only dream about the lifestyle I gave you. How ungrateful and stupid are you?'

Anger replaced Mihaela's fear directing it back sharply like an icicle snapping loose.

'You did not give me such a lifestyle! It was more like imprisonment. You took control of my life for your own needs. You used me and my future was nothing to you if, at some time, you no longer needed me. So, what if I left! I was bored with you! I despise you!' She spat in his face.

Sergiu held her face tight gripping her jaw with one hand; her spit ran down his cheek. 'I own you! You owe me. Let's not forget that. Now you give me no choice but to drag you back or destroy you!' He loosened his grip.

'What do you mean by destroy me? You don't own me and I don't owe you anything!' She spat at him again.

He struck her harder, knocking her from the chair. Christine tried to help her but Sergiu pushed her away as he planted Mihaela firmly back on the chair.

'You know why I came, Mihaela? I want to punish you for being a lying slut, for making me a fool in front of everyone. Yes, I know about your lover, doing business behind my back.

Mihaela protested. 'He was a lover, not a client.'

'No, he was not! He kept you for himself. He gave you money. I know what lies you told him that you needed to visit your sick grandmother. What a pathetic grovelling shit he was and you used him like you use everyone.'

'It wasn´t like that, he was a regular client, like any other.'

'Wrong Mihaela, you broke the rules! Trust me. I dealt with him. He got what was coming to him. You belong to me and you do as I say! You can sleep with fifty men in one night but not fifty nights with one man! You are nothing but a whore!'

Sergiu´s voice boomed as he brought his hammer fist down on the table. Christine felt powerless and trapped. She realised he wasn't going to let her walk away from this, nor Dorin and maybe not even Rosa. Baloo began whimpering at the door. Sergiu cursed. He would deal with it quickly enough.

Mihaela argued, trying to buy time. 'I have done nothing wrong. Why do you need to interfere? You have all the girls you want. What does it matter if I choose to come back to Romania? Please, Sergiu!' She was terrified by the thought of what might have happened to Jan.

'Ah but you didn´t just come back for a holiday did you Mihaela? Instead, you played a conjuring trick, disappearing into thin air! Now you have put others in danger because of your selfishness. What did you think was going to happen? As I said, I dealt with your boyfriend but that is the least of your problems. There are important people asking questions and they expect me to solve their problem. Do you understand me?

'What are you talking about? I don´t understand,' said Michaela.

'Oh but you do. You are lying again, eh? You know you were seen that day on the yacht. You disobeyed my orders. You saw things you shouldn´t and then you ran away. You made a big mistake.'

'You tell me what you think I saw or heard that should make you so worried.' she spoke with contempt in her voice.

'You don´t worry me, Mihaela. I couldn´t give a damn about you. You are a piece of garbage that blew across my path, a lying, cheating, dirty little whore. You don´t understand anything, do you? You would ruin everything for a pathetic life without thinking of all the people that have food on their table because of what we do, hundreds of them, Mihaela. What do you think of that? So, you see we must keep the lions happy. They feed on those who make mistakes. They care nothing about you.'

'You forget, Sergiu, that I am not alone in this. Who do you think brought me to this place?' She was thinking about her brother, thinking that because she told him everything, it would keep her safe. Sergiu laughed. He stood half a meter before her with his back to the barred door and casually lit a cigarette.

'You mean that sentimental policeman brother of yours? He has less influence than you think. You are probably an embarrassment, a thorn in his side. He doesn´t worry me! I would probably be doing him a favour disposing of you, to remove a stain from his perfect career.

Mihaela was trying not to look as terrified as she was feeling. 'You are the one that uses people, getting Christine to do your dirty work for you.'

She looked at Christine. 'He planned everything didn't he, the letter, the reason to get me here on my own? He threatened you, didn't he?'

Christine nodded. 'I'm sorry, truly I didn't know, he gave me no choice. He has Dorin.'

'Shut your face bitch!' ordered Sergiu.

'It's okay Christine. I realise that now and I am sorry too.' Mihaela turned her attention back to Sergiu.

'You bastard, you are nothing but a bully with a small penis. Everyone knows it, laughing behind your back. Look at you, you look ridiculous! You said it! They have made you feel a fool and you think by wasting time coming after me that will change? I don´t think so!'

Sergiu put his cigarette to one side in a bowl on the small table and leaned into Mihaela's face, his expression fierce as her comments eroded any chance of saving herself. He sat astride her trapping her under his weight.

'Just like old times, eh, Mihaela? With one hand, he

began stroking her gently on the cheek. She turned her head away from him. He brought up his other hand, turning her head towards him and stroking her. He moved his hands down her upper body, caressing her breasts and muttering 'dirty little whore, dirty little whore, no one speaks to me like that!' He brought his hands back up to her throat and then he began to squeeze. Her eyes began to bulge and she couldn´t breathe, she felt as if she were drowning, struggling uselessly below Sergiu's frame. She knew she was losing consciousness.

Christine couldn't believe what was happening. She had to do something. She could try to escape but she wouldn't make it. Sergiu was more than a match for her even if he was distracted by Ana and she couldn't just abandon her. Her heart was racing. She began to panic, feeling frantically behind her for a weapon, finding a heavy iron skillet. She had just one chance. In one move she gripped the handle stepping forward and took a big swing, her eyes fixed to the target in the shape of Sergiu's head. She made sure she followed through with all the strength she could. The metal connected with the side of his face and he toppled over, his bulk crashing to the floor and taking Mihaela with him. She lay pinned under his legs, barely conscious and unable to move.

The collision scattered the remaining furniture and Sergiu roared in anger. The impact of the skillet left him dazed as he struggled to pull himself up amidst the tangle of chairs and the table. Christine moved in quickly for another strike, feeling the adrenaline surging through her. She stood above him; her legs straddled for balance and with both hands raised the skillet above her head, bringing it down onto the top of his skull. This time Sergiu seemed to pass out. She dropped the pan in shock, catching her breath, staring at him as blood began seeping onto the floor.

For a few moments, she was oblivious to anything, unaware of the lit cigarette lying in a pool of kerosene from the broken lamp. The liquid ignited with a spontaneous pop and the flames began to reach out, following the splatters of fuel. They feasted on the fabrics and dry wood and began licking their way up the walls of the hut and to the roof above.

The room quickly filled with smoke and heat. Christine became disorientated and dizzy, fumbling for the bar to the door as the flames spread. She managed to slide the bar out and kicked the door open, looking back in panic. It was hard to see anything but she could hear Mihaela moaning and beginning to cough. Sergiu lay motionless beside her. Somehow Christine managed to grab her by the arms and drag her into the daylight, the two of them tumbling down the steps onto the grass below. Mihaela's left ankle and foot were at right angles to each other and bone was sticking out. Baloo was barking incessantly, keeping close as Christine half carried, half pulled, a semi-conscious Mihaela away from the fire.

They were forced to pause after only ten meters to recover when a huge roar caused Christine to turn towards the hut. She watched in horror as a demonic creature emerged from the hellfire, his clothes alight and his face distorted. As he stepped down, she saw the gun in his hand. Baloo turned to defend thembut Sergiu reacted automatically, firing two shots as Baloo sprang toward him. The dog collapsed on the second shot with a piercing howl, a mound of black fur lying still on the grass.

Christine saw the blood coming from Baloo's head and tried again to pull Mihaela up but she had no strength left. 'Run Christine!' Mihaela gasped, as Sergiu bore down on them but Christine couldn't leave her. Sergiu threw himself in a rugby tackle, bringing them both down again. Christine kicked out at him, striking him frantically with her fists but she was hitting a wall. His hands were clutching at Mihaela's throat. Above his curses, Christine became aware of the sound of other voices and shouting. She was sure Mihaela was on her last breath when a black shadow, like the grim reaper, suddenly swooped upon Sergiu and his cries now came from teeth sinking into his flesh. Baloo's head shook violently backwards and forward biting into Sergiu's shoulder, shredding skin, ripping tendons and crunching bone, his giant paws clawed at Sergiu's body. Someone reached for Christine pulling her backwards away from the carnage and she watched as Mihaela too was pulled back. She heard Mattei shouting out commands to Baloo who now had the taste of blood and didn't want to let go. Mattei wasn't strong enough to pull Baloo away but as more people arrived the dog relented and drew back.

Christine sat huddled on the grass, shaking and crying uncontrollably. She realised it was Maria's husband who pulled her back and she clung to him as he kneeled beside her, wrapping his arms around her.

'Rosa, where is Rosa?' she begged.

'She's fine, with Maria at Casa Flori. Do not worry.

What happened here?' David asked trying to calm her but Christine was becoming hysterical.

'Dorin, oh my god, Dorin! Someone has to look for him!'. She wasn't making any sense, something about Dorin in trouble, in her home, beaten up, a man watching him. Her words came out all muddled.

'Him!' she pointed wildly at Sergiu's body. 'He has him hostage, please someone has to go there now!'

Mihaela turned her head towards Christine. She heard her desperate attempts to explain Dorin was in danger. Now she understood how Sergiu had set a trap for them both but she was unable to help, her voice reduced to a hoarse whisper from the effects of the smoke. Christine could see Mihaela laid out on the grass, covered in blood. Their eyes met and Mihaela tried to mouth the words, 'I know, I understand.'

Mattei and Alex were doing their best to make a support from sticks and Alex's tee-shirt for her ankle. David tried his best to reassure Christine. 'The police are coming, everything will be okay,' he said stroking her hair. He couldn't understand what she was trying to tell him. No one knew what was going on.

David had been at Casa Flori when Mattei returned with Rosa and Alex. They joined him on the terrace along with Sasha and Brigit. They were enjoying a drink as the girls played in the garden when Mattei heard Baloo. He knew something was wrong by the way the dog was barking. He was sure Christine would have taken him with her to the cabin and then suddenly they could see smoke. No one knew where Ana was but if she was not at the hotel she could be up there to. Something was very wrong. They didn't hesitate, with David grabbing the keys of Maria's

Opel Zafira. 'Call the Fire Protection Services, Maria,' he shouted as they hurried to the car.

It took fifteen minutes to make it up the rough track to the burning cabin. They arrived at a scene in chaos, with local people from the hamlet helping the Forest Fire Protection services beat out the flames around the hut. Blue lights flashed and sirens wailed as three police cars approached, followed by two ambulances making their way steadily up the cart track.

By the end of the afternoon, the shepherd's hut was nothing more than a dampened bonfire. Sergiu had been loaded into one of the ambulances, heavily bandaged and peering like a snake through one eye at Mihaela. She didn't look at him. A policeman was leaning in close to her, writing notes and then began tapping a number into his mobile phone. Christine went over to her, hearing the policeman mention Dorin's name. 'Please, tell them to find him now!' she begged. Mihaela could only nod as she was stretchered up ready to go in the second ambulance. From the dense woodland above, Sergiu's driver watched through binoculars as the scene unfolded. There were too many people around. He turned and ran.

Christine refused to go in the ambulance. 'Don't let them take me!' She pleaded in desperation clinging to Mattei's tee shirt. She wanted to be with Rosa and she needed to know Dorin was safe. Finally, exhausted and heavily bruised, she was persuaded to go back to the farmhouse with Alex, Mattei and David, reassured that her daughter was in safe hands.

Maria was waiting with the local doctor and

helped to bathe her before she was given a sedative to make her sleep. Alex took Baloo to the vet in Bran. David looked after Rosa, Sasha and Brigit. There was a hotel to run and Mattei reluctantly headed back to Casa Flori with Maria. Alina, the housekeeper, would stay with Christine until he returned. There was nothing more he could do; she was sleeping.

Razvan was not expecting a sudden call from the Brasov County police in the late afternoon. He reacted quickly, making several calls. After an assessment that Mihaela's injuries were not life-threatening, he made sure she was transferred to a private room with a police guard at the main hospital in Bucharest. They could not take her to the same hospital as Sergiu. He informed the Brasov police to place Sergiu under immediate arrest, with an armed guard, whatever his condition. Lastly, he called his superior to inform him of events and tell him that Sergiu had been taken to Brasov's Military hospital and was in intensive care. His Superior was polite enough to ask after his sister but could hardly contain his satisfaction that Sergiu was alive and in custody. He would take control now and issue an armed team to go to Christine's home in search of Dorin and report back to him.

It wasn't good news. In the early evening, armed police arrived at Christine's address, expecting a fight and stormed the building, bypassing a few residents who quickly closed their doors. The team smashed down the entrance to the apartment only to find it empty of any living thing, apart from the flies that buzzed in triumph over Dorin's stinking body, lying in a pool of vomit, in the heat of the closed room.

Their guess was his captor abandoned the place

when he discovered his hostage was dead. An initial autopsy confirmed Dorin died by drowning, falling unconscious, unable to react to complications caused from internal bleeding as a result of injuries sustained from a beating. Razvan accepted the task of informing Christine and providing an explanation of events to those affected.

As dawn was breaking the following morning, Razvan stepped out of an unmarked car, taking in a deep breath as he made his way up to the farmhouse door. Mattei was already awake, making coffee and Alex got up when he heard voices. They had sat on the porch the previous night trying to make sense of things but unable to make any connections.

Christine was still asleep and so Razvan accepted the steaming cup of coffee Mattei handed him and began to unravel the mystery which culminated in Dorin's tragic death. He chose his words carefully, apologising and accepting full responsibility for exposing anyone to danger through his attempts to protect Mihaela. His sister was an innocent, caught up in an underworld that was an indiscriminate virus that knew no boundaries. He promised they would see justice for Dorin, Christine and Mihaela.

Mattei and Alex listened to Razvan's account, wanting to know more but Razvan felt he had said enough. He excused himself to go to Christine, closing the door to her bedroom. The farmhouse filled with the wail of sorrowful sobs.

35

Ashes to Embers

Two weeks later, Christine buried her husband in Cimitrul Tudor Vladimirescu cemetery in Rahova. The ceremony was simple, just like their wedding day with only a few traditions afforded. The plot had been expensive. There was no embalming of the body, no procession of mourners to the graveside. Dorin had been placed in the coffin by the hospital and the lid sealed. Christine had bought a blue suit for him. She knew Dorin would have hated it but she preferred to think of him laid to rest looking as smart and happy as she remembered him on their wedding day.

She had chosen a carved wooden cross with a pointed tin covered roof that would protect it from the rain and added her own hand-painted flowers in bright geometric shapes with a framed photograph of Dorin placed in the centre. It looked cheerful amongst the other crammed grey tombstones with their plastic bouquets in pewter vases and statues of crying angels.

Mattei and Katerina looked on as they lowered Dorin's remains into the grave with the customary even number of chrysanthemums placed on top of the coffin lid. Christine added a flower crown, sent by Ana. They stood together for a few moments holding their lit candles and made a toast with a glass of wine each. There were no speeches, no celebratory wake.

Christine had stayed with Mattei until the time for the funeral with no wish to return to the apartment in Rahova, She did not want to be reminded of Dorin's suffering in his final moments. Instead she abandoned their things and accepted Katerina's invitation for her and Rosa to stay. Lucia wanted them to come home to her but Christine felt unwilling to burden her so soon after Dorin's death. Deep within, Christine knew she could never have changed Dorin but she carried the guilt of being unable to save him.

Rosa had been protected from the real drama of why the holiday was extended, surrounded by her new family but after several days back in Bucharest, Christine felt she needed to return to Lucia's. Lucia's health was rapidly deteriorating as the cancer took hold and they would have little time to be together. She made a bed for herself and Rosa in the living room and cared for Lucia who was now bedridden.

Four weeks after they moved in, Lucia passed away. On her final day, Lucia calmly held Christine's hand, her thinned hair made bright with the ribbons she loved, her wasted body wrapped in her favourite multicoloured coat.

'Can you feel it, Christine that I'm not leaving

you?' she whispered, barely audible. Christine leaned close to her and smiled fondly, squeezing her hand in response and stroking her hair. Her lovely eccentric Lucia filling her with hope and then suddenly she felt a warm current of energy transfusing into her.

'I will always be with you,' Lucia mouthed before she closed her eyes for the last time.

It was the darkest period in Christine's life. Within two months of the events at Casa Flori, she had buried her husband and the woman that was an angel to her in life and continued to be her inspiration in death. She went back to what she loved, what gave her solace and began painting again. Lucia's home was now hers and Rosa's.

Over the next few months Christine met up with Ana several times. She never imagined she would have anything in common with her but after everything they had been through somehow there was a bond. For Ana, Christine's unselfish actions had saved her life and whatever happened in the future she would not forget that. She was living at home with her parents, who felt they had failed their daughter in some way and were determined to cocoon and protect her. For a while, she enjoyed this new attention during the time it took for her wounds to heal but deep down, she was feeling stifled again.

In early spring she arranged to meet up with Mattei and Christine at Esperanto, a popular restaurant in the city centre. Whenever the three of them were together they called her Ana. They had never known Michaela. They preferred not to know and few details had been shared of her previous life despite all the police attention following the arrest of

Sergiu and Dorin's death.

Life had become normal again, and Ana now had her freedom. She laughed with Mattei and Christine, telling them how her parents were treating her like a little girl, trying to persuade her to become a school teacher of all things. Neither could imagine her as school teacher. Mattei asked what her plans were. She didn't know but she knew living with her parent's wasn't what she wanted. She was ready to move on.

'You could always come back to Casa Flori,' Mattei suggested. He still had feelings for her but kept them to himself. Alex had been right; there was something about her that kept her at a distance. Ana was all about preparing for the unexpected. She missed them all and the hotel but after everything that happened, they would understand she needed a fresh start. As far as she was concerned, mountains were for climbing so you could see the view from the top and what was beyond held more excitement for her now. She promised she would visit again, 'As a guest!' she laughed. Mattei secretly hoped that whatever she was planning one day she might appreciate people mattered more than places.

Endless police reports lay piled on the shelves of bureaucracy in the aftermath of the destruction of the shepherd's hut. They were deliberately buried in administrative delays and under a press blackout for the convenience of continued intelligence gathering.

Sergiu remained in a prison hospital for over three months undergoing several painful skin grafts to burns and the deep lacerations caused by Baloo. His face would be permanently autographed with scars from the dog's claws. Eventually, he was moved to the maximum-security Penitentiary in Gherla, four and half hours north of Brasov, locked up with nearly 15,000 other inmates, and awaiting trial.

He had two objectives, firstly to stay alive, building protection against his former bosses, starting within the prison walls and secondly to work on getting himself out. He had not been caught murdering anyone. He was a victim himself, albeit from a dog. He would zigzag his way through the legal system, negotiating an amnesty with the intelligence services by feeding them whatever it took to gain an advantage over his enemies. It would take patience and planning but prison was the ideal place to rebuild his reputation and he still had unfinished business. He was sure he would be out within a year. The fire was not out, yet.

Epilogue

Chameleons

Changing Colours

There was a gathering in the gardens of Casa Flori. Each person held a glass of Champagne, raised in celebration for the opening of Gallery Lucia. The buildings that once housed Ana´s room were converted, not to a sauna room but into a working art studio. The space had been extended to include a workroom to host classes in drawing and painting and a second larger room to exhibit the work of local artists, guest's paintings and traditional handicrafts. Christine´s paintings took pride of place.

She stood in the sunshine next to her brother. She no longer had dark circles under her eyes. Her hair was glossy, thick and wavy about her shoulders and her once thin frame now cut a shapely suntanned figure in a floral sundress. There was no hesitation to see she and Mattei were brother and sister. She ran her fingers through Rosa's hair, full of bright ribbons and looked to each of the faces before her. All the people at Casa Flori were her family now. She smiled at Julia with whom she had been reunited, respecting Lucia's wish that she should make peace with her past. Alex was fussing over Baloo, fondling his big head which still carried the lump of the one bullet that had pierced his scalp the year before. Mattei made a short speech and they all clinked their glasses, 'To the continued success of Casa Flori, our new venture and to absent friends.'

At the same moment the group in Casa Flori was celebrating, a young woman took up a seat under the shade of a sun umbrella on the terrace of the Le Negresco Hotel in Nice. She seemed very at home in the elegant surroundings on the French Riviera. The hotel was famous for welcoming the jet set, artists, politicians and Royalty since opening its doors in 1913. She ordered a freshly squeezed orange juice and began writing postcards which she had taken from her Louis Vuitton clutch bag.

She was a beauty, with a cache of shining fiery auburn hair and smooth milky skin. She crossed her long legs and adjusted her dress in a ladylike way, catching the attention of the man sitting a few tables opposite her. He was alone and similarly ordered fresh orange juice. He was admiring her and she knew it. He noticed how her Versace shift dress in Mediterranean blue matched her eyes. It flattered her figure without being clingy. He liked classy women. He did not think she was French. There were no rings on her fingers, only a pair of silver Cartier studs in her ears and an unusual silver locket around her neck.

She glanced over to him and smiled in politeness. He couldn't resist making his way over. 'You are alone? May I join you? It seems a shame not to enjoy some company on such a glorious afternoon. I am

Robert,' he said, in English buttered with a French accent. He extended his hand in greeting.

She made a calculated hesitation before lifting her hand to his and then invited him to sit next to her, removing her handbag from the adjoining seat.

'My name is Ariana, pleased to meet you, Robert,' although she already knew who he was, she had done her homework. He was an art dealer, divorced, without children and the owner of several properties on the Riviera including a yacht. He was a regular at Le Negresco.

'I hope I wasn't disturbing you,' he said, glancing at the postcards.

'No, I don't mind at all!' I was writing some cards to friends. I wanted to wish them luck. One of them is a talented young artist and she is exhibiting in a hotel I was working in.'

Robert's interest was naturally peaked.

'How interesting, perhaps I have heard of her. I am an art dealer. Which hotel?' he asked.

'I don't think you would know her and the hotel is in Transylvania. I was working there as a manager for a while. That is where we met,' she replied.

'That must be a beautiful part of the world, very unspoiled I hear. So, what brings you to the Riviera, Ariana?' continued Robert.

She smiled flirtatiously; her blue eyes fixed on his. He wasn't handsome, but he wasn't unattractive either. He had style, that certain French look of quality. She began to play the game she knew so well.

'I have always wanted to come here, to be by the sea. I was ready for a change from the mountains and I have no ties, so I thought, why not? I'm looking forward to exploring and perhaps I will make new friends!'

Robert was happy to be the first new friend, easily flattered by her interest in what there was to see and do on the French Riviera. He loved nothing more than to talk about himself and impress her with his local knowledge.

She leaned closer to him, eager to listen, toying with the alpaca locket around her neck with its enamelled pink rose and engraved initials 'A' and 'C'.

Printed in Great Britain
by Amazon